THE BURNING TIME

Also by David Mark

Novels

THE ZEALOT'S BONES *(as D.M. Mark)*
THE MAUSOLEUM (aka THE BURYING GROUND) *
A RUSH OF BLOOD *
BORROWED TIME *
BLOOD MONEY
INTO THE WOODS
SUSPICIOUS MINDS *
CAGES *
DARKNESS FALLS
ANATOMY OF A HERETIC
THE WHISPERING DEAD *

The DS Aector McAvoy series

DARK WINTER
ORIGINAL SKIN
SORROW BOUND
TAKING PITY
DEAD PRETTY
CRUEL MERCY
SCORCHED EARTH
COLD BONES
PAST LIFE *
BLIND JUSTICE *
FLESH AND BLOOD *

* *available from Severn House*

THE BURNING TIME

David Mark

SEVERN
HOUSE

First world edition published in Great Britain and the USA in 2023
by Severn House, an imprint of Canongate Books Ltd,
14 High Street, Edinburgh EH1 1TE.

severnhouse.com

British Library Cataloguing-in-Publication Data
A CIP catalogue record for this title is available from the British Library.

ISBN-13: 978-1-4483-0939-9 (cased)
ISBN-13: 978-1-4483-0940-5 (e-book)

All Severn House titles are printed on acid-free paper.

MIX
Paper from
responsible sources
FSC® C013056

Typeset by Palimpsest Book Production Ltd.,
Falkirk, Stirlingshire, Scotland.
Printed and bound in Great Britain by
TJ Books, Padstow, Cornwall.

Praise for the DS McAvoy novels

"An involving, nail-biting police procedural from a masterful storyteller"
Kirkus Reviews on *Flesh and Blood*

"A hair-raising procedural [that] highlights unselfish love, sacrifice, and man's inhumanity to man"
Kirkus Reviews on *Blind Justice*

"Deliver[s] the kind of grisly torture and murder scenes that have rightly linked Mark's work with that of Val McDermid"
Booklist on *Blind Justice*

"Polished prose, lovable recurring characters, and a stunning revelation make this a mystery to savor"
Kirkus Reviews Starred Review of *Past Life*

"A fine police procedural . . . Ian Rankin fans will be pleased"
Publishers Weekly on *Past Life*

"[Mark is] on the level of Scottish and English contemporaries such as Denise Mina, Val McDermid, and Peter Robinson"
Library Journal Starred Review of *Cruel Mercy*

"To call Mark's novels police procedurals is like calling the Mona Lisa a pretty painting"
Kirkus Reviews Starred Review of *Cruel Mercy*

About the author

David Mark spent seven years as a crime reporter for the *Yorkshire Post* and now writes full-time. A former Richard & Judy pick, and a *Sunday Times* bestseller, he is the author of the DS Aector McAvoy series and a number of standalone thrillers. He lives in Northumberland with his family.

www.davidmarkwriter.co.uk

For Eli and Artemisia. As am I.

Acknowledgements

A quick note of thanks to the good people of Blanchland, who tolerated the writer in their midst with a mix of curiosity and forbearance. It was a pleasure to live among you. I made the happiest memories of my life amid those honey-coloured stones. Richard, Tracey, Ned, Ann, Kenny, Dawn, Cliff, Tim, and Jude . . . good neighbours, good friends.

And a special note of thanks to Colin Laidler, who took me into the depths of Hell in the name of research. You're a gentleman.

Thanks to you too, dear reader. You follow me into the dark places and in so doing, help me find the light. You mean so very much to me.

'Witches who in this way sometimes collect male organs in great numbers, as many as twenty or thirty members together, and put them in a bird's nest, or shut them up in a box, where they move themselves like living members, and eat oats and corn.'

Heinrich Kramer, *The Malleus Maleficarum*

'By the pricking of my thumbs, something wicked this way comes.'

William Shakespeare, *Macbeth*

PROLOGUE

10 February, 8.34 p.m.
Wilkinson Lodge, Bale Hill, Weardale, County Durham

Call him Ishmael.

He's seated in the only chair that the cats won't go near – the one place in the cramped little living room that's reserved exclusively for the man of the house. It's a scabby patchwork of green and mould and wrinkled leather. It's gaffer-taped and superglued and there's something that might be cress growing out of one of the arms. Anybody with the strength of character to rummage around in its crevices could earn a fortune in loose change – most of it in currencies long since discontinued. It was worth a lot of money, once. So was he. Ishmael has long since accepted that he and the chair are irrevocably bonded. They could be twins, conjoined at the arse.

'. . . My hand's gone all the way through the baguette, Daddy – look it's a bracelet, look – that's really warm, actually . . . why don't people wear bread, Daddy? Bread shoes would be sooo comfy . . .'

Ishmael settles into his chair. There are creaks and squeaks and the twang of springs readjusting themselves. They might well come from his knees.

Twins, he thinks, and smiles. It's a joke he makes when they have new company. He's got a stock of favourite lines; of choice phrases – lines that make newcomers laugh. He pulls them out at random whenever somebody new pops around for a can of ale or a slurp of hooch. He's entertaining company, is Ishmael. Garrulous, when the mood takes him. Whimsical, even. He writes poetry from time to time. Writes lyrics for songs that his fingers are too sore to play. Scribbles down ditties and limericks and ripped fragments of prose, stuffing them in the big old camel-skin notebook that he keeps beneath his pillow and which has followed him around the world and back again.

'. . . she seemed so cross, Daddy. You will say sorry, won't you? She knows it's not your fault but "sorry" won't hurt, will it . . .?'

He glares into the fire. Tries to remember what it was he did or didn't do. Can't quite grab it. Can't disentangle his thoughts from his memories from his dreams. Not much of a catch, these days. Fifty-one. Lanky and gaunt; skin the colour of old newspaper. Gold tooth and neckerchief and looking like a kid in his dad's clothes as he shivers inside his big old sheepskin coat and tries not to look like he's an addict tweaking for a hit. But he's still got something about him, even now. Still some lingering residue of allure. Even as the oldest dad at the school gate, he knows he'll get an admiring glance from whichever yummy mummy opens her Cath Kidston case and puts his number in her iPhone. Whatever '*it*' is, Ishmael Piper has always had it in spades. He's got the charm of the public schoolboy blended with the twinkly patter of the rogue. And the name helps. The name and the earring and the half-remembered headlines about his days as a spoiled little rich boy and true *enfant terrible*. He could have gone far, could Ishmael. Could have been a contender. World was his fucking lobster, once upon a time.

'You're not listening!'

He's not, no. He's drifted off again. He's been losing himself a lot recently. Been drifting back into bad habits; thoughts sliding down the well-worn grooves in his brain like a needle on vinyl. He could blame the Huntington's. He won't.

'Sorry, sugarbun. Say it again.'

Her name's Delilah. She's heard all the bloody jokes, thank you very much. She's only seven, but she knows that grown-ups are all tuned in to pretty much the same frequency and she's gotten used to hearing piss-poor renditions of the Tom Jones classic every time she's introduced to somebody new. She just smiles. She's got a nice smile, has Delilah. Big blue-grey eyes and a tangle of caramel-coloured curls. She hears the name Shirley Temple a lot but, despite his promises, Daddy has yet to show her a picture. He'll get round to it, when he gets a chance.

Delilah is patient with Daddy. He hasn't been well recently. He hasn't had the energy to play. He's skinnier than he used to be and he shivers a lot. When he takes his shirt off there are blue veins all across his chest, peeking out from amid the labyrinth of old scars and indecipherable tattoos. Mummy Number One says that Daddy is getting better. Mummy Number Two – whose name is Heloise – says he's getting worse. Delilah prefers Mummy Number One, but she's angry with Daddy, so Mummy Number Two is getting him all to herself. Delilah isn't sure Daddy likes either of them very much. At least Uncle Felix has told her the truth. He'll die one day, just like she will. Everybody dies. It's what we do before that happens that counts. She loves Uncle Felix. Loves his daughter, too, and his daughter's boyfriend, and his daughter's boyfriend's dog. She doesn't think about Uncle Felix's wife much at all. Daddy does. Daddy sometimes seems like he likes her more than he likes Mummy Number One and Mummy Number Two put together. And, as Uncle Felix says, Daddy puts them together a lot. Felix's wife is called Hettie. She and Felix help Daddy stay in control of himself. They take care of his money worries. Stop him making bad decisions the way he used to. He's grateful to her. Defends her whenever Mummy Number One calls her a grasping bitch.

'She'll come back tonight, won't she? You didn't mean it. And I want her to hear me practise.'

Ishmael gives her his full attention. Flashes the smile that knocks years off him. Looks at her with such pure and perfect love that she can't help but put her plump, sausage-meat arms around his neck and press her face against his until their cheeks squish together and their lips pucker into matching trout-pouts.

'I'm watching,' he says, when she lets him go. 'Listening, even. Whatever it is you're wanting from me, that's what I'm doing, I swear.'

He is, too. Watching and listening and giving her the closest thing to his full consideration that any bugger has the right to expect. He's feeling all right. The sound of the rain pitter-pattering against the glass provides a pleasing echo to the crackle and snap of the burning coals in the open fire. He can hear one of the cats purring somewhere nearby. From time to time he fancies he can hear a low, poteen-addled snore from the little, low-ceilinged bedroom overhead. Life's OK, for a while. Life's worth living, here at the death.

'Daddy, you will blow it into the bottle, won't you? If she comes back, can you imagine?'

Ishmael realizes that he's started rolling a cigarette with his left hand: dirty fingers pulling a pinch of glorious Samson and Virginia from his little leather pouch. A second cigarette paper dangles from his lip like a flag of surrender. Mummy Number One used to make him smoke outside. Used to make him toddle across the yard and over the long grass and out into the heather if he wanted to treat himself to a cheeky spliff. Used to make him duck under the wall at the mouth of the mineshaft, huddling there in the damp and the dark like a hobbit with a habit. She didn't want him setting a bad example. Didn't want to be able to smell the nasty stuff in her hair or on their daughter's pyjamas. Changed a bit from the hairy-pitted, blue-dreadlocked hippie who introduced herself to him by climbing on to his shoulders at an AC/DC concert and rubbing herself off against his skull. Middle-class, now. Worried about what the neighbours will say, even though she and Mummy Number Two are talk of the bloody village. Makes up for her bohemian tendencies by juicing all the decadence from their lives. Smoking weed in the bloody mineshaft! He's appalled with himself that he ever agreed. She's relented since he started getting worse. She lets him stay indoors if needs be to numb the pain with a few drags. But she insists he blow the smoke into the empty bottle of supermarket cola on the windowsill. He agrees because he loves her. She asks because she loves him back. She wants to keep him alive, she says. Wants to get as much time with him as she can. She says it with such sincerity that he sometimes forgets that she's spent the past few weeks trying to kill him.

Paranoia, he reminds himself. That's all it is. A lifetime of smoking things you shouldn't, coupled with a nasty dose of fatal illness. Huntington's affects the brain as much as the body. He can't trust himself any more. He has terrible thoughts. Dark thoughts. Sees things the way he did when he was on the smack.

Sometimes he has to go and lie down in the crystal garden, the cavern of wonders, out there by the shaft. He calls the rear of the property his Museum of Unfinished Projects. It's a graveyard to his fallen enthusiasms, cluttered over with the paraphernalia of his lost interests. He was going to turn the mineshaft into a tourist attraction, for a while. Spent a fortune on paraphernalia: helmets and ropes, shovels and supports. Bought half a tonne of rocks and minerals to return to their rightful place beneath the ground. He had plans to hold acoustic evenings and séances, poetry readings and silent banquets in the great twinkling caverns beneath the ground. Health and Safety scuppered it. The crystals are dumped out by the chicken coop, next to the bags of cement and hardcore that were part of his long-forgotten plan to build a stargazing pod. It had seemed like a good idea, at the time. But then, so had heroin.

'Right, that's it. Showtime.'

She clears her throat. Takes two purposeful strides to the centre of the square, low-ceilinged room and takes her place at the centre of the tattered rag-rug as if it were the stage at the Albert Hall. She's lit from behind by the smouldering coals in the hearth; a dusky purple light bleeding out through the cracked glass of the cast-iron fireplace and casting her ragdoll shadow on the timbered roof and choppy walls. On the sofa, two of the cats wake from their slumber and take a look at the performer as she limbers up and does her breathing exercises. They give one another the knowing look of those who have survived past trauma. Soundlessly, they extricate themselves from the pile. Ishmael smiles as they slink towards the kitchen door, leaving their less experienced brethren to slumber in blissful ignorance atop their mountain range of cushions and coats, blankets and boxes; the sofa itself all but invisible amid the hessian bags of half-begun knitting projects, and the split bin-liners full of ribbons and rags.

Another cough: for effect this time. Then the bow, and the curtsey, and the star-jump, just for effect.

'Hello, Reception Class. Hello, Mrs Blazey. And a special hello to you, Miss Swantee. My name is Delilah Piper. I'm very pleased to be joining your class. Mrs Blazey asked me to think of some things that I would like you all to know about me, so we can hopefully become friends. She asked me to think of three things I like about myself. It wasn't easy, but I've managed to whittle it down . . .'

Ishmael's grinning as he watches her. He's a dad of five, but this one's the best. This one's perfect. This one's not just worth dying for, she's worth living for, and that, in Ishmael's estimation, is as close to miraculous as it gets. He takes a polythene pouch from inside the tobacco wallet. Holds it to his nose and takes a sniff. It's pungent and rich: an olfactory explosion that makes his skin break out in goosepimples and his tongue feel two sizes too big for his mouth. He takes a pinch from the bag. Crumbles it into his disassembled cigarette; his fingers acting from muscle memory alone.

'. . . I get my eyes from Mummy Number One. Her name is Joy. I would like brown eyes like my daddy, but I suppose I can't have everything. I do get my brains from him, according to Mummy Number Two. Mummy Number Two is called Heloise. She's French. She comes from a place where they grow mussels on ropes in the sea. Mussels like the shellfish, not like on your arms. I never lived inside her but she's still my mummy. I get my *vocabalabalabuary* from her . . .'

She stops, waiting for the laugh. Ishmael obliges. She gives him a look that tells him he was almost a fraction too late and that if he lets her down on the day, she'll take a hammer to his knees. It was Heloise who told her that saying vocabulary wrong would be a good idea. Ishmael didn't disagree. Ishmael rarely disagrees.

'Mummy Number Two has been teaching me at home since I was very little. I would have liked for her to keep teaching me at home, but . . .'

She stops. Wrinkles her nose and gives her dad a hard look. He smiles at her from behind his spliff.

'You said you wouldn't inside,' pouts Delilah. 'Mummy will be really cross.'

They both know which mummy she means. They have long since stopped seeing the humour in her name. Joy's the buzz-kill. She's the mood-hoover. She's the grump. She's as much fun as sand in your butt-crack and she's the reason Delilah isn't allowed to be home-schooled any more.

Ishmael gives his daughter his naughtiest smile. For a moment he's handsome. With his soft eyes and crow's feet, his stubbly, wolfish features; his earring and his curly sugar-dusted hair – for a moment he looks like the young man who used to be able to charm his way into and out of anything he chose.

Delilah finds herself smiling back. She flicks a look at the dirty, rain-speckled window beside his armchair. There's an oil lamp on the sill: its insides clogged up with burned-down tea-lights and the waxy corpses of spiders and flies. She can see his reflection in the dark glass. He looks like he's made of water. She squints through him and out on to the moor. There's a storm brewing: clouds massing above the lip of the hill. There's a violet tinge to the sky; the brooding thunder-heads seamed with the mingled hues of foxglove and heather. It seems to get darker as she stares. She thinks of a black-smeared paintbrush being dipped in clean water.

'Sheep will be bleating about this for days,' says Ishmael, as his daughter comes to his side. She plays with the curl of his hair at his neck. Runs her thumb along the mucky silk of the red handkerchief at his throat, plucking at the strings of his necklaces and chains as if strumming a lute. He puts his arm around her. Pulls her close and presses his face to the crown of her head. Breathes her in. Breathes in soap and mildew, coal dust and cats. Breathes in his own sweet marijuana and the lingering meatiness of whatever it is that's unhurriedly decomposing in the slow cooker.

'What's that, Daddy?'

She's looking past him. Looking through the glass. Looking out past the chicken coop and the wood-store and the little lean-to outhouse where he stores his tools and his pallets and where sacks of fertilizer and cement lean against one another like drunks at a bus-stop. She leans forward. Squints, theatrically.

'What's what, sugarbun?'

Delilah puts a hand to her brow, the way people do in her storybooks. She can barely make out the outline of the old tower: sticking up like a mid-finger – an exclamation point visible for miles around. She's played in its dark, gloomy hollows since before she could walk. She can call its smell to

mind from memory: wet stones and funky moss; dead animals
and sheep-poop. She'd like to be out there now. Would like
to be hunkered down with her daddy and one of her mummies,
cuddled up beneath an oilskin and drinking hot chocolate from
a Thermos, tasting the static on the air.

'There's somebody on the moor.'

Ishmael can already feel the drug dulling his senses. He
feels delightfully sluggish and numb. There's no pain, or at
least, none that matters. Nothing to worry about for a little
while. Not a single damn problem in his head. He deserves a
little bit of this, he tells himself. You work hard, mate. You
do your bit and more besides. You're good at this. You do
what's asked of you and you do it with a smile on your face.
Go on, son. Close your eyes . . .

He hears a voice that terrifies him. It's been talking to him
for as long as he can remember. It's quiet. Well-spoken. It's
charming and oh so reasonable. It's at once his comforter and
his abuser; his confidante and agony aunt. It's the voice that
tells him to do things that are bad for him.

*She's going to ask you to go and see if the people are OK,
Ishmael. She's going to ask you to get up from this lovely
warm chair and pull your boots on and toddle out on to the
moors. Look at it, Ishy. Look, my boy. The rain's blowing in
sideways. You'll catch your death. Sit and smoke and let it all
go. You've got enough to think about. You've got problems
they don't even know about. Smoke it down and light another.
Maybe call the lovely girl at the posh hotel, eh? She's taken
a shine to you, I can see that. And she knows a guy who knows
a guy, as they say. He can score. A little smoke of the brown
stuff, just to take the edge off, eh? You've been so good. Fought
so hard. You've been under so much pressure, Ish. How fucking
wholesome do they want you to be . . .?*

Ishmael pulls himself out of the chair. His head's reeling,
as if he's just stepped off the waltzers. Fuck, that weed was
strong. He blinks, rapidly. Closes his eyes and tries to centre
himself but he feels himself falling over behind his eyelids
and has to reach out to Delilah for support. He opens his eyes
and finds himself still static, still rooted to the floor, even while
part of his consciousness is looking up at him from the rag-rug

and another peering down from the low, chocolate-coloured beams.

'I need some air,' he mutters, and drops the unsmoked end of the spliff. Treads it into the carpet. Feels himself reeling. 'I need to think. To remember . . .'

'Daddy? There's definitely somebody out there? Do you think they need help? Remember the story, Daddy? Remember what you said about the mine and the man who went up there when he was sad? Tell me again. I can do it for show-and-tell at school, if you let me see it . . . if you let me see the thing . . .'

Ishmael totters past his daughter and blunders his way towards the kitchen. He feels too hot and too cold all at once. He can't seem to make his thoughts stitch together. He fumbles in the pockets of his padded lumberjack shirt. Finds his phone and squeezes it in his fist. He's not supposed to go outside, though he can't remember why. He's ill, he knows that, but the name of the condition escapes him. He knows he's in love with somebody, and that somebody wants him dead, and he knows that he's rich and he's poor and that he's trying to be a good man without knowing what such a thing really looks or feels like.

'Are you going to help them, Daddy? Can I come? Should I get Mummy Number Two?'

The rain's rattling the glass, now. The first growl of thunder rolls in across the moor like the rumble of a waking god.

'Daddy . . .'

He looks down at his feet. No shoes. Mismatched socks: a hole in the big toe; the nail painted green as grass. He grabs at his neck as if suffocating. Holds his tangle of medallions and trinkets in his fist. Stumbles across the bare flags of the kitchen and clatters into the back door, scattering cats and stumbling over shoes; old coats falling down from the lopsided pegs.

'Daddy?'

He looks back. She's framed in the doorway, watching him. 'Daddy, you shouldn't. Or I'll come. Yes, I'll come . . . stay there, I'll get my shoes . . .'

She disappears back into the belly of the house. Ishmael

opens the back door. Steps out into the swirl of wind and rain. Feels the fizz of hot metal and electricity in his hair, on his tongue.

They'll have a wrap, lad. If it's who you think, they'll sort you out. Pop out, get your head sorted – come back and be Dad of the Year, yeah? You've earned it . . .

He clatters out into the rain. Slips and slithers across the wet grass towards the wooden fence beyond the chicken coop. Puts his hand out in front of him. It's warm. It's red, as if he's been pulping elderberries through muslin.

He staggers on. Staggers on towards the mouth of the mine. Stones puncture the soft flesh of his feet. The twists of burned heather tug at the sodden hems of his trousers.

He blinks as his eyes begin to sting. For a moment his head clears and he suffers a terrible moment of self-awareness. There was something in that joint. This isn't right, Ishmael. This isn't you. Get back inside, eh? Eat a banana and drink some water and sit yourself down until it passes. Go back, eh? Go on . . .

A few more steps, lad. That's it. They'll be waiting, like before. You could be a hero, if you do this right. Save the day, like last time. They'll all look at you like a fucking king. You deserve that. You're Ishmael Fucking Piper. You're too fucking rock-and-roll for this domestic shit. Get high, son. Get yourself on the stairway to Heaven and don't let anybody stop you . . .

Ishmael stands still. The rain pummels his face. He looks down and sees blood leaking, blackly, on to the grey stone at the lip of the mineshaft. There used to be a No Entry sign, back when they first moved in. Used to be a fence up and a big metal grid nailed across the big black hole. He tore it down. He doesn't believe in boundary lines. Thinks of ownership as theft.

'Daddy?'

He slaps himself in the face. Does it again. Turns back to the house. He's left the door open. He can make out the little outline silhouetted in the frame.

'Delilah . . .'

He spits. Tastes blood. Tastes iron. Tastes the salt of his own sickness as he gives in to a great hacking bout of coughing:

doubling over, gasping for air; eyes popping, mouth open – strings of saliva whipped away into the rain and the wind and . . .

He looks up.

And then the ground is rising to meet him. There's a sudden pain in his side. It feels as if his brain has sloshed against the inside of his skull. Feels like he's driven at full speed into a wall. He can't decipher up from down. There is a moment of freefall, a sensation of merciless impact. And then his skull is smashing into the jagged, copper-seamed rock; the bone splintering; flesh tearing – one eye rattled loose by the violence of the impact. There's a sound of gentle avalanche – of earth and stone and ancient bones tearing themselves loose from the soft ground. The split sacks of cement slump over one another and topple down – spilling their ash-grey innards over his prone, helpless form. It adheres to his skin. Coats him. Darkens as it begins the process of encasing him in stone.

His blood-filled eye twitches. He stares through the darkness, blinking weakly. Sees the first wisps of smoke. Sees the red flowers begin to bloom at the window, at the door.

He tries to move. Tries to breathe. Tries, desperately, to live.

A memory surfaces: a random impulse fired by synapses in a dying brain. He thinks of the man who came to his door and told him things he did not wish to hear. Thinks of the recording. Of the mine. Of the place beneath the stones. He feels a sudden urge to pray. Eyelids flickering, blood in his throat, he remembers the times he sought out his own death. Thinks of how hard he fought to get clean. To get better. To get good. Wonders, whether he deserves this. Christ, Felix is going to be so fucking angry with him. Joy, too. Joy and Heloise and Big Harry and all those who toasted his good health as he conquered his demons and swore he'd become a decent man . . .

His last word, a whisper upon red lips:

'Dad . . .'

His last breath rises, wetly, into the dark sky.

So does the smoke.

Then there is just the sound of crackling flames, and falling stones.

ONE

The heart is a knuckle of charred tissue, blackened gristle. Heat rises in helixes of greasy foulness from the pulp that sizzles and spits upon the iron griddle. Ingle presses a hand to his mouth as he leans into the fireplace – fearful that the vapour climb inside his mouth, his nose – colonize him like those that have come before. He uses the tongs to flip the charred meat on to its side. One of the nails slides out of the mess of blackening offal. He wonders if it is a sign. All things seem to be, when viewed in retrospect.

He moves back from the hearth. Sits back in the rocking chair and watches the meat burn. He glances at the clock on the little table at his side. He has another few moments before the heart burns itself into nothingness. He has done this many times before. He sometimes permits himself to feel a fleeting pleasure in the familiarity of repetition – to allow his muscles, his digits and limbs, to go through their individual ministrations without need for the interference of any higher consciousness. He permits himself to be a mere observer, to drift above his own corporeal form like a kite tethered by a dancing string. Reduced to the level of onlooker, he does not register the feeling of blood upon skin, nor shudder at the sound of the cracking bones, the rapidly cooling warmth of innards exposed to cold air; the deft sifting through the purples and reds and greys of delicate innards: the twist and pull and pop of the little red heart, freed from its prison of white bone with the ease of a strawberry plucked from the bush. He simply watches. Watches his own likeness press the heart to the glittering stone and push the iron nails through its middle, again, again: cocktail sticks skewering hot olives. He only returns to himself once the heart is on the griddle, oozing blood, fat, grease, charring and sizzling against the ancient black metal.

He picks up the hand mirror from the table. He looks straight into his own eyes, watching as his face becomes a blur of its component parts. His blue eyes swim in the pale, yellowed batter of his pocked skin: lips a livid red scar, nose hooked like a beckoning finger. He cannot stand to look at himself with any degree of clarity. Despises his own reflection and the ruination these months have wrought upon once-fine features. He knows himself to be a collage of scars and lesions, gristled warts and weeping sores. He no longer examines them. He no longer applies the creams. His well-being is in the hands of a different power now. He has given himself over to the entity. Given himself over to the old ways.

He looks up as a hiss emerges from the rancid hunk of meat upon the griddle. It is a new sound, like a whistle between missing teeth. Instinctively he tongues the rounded, three-pointed incisor in his top lip. It is a comfort to him. So too the chicken claw that he wears on a cord around his neck. He allows himself a moment's excitement. Perhaps it will be today. Perhaps, this time, he has got everything right. Perhaps, at last, the ritual will yield results. He hopes so. He has no more chickens to slaughter.

He looks into the hand mirror again, forcing himself not to focus on the upper left portion of the glass. It is always the upper left portion of his vision where she appears: a sensation, a whisper, a glimpse. Over the months he has assembled the flickers into something close to a likeness. He fancies he would be able to sketch her, if such a thing might be permitted. He sees her as she was in her youth: chipped-jade eyes, fine features, angular jawline and elegant neck, all framed with ringlets of bouncing black hair. She wears the diadem: the gleaming purple stone glaring out from the centre of her fore-head like a third eye.

He feels the excitement dissipate. Dwindle. Die. He has killed another bird for nought. He has failed again. Failed himself. Failed her. This is the sixth chicken heart he has given over to the flame in his search for answers: all torn from the still-warm mass of flesh and feathers and bone; all hammered through with pins and nails; all tossed upon the skillet to sizzle and twist. The ritual is a simple one. While the heart burns, his persecutor should present themselves at his door, their mouths dry, tongues swollen, begging for water. It is a spell that has been used for centuries, a guaranteed way to identify a persecutor. But no witch has knocked at his door. Nobody has knocked upon the door of his little cottage in a very long time.

He breathes out, long and slow; breath rattling in his lungs. He stands up, dizzy, off-balance, his bones and muscles registering their familiar aches. He feels crushed by the weight of her, feels as though his body is being squashed and moulded like warm wax by the constant pressure of the liquid darkness that fills the house. His ears ring, as if he were underwater, out of his depth; as if there were not enough air within him to see him back to the surface. He sways where he stands, his dirty feet planted in the cold, wet soil that he has scattered upon the circular rug in front of the fire. He makes fists with his toes, kneading the soil, squeezing it, compacting it. He dug the earth from her grave on the night of the last full moon, giggling, gasping, thinking himself a madman as he bent and rose, bent and rose, the white light of the great lunar eye reflecting in the glinting silver of his spade. She had been pleased with him, he had felt sure of it. The air in the house had felt brighter, lighter. She had permitted him to eat. He had gorged himself on fistfuls of dried food: cereal, pasta, grain, crunching bloodily through their hardness, swilling down pulses and grains with great choking glugs of honey from the jar. There was no purging. He ate and was filled. Rested and was content. She will punish him for this failure, of that he has no doubt. She will show him the things he does not wish to see. She will scream inside his skull as he strives for sleep. She will show him what he did; what he is; what he is not.

A new sound penetrates his thoughts: a noise so unexpected, so incongruous, that at first he had glanced through the dirty windows towards the skies, as if expecting thunder. It takes him a moment for his brain to disentangle itself – to match up the throaty grumbling din with an image in his memory.

It's a car, he tells himself. It's a visitor . . .

He squats in front of the hearth and fidgets with the embers. They are grey and powdery on the outside but still blood-red

within, like bisected figs. He takes a handful of the papers on
the mantel and twists them into kindling, pushing them deep
into the glowing ash. He sits back on his heels and looks into
the pan. The heart twinkles like iron ore. He feels the heat of
the flames upon his bare legs. Reminds himself that there are
conventions to be observed, social niceties to be maintained.
He pulls a knitted blanket from the back of the chair and
covers his nakedness in its itchy folds. He glances around the
room, as if seeing it for the first time. The sofa is rotting,
sagging inwards: tufts of fur sprout from the slashed fabric
like dead lambs. Books and papers are piled high: great
tottering towers of yellow newsprint, with their bad, unwashed-
skin reek. Bouquets of dead flowers hang from the low,
soot-blackened timbers like garlands at a ghostly wedding,
grey petals falling from dead stems like flakes of ash. The
floor is a dizzying mess of sigils and scribbles, chalked
inscriptions smudged across the damp wooden floorboards,
constellations of pentagrams carved deep into every surface,
dotted here and there with puddles of stinking yellow wax where
the guttering candles have devoured their blackened wicks.

The knock upon the door is brisk. Businesslike. It is not a
knock to be ignored.

He rubs his face with his hands and feels the grime flake
on to his chest like ash; like snow. He scratches at the warts
upon his brow, his wrist twitching as his pulse connects with
the gnarled growth above his eye: an arachnid egg-sack hanging
low to occlude his vision.

The knock again. Louder now. More urgent.

They must be so thirsty, he thinks. Must be so very desperate
for water.

For a moment, he fancies he can hear a voice in the recesses
of his head. He hears the distant whisper of the man he once
was.

*Don't. It's not true. You're ill. You need help. Take your
pills. Call the number they gave you. Tell them what
you've done. It'll be hard, but they'll understand. It's not
your fault . . .*

He shakes his head and the words disappear into the blackness that surrounds him. He glances into the hand mirror,

prone upon the little table. Sees movement in the top left-hand corner. Feels her hunger. Sees the redness in her ravenous smile.

He answers the door as the knock comes again. Pulls open the ancient wood and lets the trapped fug of burnt meat and fat and iron wrap his abuser in its greasy folds.

His visitor steps back, raising a hand to her nose. Her brown eyes are angry, pupils hard. She's pale-faced, red-haired: long tresses tied back in a braid. She wears a waxed jacket over a business-suit, hands clad in soft, cream-coloured gloves. There's an expensive-looking car parked on the little patch of broken ground. The road stops in a jagged gouge of splintered tarmac and stone: an ugly, shark-toothed wound. Behind her the sky is a great smear of grey and the air is speckled with a misty rain, a billion tiny raindrops hovering like flies.

'Mr Ingle,' she asks, flashing an angry glare to her left as one of his talismans catches in her hair. It's a crucifix of rowan twigs, bound together with red thread. It does not sizzle when it touches her skin. He finds himself marvelling at the extent of her powers. Wonders whether he will be strong enough, righteous enough, for the trials they must both endure. 'Mr Ingle, I've been trying to call you for several days. I need to talk to you about the death of Ishmael Piper.' The words catch on her tongue as she looks him up and down, as she drinks in his rancid appearance, his mildew and meat smell. For the first time, something close to fear takes her features in his fist.

He takes the spade from where he left it when he came back from the entity's grave. Curls his bone-white fingers around the handle. He does not have much strength left but he knows his task to be righteous, noble; his actions blessed.

He smashes the flat side of the spade into the side of the witch's head. She drops like a puppet: strings cut in one perfect swipe.

He takes a moment to catch his breath. Looks up to the moon as she emerges for a moment from the wall of purpling, blackening thunderclouds. There'll be a storm, he thinks. A storm to cleanse. To wipe away the darkness, and to begin again.

He takes her by the ankles.

Drags her over the threshold of his little cottage: blood upon the stone.

Pulls her by the ankles into the room where the entity waits.

Kicks the door shut.

And night falls.

TWO

Three days later . . .

'That's it. Aye. Oh aye, Jesus, just like that . . .'

Roisin McAvoy stands in the doorway, wreathed in steam, a white towel wrapped around her head and another tucked beneath her armpits. Her dark hair drips water on to her toes. She glowers at her husband's big, broad back and watches as he makes himself feel better. He's naked from the waist up, sweat-soaked and goose-pimpled – one hand on the wall. He would be staring out of the pretty little square windows if his eyes weren't closed in ecstasy.

'Deeper. Aye, go on. That's the badger.'

She stifles a giggle. Drinks him in. He's seen violence, this man that she loves to her bones. He's suffered at the hands of bad men, bad women. He carries the livid inscriptions of his twenty years as a police officer. There's a great mottling of scar tissue and bruising up his left flank, as if he's been gripped in the mouth of a great white shark then spat out for being too tough. She feels her fingertips tingle as she mentally traces the familiar contours of his scar tissue. Feels her lower lip prickle as she recreates the sensation of her mouth upon scorched flesh.

He's making soft moaning sounds – muttering to himself the way he does when she's giving him a treat.

'Aye, that's magic . . .'

She can't keep quiet any more. She needs to see his blush.

'I take it you're enjoying your new toy? Feck, you haven't spoken to me like that since I did the thing with the champagne and the marshmallows.'

McAvoy whips around, face beetroot red. Even his bushy, red-grey beard seems to be blushing.

'Does the job,' he mutters, unwrapping the massager from his neck and dropping it on to the hard-backed chair at his side. 'Honestly, I felt it touch my soul.'

Roisin grins. Shakes her head. 'I feel like I've bought my
own replacement! This must be how the lassies at Tesco feel
when they have to tell customers to use the self-service tills.'

McAvoy wipes the sweat from his face and pushes back his
thick mop of fox-fur-coloured hair. The tail-end of an ugly
ridge of scar tissue peeks out from his hairline. It has a twin
in the inch-thick line of pinkness that hems his beard.

'It's purely physical,' says McAvoy, with a little smile.
'There's no intimacy. It's strictly utilitarian, I swear.'

Roisin drops her towel. Unwraps the other from her head
and starts patting the moisture from her slim, tanned arms.

'Replaced by a shiatsu machine,' she mutters. 'Cast aside,
so I am. Kicked to the kerb in favour of a younger model. A
younger model without a head. Or limbs! I mean, feck it,
Aector – I do at least have limbs.'

McAvoy sits down on the edge of the bed. Stares at her
with the same intensity and adoration that he has looked upon
her for the last fifteen years. 'Not replaced, my love.
Augmented.'

She gives him the look that he loves – one eyebrow raised,
her little nose slightly wrinkled; a curl to her lip like a cat
about to pounce. 'You've said "utilitarian" and "augmented"
in the past two minutes, Aector. Are you practising? Getting
out the old public-school vocab to impress the arseholes?'

McAvoy sags, shoulders lumping. He nods, guilty as charged.
He reaches over and picks up the shiatsu machine and strokes
it like a cat. It was a birthday present from Roisin and the kids
and he's slowly started falling in love with it. McAvoy isn't
in the habit of complaining about his aches and pains, but his
last encounter with violence has taken its toll on a body
already visited by too much suffering. His neck and shoulders
are in a state of constant throbbing tension and he feels like
he has a migraine more often than he doesn't. His body doesn't
really feel like his own. He's always been a huge great lump
of a man: a Highland warrior who's stepped down from a
gilt-edged frame, shed the tartan and put on a suit. But he
hasn't yet begun to feel strong again. Even making a fist
seems to make his arms ache. For the three days he managed
to go back to work, it took all of his strength just to keep

from crying out each time he had to raise himself from his seat. His boss sent him home for the good of everybody else's health. None of the other members of the Major Incident Team could stomach seeing him suffer in silence. Colleagues only too quick to phone in sick with everything from a runny nose to a split toenail had to watch as he endured his broken ribs and ruptured oesophagus, his hairline skull fracture and dislocated fingers, with a Christ-like forbearance. He was proving bad for morale. *Go home*, they said. *You're making us look bad.* He'd have fought the instruction if his boss weren't also his best friend. DSU Trish Pharaoh had given the instruction from her own sick bed – convalescing poolside at a hotel in Taormina, Sicily. She felt no guilt whatsoever about taking as much time to recover as she was permitted. Their last investigation had nearly killed them both. Nobody was going to thank them for it, so they might at least spend a few weeks putting themselves back together on full sick pay. McAvoy has only recently been appointed a full detective inspector. He feels guilty that he's not providing value for money. He felt the same when he was a detective sergeant – even when receiving his second Queen's Police Medal for Valour.

Now into his third month of sick leave, he's beginning to forget how it feels to be a police officer. He's spending most of his time with the shiatsu machine kneading and whirring and oscillating its way around the lumps and bumps in his neck, listening to audiobooks and trying not to feel sorry for himself. He likes being home, though he can tell Roisin is starting to get a little tired of having him under her feet. He wears a size twelve shoe and she wears a size three. He's a lot of man to squeeze into their little waterfront fisherman's cottage in East Yorkshire.

'They'd love this,' says Roisin, gesturing at the room. 'They'd be sword fighting, don't you think? You see the suit of armour in the fireplace? I swear, one too many espresso martinis and I'm climbing in that and going mad with a claymore.'

McAvoy grins. Lies back. The cushions are feather-filled and sumptuous and fold themselves around his big, ursine head. A moment later, Roisin is in his arms, one leg snaking around his, her head in its familiar nook. He kisses her head. She's used some unfamiliar shampoo and she doesn't smell the way she should.

'I won't use it again,' she mutters, reading his mind. 'It's for women who have a favourite type of lettuce.'

'It's nice,' mutters McAvoy. 'Just not you.'

She sniffs at his beard, an animal scenting its own clan. 'You're still you. Bergamot and sandalwood and a touch of spilled cappuccino.'

McAvoy laughs. Holds her closer. Roisin makes her own herbal potions. She's been doing so for years but in the past few months she's started selling online. It's proving lucrative. Her little bottles of lotions and potions are now available in a chain of mid-range hotels and from a stockist in Covent Garden. A couple of broadsheet newspapers have sought out interviews with her in the past few weeks after an actor once tipped to be the next James Bond swore that her blend of beard oil was the only thing that could tame his woodsman tresses, and that the concoction had an effect on the opposite sex that he would ordinarily have needed a litre of pheromones and a new Lamborghini to achieve. McAvoy's so proud of her he could burst. Roisin finds the whole thing rather funny. She won't be giving any of the interviews. She certainly won't be promoting herself or flying too high above the parapet. She may be a copper's wife but she's a Gypsy to her bones, and no self-respecting Pavee woman would ever willingly court the attention of the taxman.

'Bit posh, isn't it?' asks Roisin, settling herself and looking up. The room is called The Buttery and sits on the top floor of a little house overlooking a quiet, gravel-lined courtyard. Much of the little medieval village seems to belong to the luxurious hotel that dominates most of the old marketplace, though there are cottages here and there rented out on long-term lets. It's all red doors and hanging baskets, old anvils and higgledy-piggledy walls; the stones cleaved from the old abbey that once dominated this quiet pocket of rural north-east. There's a church and a tea room and a post office, and would be impossibly beautiful if not for the car showroom of big

Range Rovers and Porsche Cayennes blocking the view of the historic buildings and tucked up bumper-to-bumper on the too-narrow road.

'He was never going to book a Wetherspoon's,' growls McAvoy, trying to keep the scowl off his face. 'Has to be seen to be expensive or what's the point of doing it?'

Roisin tweaks his nipple. Slaps his chest for greater effect when he doesn't yelp. 'You said you'd try to enjoy yourself.'

'No, I said I wouldn't spoil your fun.'

Roisin sighs. She takes a tuft of his chest hair and twists it. A diamanté star dislodges itself from her thumbnail and disappears into the thicket.

'Sorry,' he mutters. 'I'll try. I will. It's just . . . I don't know . . . so much unsaid. Or maybe it's been said and I missed it. Or maybe nobody has anything to say because none of it matters anyway. I just don't belong. I never did.'

Roisin strokes his beard. Puts her fingertips to his lips for a kiss and then rubs them against her own. 'Nobody's going to get a chance to make you feel bad, my love. I swear, one sour look from that mardy bitch and she's going headfirst into the trifle. I don't give a feck if it is her birthday.'

McAvoy squeezes her. He can't decide if her presence makes her feel more comfortable or more anxious. He's been trying to work out the answer to that conundrum for years.

'Feck, this is like sleeping on a fax machine.'

McAvoy purses his lips, embarrassed at the sounds his stomach is making. He's famished. He's always famished. He glances down the bed. There's a complimentary packet of fudge next to the Nespresso machine. He has big plans for it later, but he knows he'll get told off if he starts snacking before their evening meal. They're eating at eight p.m. He's got three hours to wait until he gets his hands on so much as a slice of sourdough.

'You're not having any,' says Roisin, drowsily. 'The starter you wanted is nine quid. I know we're not paying for it, but you are bloody well going to appreciate it, my lad. You are going to eat every mouthful. I don't know what a goat's cheesy crottin is, but I refuse to allow that goat's sacrifice to be in vain.'

'I'll eat it even if I'm full of fudge,' pouts McAvoy.

'But you'll want the fudge when you come back.'

'I might not.'

'Shush.'

Her breathing changes. He feels her settle against him. Holds her. Loves. Listens to her breathing. She's been so much better these past few weeks. She suffers from a recurring flu-like condition common to people from the travelling community, and for much of the year she's been too exhausted to do much more than keep the kids fed and clothed. They spent some time in the outdoors a few months back and it seems to have revived her spirits. She's ten years younger than McAvoy and, at the moment, with his aching bones and tired eyes, it feels like an age gap that's getting bigger. His thoughts begin to drift into a familiar groove. He wonders what his bloody mother will say when she sees his new injuries. Wonders what she'll make of the dress that Roisin has bought specifically for this grand occasion: its hemline eye-wateringly short and designed to create a cleavage that should be home to shepherds, goats and singing nuns. He knows that the next few days will be excruciating. He sees very little of his mother and was genuinely astounded when her husband called him out of the blue and told him that it would mean the world to her if he could come along to her seventieth birthday party. McAvoy hasn't even recognized the voice of the man who paid for his education and who seduced his mother away from his father when Aector and his brother were just children.

McAvoy closes his eyes. Remembers the absurd, awkward conversation he'd endured with Crawford Darling: entrepreneur, philanthropist, venture capitalist and prick. *Ploppy*, to his friends – the origins of the less-than-dashing nickname remembered only by the hyper-wealthy geriatrics who endured boarding school alongside him. His mother's husband. His *stepfather*, though he's never been able to use the term without disgust. McAvoy hadn't recognized the number, but he'd identified the breathy, BBC World Service voice as soon as he'd spoken. He'd called him *Eck*, the way he'd done when he was a boy. No apology for the years since they'd last spoken. No enquiry as to his health, or his happiness, or whether more children had been added to the brood. Got straight down to business, the way he always did. Cecilia's birthday, that was the thing of it. Important. Significant. Momentous, in point of fact. Told him that seventy was a big number, and that by the time another ten years had gone by, they'd probably all be too doolally to even recognize each other. It was now or over. A chance to mend bridges – to bring the whole family together and celebrate Cecilia's legacy. Retirement party too, of a sort. Booked a big old sprawl of a place in Weardale.

'. . . *Know it, do you? North Pennines. All heather and deer and miles of not a lot. Felix's back yard, as it were. Booked the whole bally place for the weekend. Bring the lady-friend, yes? No children, m'fraid, but a chance to have a bit of luxury and some good food. Can't be easy on a policeman's salary but don't worry, all on me. On the company, as it were. Say you'll come – your brother was a damn stick-in-the-mud and made his feelings known, but you always were the more reasonable of the Highland cuckoos – that silly business at school notwithstanding . . .'*

McAvoy had just stood there, gulping like a dying carp. For a while, he was ten years old again and the mother who'd buggered off when she lost interest in family life was driving up the track to the family croft, a mile up the glen from Loch Ewe. She was in the car that her new lover had bought for her: plush and expensive and utterly wrong for the cold, rugged landscape that she'd ditched in favour of a big house and a rich man's bed. She was coming to take him away. She was coming to give him a chance at a better life. He deserved more than the whitewashed, tumbledown building where his father and grandfather had eked out a living since before the war. She had a big house, she said. She could give him whatever he wanted, she said. He could go to a school that would give him a chance at a future that would be forever out of his reach if he stayed here, drawing his pictures, writing his little poems, catching fish and swimming in the loch and being no different to all the McAvoys that had come before. He's never forgiven himself for agreeing to go with her. Still can't believe that she thinks he was swayed by what she had to offer, rather than just a desperate desire to be with his mum. Three months after following her, she and her darling husband sent him to boarding school. It would be years before he found anything or anyone that felt like *home*.

Roisin has taken the phone off him. She'd listened. And she'd said yes. It would be lovely to see the pair of them again and to get to know some other members of the family. She couldn't wait.

McAvoy's terrified of what the next few days will bring. The last time he saw his mother she was telling Roisin that she knew exactly what kind of woman she was and that her son would eventually see through the tits and the twinkle and spot the money-grabbing floozy underneath. She's never met her grandchildren. The last time McAvoy was in hospital she sent him some book tokens and a balloon. She's too bloody good to be true when it comes to her stepchildren, though. Crawford's son, Felix, thinks his stepmother is wonderful. She dotes on his daughter, even as she struggles to remember the names of Fin and Lilah McAvoy. She hasn't even spoken with her eldest son, Duncan, since that day outside the croft. McAvoy's father is a reasonable man, but he will not be swayed from his long-held belief that she is a succubus raised from a hell dimension and cast forth to cause maximum misery to any man who makes the mistake of loving her. Aector's brother feels the same. But Aector, ever so fucking reasonable, ever caught between a rock and an anvil, has spent his adulthood defending her from them, and them from her, and feeling at home with none of them.

He stares up at the window. Imagines the view. If the clouds withdrew and the darkness receded, McAvoy would be able to see the little snatches of the North Pennines: a UNESCO Area of Outstanding Natural Beauty. McAvoy had allowed himself a wry smile at the use of the word 'natural' in the promotional materials. He glimpsed nothing on the drive over that suggested the landscape was natural. Parked up in a layby on the A68, he'd stared upon a colossal treeless expanse of worked-out quarries and abandoned mines; a rough, rugged, erratic panorama of soft browns and sickly greens: a quilted blanket thrown over an unsightly mess. McAvoy had felt a distinct unease as he gazed upon the Dale. He recalled similar

sensations in his youth; the incongruous feeling of claustro-
phobia that comes with being alone within an unexplored
vastness. Such areas have always felt laced with a sense of
menace; of something ancient, malevolent; something waiting.
The deeper they drove into the Dale, the more he lost his sense
of geography, his ability to know north from south. He'd
experienced the creeping sensation of being watched from far
away, from above, from below.

'Something in the air, isn't there?' mumbles Roisin. 'It's
like static. I can feel it in my hair.'

McAvoy nods. He would love to be a man of science.
Nothing would make him happier than to be able to dismiss
the whispers and echoes of the supernatural as so much stuff
and nonsense. But he's been a murder detective for twenty
years. He's seen evil up close. He's been led to the final resting
place of sad, delicate bones on the guidance of clairvoyants.
He's seen people killed for their old-world beliefs. He knows
better than most that the modern religions are a veneer over
something older, something deeper. In the bleak and beautiful
wilderness of Weardale, he fancies that even houses with
crosses on the wall will have an iron horseshoe above the
door, and a hagstone hanging somewhere near the bed.

'Nightmare,' he mutters to himself. 'It's going to be a
nightmare.'

In his arms, Roisin wriggles. She's primed for devilment. She
has a lot of things she wants to get off her chest. Cecilia's
seventieth birthday party seems the ideal place to unload. She
smiles, happy in her righteous slumber.

THREE

Petra's house was built as a Methodist chapel. It was designed by Samuel Sanders Teulon, and she's reliably informed that he was, like, the Balenciaga of mid-nineteenth-century architecture. It's got a sharp roof and shiny grey slates and big black railings. Its windows are mullioned, whatever that might mean, and inside it's all wooden floors and vaulted ceilings: so much varnished wood and shiny stone. There's a great chunky Bible on an ornamental lectern in the front hall. John Wesley preached here, apparently. Petra is fourteen and doesn't know with any real certainty what a Methodist is. She fancies it has something to do with the more vanilla type of sexual activity, but she wouldn't put money on it. Nor does she know who John Wesley was, or is, or might still become. He gave a sermon beneath a tree, or something. Attracted quite the crowd. People say 'ooh' when Mum tells them about him, so Petra presumes it's a thing worth mentioning, and so she mentions it herself from time to time. She's even told her old WhatsApp group: her friends from her old school. *Grace, Maddie, Pippa.* Best Friends for Life. They all got matching BFF bracelets when she left, promising that nothing would change, that she'd still be a part of the friend-ship group; she'd still be invited to the parties and the sleepovers and the trips away. It hasn't worked out. They haven't replied. They haven't even checked in. She's pretty sure they've started a new group, just the three of them. And she's got so much to tell them. So much she wants to say. She doubts John Wesley will be the name that changes their approach to her, but she's willing to try anything at this stage. Even the tree. She's far more familiar with the tree. It rises above the little stone wall just next to the curve in the road. It faces the old pub, which sits side-on to the clogged little stream that runs through the little patch of woodland that surrounds the chapel. Dad's had a lot of the wilderness landscaped, but there are still great chunks that have yet to be tamed with railway sleepers and patio slabs and patio heaters. These are the bits she likes best. They're the bits that she thinks John Wesley might still recognize, whoever he was, or is, or might be. She'll make the time to Google him, some day. She'll even look for the old black-and-white photographs of the grim-faced, moustachioed miners who used to scrub the coal from their hands and faces to come and worship in the cold, draughty space that is now her pink and purple bedroom. Just not today. Stuff to do. Always stuff to do.

Petra's surname should be Darling, like Felix. He's a bit funny about her taking ownership of a name that opens doors and greases wheels – talks about how it's an honour, a privilege, and has to be earned. She's a Brett-Fethering, like her mum. She doesn't think Darling is much of an improvement, but Brett-Fethering is a mouthful she's tired of chewing through – especially when her cursed middle name is thrown into the mix. Petra Calpurnia Brett-Fethering is not, she admits, a very gangster name. It's not cool. It's not edgy. Her ex called her Petey for a while, but it never really stuck. He never used her name much anyway. Called her 'sweets' when he was pleased with her. She liked that, even as she told the empty air of WhatsApp that it was cringe.

Petra's sitting on her bed, fiddling with her new guitar. She's wearing her running gear under her big, fake-fur hoodie. It reaches down to her knees. The guitar used to belong to Uncle Ishmael, and his father before that. It's purple, and she likes how it feels tucked under her arm. It's an electric guitar but she hasn't plugged it into the amp. She's not even strumming. She likes moving her fingers over the strings – the pads of her fingers finding the same grooves worn by Ish, and his dad, and a half-century's worth of legendary session musicians. It smells of polish and metal and weed. It's worth a fortune, according to Daddy, and Daddy knows a lot about money. He looks after money for rich people. He runs a company called Felicia Holdings, which invests people's savings into companies that are on the rise. Mum does something similar, though it's smaller and doesn't seem to take very much work. She helps people who aren't very good with their money. She ran

a service for Uncle Ishmael. Saving him from himself,
was the way Daddy described it. She had responsibility for
his estate and provided him with an allowance to live on. It
was an arrangement that suited everybody, and stopped him
going off the rails the way he did when he was younger; a
druggie no-hoper living in a squat and pissing his inheritance
up the wall. Daddy got him sorted. Got him clean. By the
time Ishmael died he was finally living well. She supposes
that's what grown-ups mean when they talk about God having
a perverse sense of humour.

She plucks a string. Tries a chord. Leans in to a wailing
guitar solo, just like Ish's dad: the late, great, devil incarnate:
Moose Piper. She wonders if she can pick up some of his
magnificence through osmosis. She's supposed to put white
gloves on if she wants to play it. It's going to a museum in
London soon. It's going to be imprisoned inside a Perspex
case. She hopes she gets a chance to bash out a power solo
with the amp cranked up to eleven before she has to say her
goodbyes to it, and in her way, to him. Ish was never really
famous, but his dad was. Famous in a way John Wesley could
probably only dream of. Ish's dad was Moose Piper and he
was a Fucking Legend, according to the internet, and people.
He was in The Place. He was a Proper Fucking Rock Star.
He drank with David Bowie and partied with Roger Daltrey
and slept with groupies and movie stars and once shot himself
in the head with a tranquilliser gun on live TV. He did coke
and smoked weed and got arrested for smashing up hotel
rooms and driving cars into people's swimming pools. He
drank a gallon of vodka a day and was once pictured with
blood pouring from his mouth while midway through a guitar
solo, his pancreas having exploded mid-set. He died before
Petra was born. She's made the time to Google the particulars.
She knows all about the man called Moose, and the paranoia
that swallowed him up in his last years. Died of fright,
according to the stories. Heart gave out as he was performing
some exotic summoning ritual with a rabbi and a ukulele
player, trying to draw out the evil spirit he'd convinced himself
was haunting his plunge pool in Beverly Hills.

That was in 1999. Ishmael was already off on his own

adventure at the time: deep into the drink and the drugs and the decadence that it would take him another decade and half to claw his way free from. She's heard the locals call Ishmael's death 'untimely'. Heard them say it was 'such a bloody shame'. One even called it 'a kindness, in its way'. Petra doesn't agree. Ishmael might have been ill, but he wasn't dying. He could have been around for years. He could have seen Delilah grow up. He could have played a love song at Petra's wedding. But he's dead, his body six feet beneath the wet soil of St Mary's, while those he loved and who loved him back fight like cats in a sack over who gets what. She sometimes wonders whether they even care who killed him. She knows for a fact that none of them give a toss about Heloise. Just another bit of fluff, according to Daddy's solicitor, when she'd listened at the window to his study. A shame, but not germane to the issue at hand . . .

Petra had Googled the word 'germane'. She'd Googled Heloise, too. And he'd been right. The papers barely even mentioned who she was. Just a woman. Just the girlfriend. Just the lass in the bed upstairs, her lungs full of smoke, her skin and hair ablaze as the roof caved in and buried her in a maelstrom of fire and brick and stone. Heloise Guillou, originally from the little oyster-picking commune of Cancale in Brittany. She played the harmonium and had blue dreadlocks and Petra had always thought her singing voice was better than anybody she was supposed to have heard of. She was a little witchy. Made potions and amulets and cast the occasional charm. Enchanted Uncle Ish, that much was true. Delilah loved her nearly as much as Joy. Heloise. Dead at twenty-nine.

'Petra, I can see Georgia outside! She's flashing her light!' Daddy calls from downstairs.

Petra puts the guitar down, carefully, on her bed. She checks her reflection in the mirror on her sloping ceiling. Big eyes, good skin: hair in a tight tangle of coal-dark curls. She supposes she's pretty, if such things are important. Her old friends used to tell her she was beautiful, but she told them that they were, and in truth, Pippa looked like something that should live at the bottom of the ocean. There's a girl she goes to her athletics club with who could pass for a blobfish if she took her glasses off and pulled a sad face, but Petra's a nice person, and would tell her, if asked, that she's gorgeous. They used to say different things in their private WhatsApp groups, of course. Snapchat too. That's how it's meant to go, after all. There's what you say with your public face and what you say in the privacy of your own intimate friendships. She can say what she wants to Georgia, who's waiting outside for her now. Georgia's her new best friend and closest mate and Total BFF and confidante. She's her amigo, her intimate, her coun-sellor and consigliere. They've been close for almost eight months now and she can't imagine there'll ever be a time when she doesn't tell her everything, or near enough. Georgia would help Petra get rid of a body, if she asked. She'd withstand torture for her. She'd give her an alibi. She'd do time for her. Georgia has promised all this, and more, and Petra believes her. She'd do the same for her, after all. Georgia's been there through the bad times. And there's been nothing else since Ishmael and Heloise died, and their little sugarbun got herself hurt. Everything's been horrible since. Nobody's got time for her. None of the people she likes are being nice to each other any more. They're all fighting. Arguing. It's all solicitors and accountants and laptops slammed shut; whisky tumblers hitting walls and cars peeling away in screeches of rubber and grit.

'Petra! She's waiting!'

Petra switches her bedroom light off, the way she's been told to. Mummy and Daddy aren't made of money, after all. *And there's the environmental impact to consider, Petra. Did you know that . . .*

Petra moves quietly down the big wide staircase. Daddy's in his studio with the fat little lawyer and the police officer with the hair that doesn't seem to know where it wants to part. Mummy's in the living room, doing yoga in front of the TV: slouch socks and Lycra, lurid pink headband and noise-cancelling headphones. There's a protein shake on the coffee table: some spinachy grossness that smells like cat-farts. She's got a Toblerone for afters. Petra doesn't let herself look at Mum for long. She can't stand to let her gaze linger. She's so bloody dull, so bloody feeble, such a total waste of time. She's always got a wobble to her lip, a tear in her eye; always looks like she's about to break some terrible news. Petra can't believe she used to think her mum was awesome.

'*Petra!*' She stops outside her father's study door. She knows he has to lecture her about safety before he lets her leave to meet her friend. He always does. Waits for him to shout for her again. Puts on her sweetest expression and opens the door like a 1950s housewife about to enquire whether the gentlemen would care for a cup of tea.

Felix Darling is seated in an ergonomic desk seat: back rests and head rests and an abundance of shiny cream leather. It doesn't suit him. He looks like a burglar who's decided to log on to the homeowner's laptop and take care of his correspondence. He's a short, round man with a perfectly round head, smooth as a watermelon on top and subtly dusted with stubble around the back and sides. There's grey in his goatee and dust on his glasses and he has his hands stuffed in the front pocket of his big blue hoodie, rowing club logo almost faded away. He doesn't look like he used to. Looks like a man in pain.

'Hi Daddy,' says Petra, lingering in the doorway. She glances at her father's companions. Greenwood's still youngish, for an adult. Maybe thirty, no more. He's slim, and slight, and full of a weird kind of energy that means he can't sit still. He's wearing a tailored suit but it's wrinkled and shiny and clings to his knotty frame like crinkly Lycra. He's all edges: a triangular sort of a chap. The knot in his tie is far too big. There's a rash on his neck. Petra doesn't like him. Doesn't like the other one either. She's got a pleased-with-herself look on her face, even when she's got no right to. Looks like she's trying too hard in her Doc Martens and her flared cords and her fluffy black V-neck jumper. She's always got this look on her face, like she knows more than she's letting on. She has an ability to make Petra feel guilty about stuff she hasn't done. Petra gives a nervous little half-wave to both. Tara gives that sly smile – her nostrils flaring a little, as if she's already detecting a foul-smelling lie in the air.

'Come in, Petra – you're letting the heat out.'

Petra does as she's asked. She leans against the bookcase. It's the only part of the room that suits her daddy's personality.

It's a jumble: a big, scattered mix of new and old; kempt and chaotic. There are first editions and leather-bound classics pushed up against charity shop paperbacks. There are teacups and interesting stones and odd little ceramic creations deposited in random places on the rustic wooden shelves. The rest of the office is all clean lines and savage angles. His desk is glass; the wires neatly tucked into tubes and tacked to the wall. He has two computers set up on the desk, his laptop open between them. It looks like a child out for a walk with its parents.

'You know Greenwood,' says Daddy, waving a hand at his solicitor. 'And Tara, of course.'

Petra doesn't meet her eye. To Daddy, she's Tara, an old friend of the family. To people like Deon, she's Mrs Tara Chopard. She's important. She's deputy police and crime commissioner for Durham Constabulary and her family owns a good chunk of the Dale. She's good, apparently, though she couldn't find the house without phoning up twice for directions, and she's done her eye make-up better on one eye than the other. She looks somehow feline: a haughty cat seated on a lap she's no bloody right to.

'One hour,' says Daddy, smiling tightly. 'And I'm trusting you, yes? Trusting Georgia too. And you stick to the route. No deviations. Yes?'

Petra gives her sweetest smile. Looks embarrassed and casts her eyes down at the floor. She fiddles with the binding of a leathery book, mumbling something inarticulate about knowing the rules and not needing to hear them again.

'Sorry,' mutters Daddy. 'I'm going on, aren't I? You have your fun, yes? Proud of you. Yes. Pop back in after, if you like. Tell me how you get on. Those trainers still fit, yes? Yes.'

Petra appreciates the effort. He's trying to be like he used to be. He's trying to care. But Daddy can't think of anything other than Uncle Ishmael. It breaks her heart. She wishes she felt confident enough to give him a cuddle and kiss his cheek and tell him everything will be OK. Instead she nods her head. Watches him shift his attention back to his guests. They shift uncomfortably. Neither of them wants to be here. Neither of them wants to make small-talk.

'Cold for jogging, isn't it?' asks Greenwood, making the effort. 'Can't think of anything worse!'

'I could,' snaps Felix. 'I reckon I could think of all manner of worse things than being fourteen and going for a jog with my friend in a lovely little village after dark, Greenwood. Christ, don't you ever engage your brain before you open your mouth?'

Petra slips away. Closes the door behind her – the voices trapped inside.

Mum's waiting at the back door, looking ridiculous and jittery. 'She's still waiting. Is she not cold? I wish you'd invite her in. It seems so mean to have her standing out there but the atmosphere in the house – it's not really . . . well, it's conducive to, well, it's just not conducive, is it? And maybe a shower before bed, eh? Your grandfather will be here for brunch and who knows how busy we'll be putting our faces on for that. God, it's going to be dreadful, isn't it? Shall we just slip away? You can pretend you're poorly like we used to when you had to give a presentation . . .'

Mum holds out the luminous yellow bands that she insists Petra wear if she goes jogging after dark. Petra's never worn them. She hasn't done anything her mum has asked for as long as she can remember. She can't even look at her without wanting to shake her. She's so pathetic. So bloody wishy-washy. Such a let-down. Who does she think she is, giving her advice? Asking like she's still a baby – acting like she isn't excited about the party with the rich guests and the good food and the golden opportunity to show off how bloody splendid the Darlings are – even since they've been mixed up in all of this nasty business.

'You wear them,' snaps Petra. 'And I always shower after running. Why wouldn't I shower after running? I'd come and tell you, if I didn't think you'd start sniffing me to make sure that I haven't been out with Deon. God, it's like living in a prison! I can't breathe!'

Mummy's bottom lip trembles. Her eyes look like wet marbles. Oh God, she's such a drama queen.

'Please, Petra. I worry.'

Petra rolls her eyes. 'I don't need it. I've told you I don't need it. There's no cars on the route. It's all trees! What's going to run me over? A fox?'

Mummy drops the yellow bands on the floor by the pile of shoes. She's small. Squishy. She's got short hair and pulls faces that are too expressive, too extravagant, too characterful. She's a geek. She's so cringe. Petra can't stand her. Loves her to the bone and hates her with a passion.

'Back for eight,' says Mum.

'He already said,' snaps Petra. 'God, if you would just talk to each other, I wouldn't feel like I was living with an echo.'

'Sorry,' says Mum. There's sweat on her top lip and in her hairline. The front of her vest is moist with perspiration. She puts her arms out, hopeful for a hug. Petra can see down her sleeve. She hasn't even shaved her armpits. Oh *gross!*

Petra walks past her. Opens the back door and steps out into the cold and the rain. The darkness slaps her so many unforgiving palms. She jogs across the gravel, past Daddy's car, and on to the slick blackness of the road. She squints into the wind. Georgia's there, jogging on the spot. Her glasses are jewelled with rain: her long brown hair plastered across her face. She looks sportier than Petra, but Petra's the fitter, the faster, the stronger.

'Did you do it?' asks Georgia, huddling into her hoodie. They have a little cuddle: wetness and darkness and sweat. 'Did you? I haven't checked – I daren't.' She pulls a small, cheap-looking mobile phone from the pocket of her leggings. The screen is blue – there's a call in progress. She takes the phone. Holds it to her ear. She can hear her father. He hasn't noticed the mobile she left on his bookshelf, tucked among the clutter on his shelf. She wishes it didn't have to come to this. Wishes he'd just tell her what's happening. But he thinks she's a kid. Thinks he's protecting her from it all. He has no bloody idea.

'Here,' says Petra, and reaches into her sock. She pulls out another little phone, the screen cracked, the rubber almost worn off. It's almost an antique. Still works, though. 'Tell him we'll be there at half past,' says Petra, and hands the phone to her friend. 'Tell him what we need.'

Georgia does as she's asked. There's only one number in the phone. Georgia likes pretending to be Petra. She even puts a kiss on the end of the message. She gets a message back a moment later and hands the phone back. Petra nods, satisfied at a job well done.

'Come on, Greenwood,' mutters Petra. 'Spill your guts for me . . .'

'Is it working?' asks Georgia, eagerly. She presses her face to her friend's, eyes gleaming. She hears Felix. Hears the little lawyer. Hears Tara. They're arguing. Petra keeps telling her that her dad is sad. He doesn't sound sad to Georgia. He sounds furious.

'. . . *hasn't returned a phone call in three days! You said she was sound. Said we'd be getting somewhere by now!*'

'*She's good but she does things her own way, Felix. Very much the lone wolf, though that's because nobody likes her and she doesn't share information the way she's supposed to. But she's been thorough. I've got all the statements. But if the little weasel won't speak, he won't speak. I didn't know they had history and it's not for me to tell the chief superintendent who to appoint to a murder enquiry. But she'll get there,' Tara says. 'If Deon has anything to do with it, she'll find out.*'

'*Can't they just turn the tapes off for a little while. Lean on him a little. Deon knows something. I mean, the thought of it – him and my little girl. You could do him for that, surely.*'

'*You want to start that up again? There is no evidence of any sexual impropriety with your daughter. It was a couple of cans of Coke in a car park and a peck on the cheek, Felix.*'

'*And Joy? She just carries on as if nothing's changed, does she? Inherits the best part of half a million and all future royalties? He appointed me as executor. For God's sake, my wife has kept him on the right track for the best part of ten years. I don't want his money, you know that, but I can't just give it to the woman who might have killed him!*'

'*There's still the possibility that nobody killed him, Felix. He was ill and frail and he fell. He left a joint burning. It started a fire and Heloise perished. You're within your rights to keep blocking the will, but there has to come a point when you accept that it might just be a tragic accident.*'

'*No! He was frightened. He thought she was trying to hurt him.*'

'He had a serious illness, Felix. He was getting paranoid. And he was smoking weed. There was Spice in his system. He shouldn't even have been in charge of his little girl that night. Joy stormed out because she couldn't take it any more. She was sitting in her car on a hillside, crying her eyes out.'

'That's no blasted alibi, Greenwood!'

'They need the money, Felix. She's going to need more surgeries. They can't keep living where they're living.'

'I paid for the headstone, didn't I?'

'This "last roll of the dice" that you mentioned. Am I going to have to worry?'

'God, no. Not even my idea. Just something to indulge the old man, really. Bloody oaf's managed to land a few medals and some friendly headlines but he's still the same silly squealer he was at school. Can't think of anybody less suited to be a policeman. But if you can't set a cat among the pigeons, you can always rustle up a mouse, eh? And he looks the part. I'll bet Deon soiled himself when Saville showed him his picture, eh? God, I suppose he's here by now, isn't he? Running up a hefty tab on Daddy's good name, I shouldn't wonder. You know he married a Gypsy, don't you? I mean, how priceless . . .'

Georgia shivers as the cold and the rain leach through her running gear and adhere to her skin. She feels Petra move away from her. Georgia goes back to running on the spot, waiting to be told, waiting to be given a task she can carry out to stay involved; to stay connected; to remain a part of this. Petra is the most exciting thing that has ever happened to her. Petra, with her rich dad and her rich grandad and her dead uncle and her bad-boy boyfriend that she's not allowed to see any more because her dad thinks he might have killed his best friend and his wife up on the moors. She'd do anything for Petra. Anything.

'Shut up, Georgia. I need to hear.'

Petra closes her eyes and leans back against the tree. She feels the excitement build in her chest. By the morning, she knows she's going to have a story to tell her old friends. She'll know what it's like to break somebody's heart. And she'll have met Uncle Aector, white sheep of the family, despite his blood-splattered fleece.

FOUR

'By God, sir! Oh give that man a rosette!'

McAvoy shrinks in behind Roisin, his entire manner that of a toddler suddenly addressed by an overly friendly stranger.

'Oh yes, sir, that's a winner. It does a chap good to see somebody with a bit of snazz. Or Pizzazz. All that jazz. You're not a fan of the skinny jean either, I see? Good man, good man. Second worst item of clothing, I reckon. First is a polo neck, if you're asking. It's like being strangled by a really weak bloke, don't you think? And skinny jeans? Jesus, you're afraid to fart in case your knees swell up.'

The voice drifts up from behind the reception desk. It's warm, friendly and very Geordie and belongs to a man who could well pass for Aector's brother. He's a big pink rhinoceros in a tweed suit: shaved head bisected by a mighty quiff. His designer glasses are perched in the centre of a face that is more beard than skin. He's the receptionist and is so firmly wedged into his leather swivel chair that there's a good chance it will lift up with him if he starts to stand. He wears a loud waistcoat, louder tie, and a shirt that is positively screaming. His name badge reads, somewhat unnecessarily, *Big Harry*. He's beholding McAvoy with almost religious reverence.

'Sorry?' asks Roisin. 'Are you talking to my husband?'

Roisin's used to being the centre of attention and in her turquoise dress and sparkling purple stilettos, she certainly doesn't think of herself as anybody's sidekick or support act.

'Oh I love that,' says Big Harry, nodding again in appreciation. 'The collarless number. And the braces. Bottom button left undone, eh? A sophisticated gent. You ever watch that Edwardian dude on YouTube? He's the one who's got me dreaming of plus-fours but the little wife says that if I buy a pair she'll divorce me for looking like a twat, and I don't reckon she's lying. Still hasn't forgiven me the cowboy boots, if I'm honest.' He plonks his foot on his desk. He's wearing alligator-skin boots, complete with spurs. 'Word of advice – take them off before you get yourself comfy on the sofa. Sit on your heels for a moment and you're half the man you used to be, if you know what I'm saying.'

McAvoy finds himself smiling. He likes Big Harry. Roisin, beside him, gestures at herself and performs a little curtsey. 'This pass muster, does it, Big Harry?'

'You, milady, are a bloody bobby-dazzler,' says Big Harry, nodding. 'I'd have said so when you came in but your husband here looks like he's disembowelled a couple of people in his time, so I thought it best to keep me own counsel. 'ere, do me a solid, big man. Stick that up on the hook behind you.'

McAvoy reacts instinctively as the small, glass-fronted picture frame is tossed his way. He feels like a Labrador catching a Frisbee. He likes Big Harry's somewhat relaxed approach to his concierge duties, but wonders how it goes down with the more tweedy, V-neck-jumpered, Range-Rover-and-gundog guests. He looks at the picture in the frame. It shows a trim, handsome man with a slightly embarrassed look on his face, handing over a big cheque to the local Air Ambulance service. He's wearing a neckerchief and beanie hat and a silver earring hangs from his left earlobe, a gold tooth in his smile. There are tattoos on his hands and a tangle of leather thongs and assorted medallions dangle at his neck, disappearing into the front of his bomber jacket.

'Ishmael Piper,' says Big Harry, spreading his hands and examining his square, clean nails. He looks up, clearly awaiting a response. 'Bit of a divisive figure, God rest him.'

McAvoy feels a faint memory tickling away inside his brain and briefly succeeds in quieting the urgent demands for attention from his stomach. Wonders if it's the somewhat literary first name, or the Highland-friendly 'Piper' that pricked his attention.

'His dad was lead guitarist in The Place, wasn't he?' asks Roisin, looking at the picture. 'Handsome devil. Nice chunk of money he's handing over there. Living off the inheritance, was he?'

McAvoy suddenly remembers the news bulletin. It had been

way down on the agenda – a titbit on a slow news day. The son of legendary rocker Moose Piper, dead in a house fire. There'd been a kid involved, hadn't there? A woman, too. Ishmael had been ill. Some suggestion of an accident; some hint at suicide gone wrong.

'Some of the locals can't stand to look at him,' says Big Harry. 'Others reckon he was the second coming, or whatever type of Messiah would get to sleep with two women at the same time. Mate of mine, after a fashion. Always bought a round, helped out if he heard a sob story. I think he deserves his place on the wall – the other receptionist always takes him down. Neither of us are backing off. Anyway, he's Felix's mate and Felix has got the old lord-of-the-manor vibe down pat. He'll no doubt be in for a snifter before the night's through and there'd be Hell to pay if he wasn't on the wall. Still a bit raw for a lot of people and it doesn't help that his little lass is such an adorable little bugger. She were so beautiful. Would break his heart to see her.'

McAvoy does as he's instructed and hangs the picture on the hook. It hangs askew. He feels an unpleasant chill spread across his shoulders. Feels the need to pee.

'He's a friend of Felix's?' he asks, quietly. 'Felix Darling?'

'Oh aye – forgot you were part of the birthday shindig. Aye, best of mates. Chums, I think they'd call it. Felix is fighting a one-man battle to stop the rumours spreading, of course. No secrets in a village like this, and rumours can get themselves from Baybridge to Edmundbyers before the truth's even finished its warm-up exercises. He's buried in the churchyard. Last plot on the right. Those of us who give a toss try and keep it nice, but for others it's the perfect place to relieve yourself, if you know what I'm saying. Oh, here's Cordy. She's your waitress, or something close to it. Have a lovely evening.'

McAvoy turns to see a young, eager-looking woman in a checked shirt and dark trousers. She has short hair and wears round glasses that make her look a little like an owl on amphetamines. 'If you'd follow me?'

McAvoy suddenly wants to linger. He's got a copper's instincts and can't help but think that Big Harry has been awfully free with information about such a sensitive suspect.

He has no doubt that Trish Pharaoh, were she standing in front of him, would plonk herself on the edge of the big man's desk and cajole him into telling her the entire story. But McAvoy isn't Pharaoh, and Roisin, her hand in his, wants her dinner.

'We'll maybe have a natter later, eh?' says Big Harry, to McAvoy's back. 'Oh, while you're waiting for your amuse-bouche, have a look at this . . .'

McAvoy turns to see an old, dog-eared book flying across reception. He snatches it out of the air. It's a pinkish colour and the front cover is illegible: a swirl of smudges and hard-to-read copperplate. He peers at the cover. It's *Witchcraft Detected and Prevented* or *The School of Black Art*, by P. Buchan. McAvoy glances at Roisin. Wonders whether Harry is taking the piss.

'We've got a talk next month. Witchcraft in Weardale. Local bloke. Been badgering us for a bloody age. Not many takers yet so I'm doing my bit and banging the drum. If you've got an interest in the supernatural, should be a blast. We've got a themed menu and everything. Pumpkin soup and four other courses. If you want to know about Leddy Lister and the girls, he's your man.'

Roisin squeezes the skin on Aector's wrist. 'I'm fecking starving.'

'Thanks,' says McAvoy, and tucks the book into his pocket. 'Will have a gander.'

They're led into a dining room that wouldn't look out of place in the court of a king. It's all exposed brick and ancient wooden tables, uneven flagstones and guttering candles. Swords, pikes and ancient muskets form a lethal-looking fan upon the far wall, and a colossal wrought-iron candle-holder dangles peril-ously over a great open fire. There are half a dozen tables, sparkling with pristine glassware and polished cutlery. Cordy leads them to a table by the window. It would offer a view of the gardens and the nearby churchyard if it weren't already black as pitch beyond the glass.

'You're wanting to swing from that, I can tell,' says Roisin, grinning, as McAvoy frees her seat from beneath the little wooden table and seats her with gentlemanly gallantry. 'Thank you, good sir,' she says, and her giggle becomes a full-throated laugh as McAvoy trips over his own feet and clatters into his own chair with a thud. He finds himself laughing too, even as he mouths apologetic platitudes to the other diners.

'I'll let you have a moment then come back with the wine list,' says Cordy, standing to attention at their side. McAvoy can't help but give her a policeman's appraising glance. She's smartly dressed and her shirt has been ironed, but her dark jeans disappear into a pair of skateboarding shoes and her socks, peeking out between sneaker and trouser cuff, don't match.

'I'm not one for wine,' says Roisin, wrinkling her nose. 'His fancy piece drinks litres of the stuff. Smokes, too. Honestly, it's amazing her teeth aren't the colour of humbugs. No, pint of bitter for the gentleman and I'll have a gin and orange please. And tap water. Actually, no, we're not paying, are we? OK, expensive water, in a blue bottle. Ta.'

McAvoy flashes a desperate grin at the waitress. 'I don't have a fancy piece,' he says, wincing. 'Honestly.'

Cordy looks from one to the other. Weighs him up with a waitress's appraising eye. 'I believe you,' she says. 'Why go out for burgers when you've got steak at home, eh?'

'I like you, Cordy,' says Roisin, lifting the nearest knife and checking her teeth for lipstick in the reflection. 'I sense we're going to be bestest buds.'

McAvoy looks across the table at his wife and enjoys the look of merry devilment that plays across her features as artfully as the flickering candlelight. He reaches across the table and takes her dainty, fake-tanned hands in his great broken fists. 'I love you,' he says, holding her gaze. 'You know I don't care what they think, don't you? Whatever they might say – whatever she comes out with . . . none of it matters.'

Roisin shrugs. 'I genuinely couldn't give a shit what the old baggage thinks about me. Your dad doesn't like me much either, but he knows I make you happy and that's good enough for him. Your mother? Christ, she doesn't even deserve the name. I'm only here to make sure nobody makes you feel like you're anything less than fecking marvellous. If nowt else, it's a free fecking holiday. When was the last time we didn't have the kids? I was starting to think that eating out had to involve a Wacky Warehouse. The party's neither here nor there. It's just a chance to be away, isn't it? You and me. We never got to do much of this, did we? Wining and dining and pleasingly reclining? You put a baby in me the first time we did it. I reckon we're entitled to a couple of nights of luxury, eh? And just think, when we have sex, I'll even get to make noise!'

McAvoy turns at the sound of Cordy's polite little cough. She places the drinks down in front of them and hands them each a wooden clipboard bearing a small but exquisite menu.

'I like the schnitzel,' says Cordy, under her breath, as if imparting a fiercely guarded code-word at a border crossing. 'Oh, sorry, the goat's cheese isn't available today. We're having some problems with our supplier. Brexit, I suppose.'

McAvoy tries not to look too disappointed. He orders the pate and the schnitzel. Roisin plumps for the black pudding Scotch egg and the steak. She may be half his size but she matches him chip for chip. They talk and laugh and tell each other funny stories about the children. They listen to the rain and the wind against the glass and the clink of glasses on wood; silverware upon crockery; the satisfied chomp-chomp-chomp of denture against veal. They don't mention the dead man whose picture has been returned to the wall.

'That was amazing,' says Roisin, when Cordy scurries back to take their plates. She looks flushed and keeps throwing a glance back over her shoulder towards the bar. There are loud voices within. Loud voices and harsh laughs.

'All good?' asks McAvoy, catching her eye.

'High spirits,' says Cordy, distractedly. She manages a smile. 'Shooting party. They're not really listening to the whole "no-cigar" rule. Their bar bill's up to thirty grand so we have to rather indulge them.'

Roisin find a discarded chip on her lap and uses it to wipe a smear of poached egg from McAvoy's plate, even as it's being borne aloft in Cordy's hands. 'I can go fuck them up, if you like,' she says, matter-of-factly. 'Here for the grouse, are they?'

Maddie nods. 'Another few weeks of it yet. You'll have seen the Range Rovers?'

'At least that's something in your mother's favour,' says Roisin, chattily, directing her words at her husband. 'At least she's an animal lover.' She gives her attention back to Cordy. 'Very important lady, his mum. Did a lot of important work in Africa. Real charitable heart, that one. Marches for all sorts of good causes. Sent her son off to be tortured and neglected at boarding school when he was ten years old, of course, but it's all about the greater good, isn't it? I do hope you'll be serving at the party, Cordy – we could have a ball.'

Cordy looks at McAvoy, who gives a little shrug. He's not going to leap to anybody's defence – not when the person on the attack is the one who has spent a decade and a half repairing the holes in his heart.

'Another round, if you get the chance please. And the dessert menu, obviously.'

McAvoy sits back. Tunes out the hubbub from next door. He's on to his second pint. Roisin, never a regular drinker, is making up for lost time and has just polished off her second gin and orange. She has her heart set on a double espresso and an amaretto coffee but he knows she won't be able to sit and let her dinner settle without first popping outside for a cigarette.

'I think I'll just . . .'

McAvoy smiles. 'Want me to come with you?'

She shakes her head. 'I'll have a little toddle in the garden. Maybe make a friend. It's all very *Wolf Hall*, isn't it? If I see any hooded monks, I'll give you a yell.'

She kisses him full on the lips and heads for the big stone archway that leads to the back of the hotel. He notices that she's kicked her shoes off and is walking barefoot across the paving slabs. He watches her until she's out of sight. Only when he feels thoroughly unobserved does he pull his phone from his trouser pocket and check his messages. Fin wants him to know that everything is fine and that they're having a lovely time and that Sophia is taking really good care of them. Lilah wants him to know that Fin is a fecking arsehole who's gone power mad in the absence of their parents and is making her stick to her homework timetable like a big ginger Hitler. McAvoy grins, covering his face with his free hand. Lilah's eight now and has been running rings around all of them since the moment she could stand. Fin, not quite fourteen, endures more than any big brother should have to.

McAvoy settles back in his chair. He'd like to undo a button but fancies it would be frowned upon. He tunes himself in to the background noises the way he always does when Roisin isn't taking up his full attention. He tries to get a sense of the building. He knows there's another dining room and a snug of sorts up the giant stone staircase, its walls patterned with huge gilt-edged portraits of austere, moustachioed men and women. He has no doubt that his stepfather and his ilk will know who they are. Duke this, Baron that, Viscount The-Other. It all matters to Crawford Darling and his ilk: men of Empire; men with stiff upper lips and calcified hearts and more money than they could ever know what to do with in a hundred lifetimes. He has little doubt that Crawford used to be whipping boy for some prince or future king back in those glorious days of cold showers and life-affirming violence. Has little doubt that his eyes fill with nostalgic mist at the sound of carpet slipper striking corduroy.

'Excuse me? Young lady? Oh, sorry, young man. No, right the first time. What a world! Might I ask . . .?'

McAvoy doesn't turn his head. The voice comes from somewhere over his left shoulder. It's English. Cambridgeshire, if he's any judge.

'Yes, might I enquire whether the forecast has changed its mind at all? I've left the old gadget up in our quarters and, dash it all, I do feel as if the pressure is dropping. Our companions, you see – sitting on the tarmac waiting for the OK.'

McAvoy decides he doesn't care whether it appears rude or not. He's had nearly two pints of ale and feels positively devil-may-care. He turns around and casts a quick glance over the elderly couple seated in the glare of the big open fire. He's a stout man in a blue double-breasted blazer and neatly pressed cream slacks, old school tie and a pocket square; silvery hair so wispy it might be entirely theoretical, boozer's nose and rheumy eyes. She's short and round and is wearing an eruption of pleated fuchsia. Her feet, squeezed into wide-fitting shoes, don't reach the floor. She notices McAvoy watching and gives him a pleasant smile that's all false teeth and red wine.

'Our friends are coming by helicopter,' she says, one hand theatrically over her mouth. 'Weather can be terrible here, I don't know if you've heard. Eight days without power a couple of years back, if you can credit it. And up the valley, out towards Nenthead, the snows come in like something from a film. It's rather odd, feeling sorry for somebody who's waiting to board a private helicopter, but I can't imagine it will be much fun in the dark – not with the storm on its way.'

McAvoy pulls a face that implies he shares their pain. 'Here for the birthday party, are you?'

The lady puts a finger to her lips. 'Hush hush, now. Big surprise. Though if you ask me, Cecilia knows exactly what he's up to. No pulling the wool over her eyes. Brain like a razor. You'll be from her side of the family, I presume?'

McAvoy wishes he hadn't spoken. Cordy saves him the agony of reply.

'Weather is getting worse but there's going to be a break in the storm first thing tomorrow so your companions will be arriving around breakfast time. They send their apologies. Don't worry, we're in contact with them and the other members of the party.'

The woman turns to McAvoy, shaking her head. 'Well, looks like it's going to be a wild one. We were going to take a wander up to see Felix, but that rain's really coming down now. Will your lady friend be OK without a coat?'

'She's tough,' says McAvoy. 'Tougher than me. She likes to feel like she's part of nature. She's never happier than standing in the rain.'

'Wouldn't do for me,' says the man, with a shake of his head and a poorly stifled belch. 'Still, looker like that, you'll forgive them their little idiosyncrasies, eh? I certainly wouldn't kick her out of bed for eating pickled eggs.'

His wife shoots him a look. He grins back. She softens her expression, indulging him.

'Do ignore him. He's had a brandy and some chocolate liqueurs. He's determined to make a show of me.'

'You'll be the stepbrother, I shouldn't wonder,' says the man, fixing McAvoy with a hard stare. 'The stepson, I mean. Cecilia's lad. From the . . .' he lowers his voice, as if the place might be bugged. 'From the marriage . . . before, as it were. The Scotsman.'

'Oh, Hector, is it?' asks the woman, clapping her fleshy hands together. 'I'm Patricia. This is Richard, though you won't hear him answering to that when he's with his pals. He gets "Sally", but I'd encourage you not to ask why. But you'll know all about tricky names, I shouldn't wonder. They call you "Eck", is that right? What's it short for? Ecky Thump?'

McAvoy takes a moment. Finishes his pint. Gives a nod. He wants Roisin to come back right now.

'Good of you to make the effort,' says Richard, nodding approvingly. He's sweating a little, the flickering shadows cast by the fire smearing a gloss over his porcine, jowly face. He looks like a ham, recently glazed. 'No doubt it will mean a lot to her. You're the surprise package, I presume. All seems a bit silly to me. Seventy-nine next birthday and I'm having to keep secrets and remember who knows what about what. Most of the buggers coming down from the family seat are hunkered down in the hunting lodge up at the big house. Sheikh Something-or-other. Wouldn't do for me. Happy to be safe and warm in a nice hotel, thanks all the same. You'll be coming up for brunch, I presume? Jumping out to give Cecilia quite the surprise.'

McAvoy squeezes his hands together. He'd like Cordy to come back. He casts around for something he can say to keep the conversation going. 'I understand Crawford's son lives here, is that right?'

'Crawford's son,' says Patricia, beaming, as if McAvoy's made a joke. 'Your brother, you mean? Felix. I forget his wife's name. You'll have to walk us through the family tree. Am I right in thinking you grew up in some little shack on the moors before Crawford swooped in? They told us the story years ago, but I shouldn't wonder that you're here. Much to be grateful for, eh? Quite the philanthropist, is Crawford. Every penny he's made, he's given something back.'

McAvoy decides he'd rather throw himself in the fire than continue the conversation, and that it would lead to considerably less catastrophic results than if he started telling Patricia and Richard just how badly they've been misinformed. He pretends his phone's ringing instead. Gives an apologetic smile and turns away.

'Hello . . . hi, yes . . . no, go on, no problem . . .'

He has a pretend conversation for a couple of minutes. Ends the imaginary call only when Richard and Patricia have said goodnight to the waitress and toddled towards the stairs in a cloud of floral perfume, talcum powder and fart.

McAvoy glances around. There's nobody else in the restaurant. There are laughs and shouts and whoops coming from the little crypt bar next door. He wonders whether Roisin has abandoned him – whether he's missed some unspoken clue that he should come and find her. He plays with his phone instead. He shifts in his seat and feels the book digging into his thigh. Pulls it out and leafs through the pages. It's thin and written on poor-quality paper. There are footnotes on every page. It's a spell book. Spells to kill a mad dog, spells to draw fish together, incantations to stop bees leaving your land; enchantments to discern if a man's wife be chaste, to allay tempests, to procure love. The most recent name written on the inside leaf is Leonard Nightingale. There have been plenty of owners before. McAvoy puts the book back in his pocket. He fancies that, when it comes to otherworldly help, Roisin has got him covered.

Still bored, still looking for distraction, he fiddles with his phone. Decides to read a little about the hotel. About the village. About the storms last year.

The ninth item found by the search engine is a newspaper article from April.

House Where Rocker's Son Perished to be Demolished
He can't help it.
He clicks on the link.

A REMOTE farmhouse ravaged by fire is to be demolished brick-by-brick so that police can search the ruins for evidence of foul play.

Pressor Villas was home to Ishmael Piper, the son of legendary rock star Moose. Ishmael's body was found in the grounds of the burning building last month. The body of his live-in girlfriend, Heloise Guillou, 29, was recovered the following day.

Experts have been brought in to take down 160 tons of bricks and mortar of the isolated home in rural Weardale, County Durham.

Police have not ruled out foul play.

Officers confirmed they are preserving what is left of the 150-year-old property as a potential crime scene.

One of the walls has collapsed since the fire and it is unsafe for investigators to venture inside.

Detective Inspector Kate Saville said: 'My primary objective is to preserve evidence while being sympathetic and caring to the family of those who died in this tragedy.

'The building is unstable and will be taken down brick-by brick before we can go in there.'

It is thought that Mr Piper, who was suffering from Huntington's Disease, was found just outside the property. He had suffered serious head wounds. The cause of the blaze has yet to be ascertained but it is understood that Ms Guillou, a practising white witch, was interested in 'candle-magic' and may have been using the full moon to 'charge' her occult paraphernalia. Mr Piper's seven-year-old daughter by a previous relationship suffered serious burns to her face and hands in the blaze.

Durham Constabulary said the girl was 'traumatized' and is being interviewed by specially trained officers to establish the cause.

A team of twenty officers are involved in the investigation, along with forensic scientists and fire experts.

Scaffolders have been brought in to stabilize the remaining walls and a temporary roof has gone up to preserve the scene from the weather.

The work has been slowed down because asbestos was discovered in the building.

DI Saville said: 'At the moment the cause of this intense fire is unexplained. We have spoken to neighbours and there is nothing to support suspicious circumstances.'

Villagers in nearby Blanchland, who launched a JustGiving page to help provide clothing and support for the seven-year-old and her mum, Joy Horsley, were slammed on social media for the gesture.

One Twitter user, MaggieB58, said: 'He was a bloody multi-millionaire! It's very sad but she hardly needs the money, does she? Her dad inherited all of Moose's estate and those songs were worth a fortune. There are lots of people more deserving of a bit of charity.'

Ishmael inherited a sum rumoured to be in excess of eight million pounds when his father died in 1999. Inheritance taxes demanded by the Inland Revenue took a great bite out of the estate and Ishmael was forced to sell off the stately family home at nearby Ruffside, Weardale, to raise the funds to pay death duties. An auction of music paraphernalia, including dozens of guitars and basses, attracted huge interest when it went under the hammer in 2002.

Piper purchased an old mining assayer's property in a remote spot near the hamlet of Townfield and had plans to open up the old workings as a 'show-mine' for tourists, before red tape and planning regulations halted the project.

The former public-school pupil was a darling of the tabloids in the mid-1990s and spent several years living in squats and communes and fighting a drug habit. He credited his childhood friend, Felix Darling, with helping him overcome his addiction. Darling, a hedge fund manager, moved his family to the Dale a little over a year ago to be closer to Piper following his diagnosis with Huntington's.

FIVE

Roisin wouldn't ever confess to being drunk – not drunk *per se*, or Percy, as her daughter insists upon pronouncing it – but she's more than a little merry. Squiffy, even, if it comes right down to it. She feels a little floaty; a tad unmoored, as if she were a canal boat rising and falling on a tilting canal. She'd like to be a canal boat, she thinks, as she makes her way barefoot across the grass. A green one, with hanging baskets and her name picked out in red and yellow. She fancies she'd be quite pretty, as a houseboat. Enchanting, even, with a smooth bottom.

She realizes she's thinking drunk thoughts and makes a conscious effort to stop. She's had her cigarette and is considering another. She's cold and soaked to the skin, but it's not an entirely unpleasant experience. She's always liked the hard slap of cold against bare flesh and there's something positively erotic about the feeling of wet grass against the warm soles of her bare feet. She's glad she popped outside. She's had herself a little explore, mooching down past the picnic tables and plush umbrellas and making her way through the arbour or roses to the little orchard beyond. There were white doves cooing merrily in a little white house on a stand, keeping watch on the kitchen garden. She'd stood for a while, her cigarette smoke not quite obscuring the scent of fresh herbs and disinterred root vegetables; wet earth and fresh air. She knows there's a full moon overhead somewhere, but the clouds press down upon the horizon like a coffin lid. She hopes the sun will shine tomorrow. She'd like to take Aector to the little curve in the river that she found online and where, she's reliably informed, they won't be disturbed if they choose to strip and make waves.

Roisin stops halfway through the orchard – her foot squelching into a rotten apple. She makes a face. Wipes her foot. Imagines herself a Somerset scrumpy wench, all juice

and pulverized flesh, skirt in her knickers as she squeezes the
syrup from a batch of sour, windfall pippins. She looks up at
the rear of the hotel and can't help but feel a tingle of excitement. It's a truly exquisite building: old and sturdy, elegant
and imposing. She has no doubt that Aector is busily annihi-
lating himself inside for his inability to make her life nothing
but romance and bubble baths and lavish trips away. She never
lets on how much his sense of inadequacy upsets her. His
nearness, his love – that's all she's ever wanted.

Still, she thinks, gazing up at the soft lights that dance in
the dark, rain-streaked windows of a second-floor room . . .
*it's not the worst thing if he starts whisking me away. And,
well, some champagne might be nice. Big Harry might know
somebody who could provide a pedicure. And if they think
they're getting those towels back without a fight they can
fecking well think again . . .*

She starts to walk back to the hotel. Winces into the hard
rain and decides she'll pop to the toilets and make herself
presentable before she goes back to sit with McAvoy. Big
Harry had mentioned that Felix would be in later, and she's
got no intention of meeting him while looking like she swam
here up the Derwent. She rummages around in her memory,
trying to recall the little that McAvoy has shared with her
about the man he refuses to refer to as his stepbrother. He'd
been something in banking, as far as she can recall. Lived the
Berkshire life after university: Labradors and green wellies,
delicatessens and wicker baskets and hacking out on great
white chargers with prime ministers and tabloid editors and
people who thought they looked smart in crushed velvet
jackets. He'd made a mint then packed it all in. Moved north
to set up home with a former colleague and her little girl.
What was her name? Hattie? And the girl . . . Petrie? Proton?
Felix had a chum nearby, wasn't that how it had gone? She
grabs the tail ends of two stories and ties them together in her
mind. Ishmael was the chum. The son of the rock star. The
self-same rock star who'd died a very rock-and-roll death in
a fancy hotel, years back. She frowns, uncertain whether she's
remembering it right. She doesn't want to look a total dickhead
in front of Cecilia and Crawford, with their money and their

sprawling house and their neatly maintained gardens. She can't help feeling relieved that Cecilia has never come to visit them in their two-bedroomed cottage on the waterfront at Hessle. Roisin's proud of her family and her home. There would be dire repercussion were anybody to suggest it was all a little unimpressive when compared to what Aector could have been if he'd stayed on the path she and her husband had picked out for him.

'You can't do this to me, sweets. Everything we've got planned – everything I've done to be with you. Please. Please!'

Roisin stops suddenly, senses heightened, almost animal in her ability to blend in to the dark. She's perfectly still, immobile in a patch of absolute darkness where the gravel-lined path meets the stairs that lead up to the courtyard garden. She doesn't recognize the voices. Male. Young, angry.

'It's killing him. He needs answers. And you did say those things. You did. You knew.'

Female, this time. Well-read. As middle-class as mung beans and skiing holidays.

'He told everybody he was leaving them something. He was my mate. I wouldn't, sweets, I just wouldn't.'

'Stick to the "no comment". She still won't have any evidence. But it might make Daddy feel better.'

'Daddy? Can you hear yourself? Do you know what my fucking daddy will do to me? What he'll do to you!'

Roisin moves closer to the wall. Tries to get her bearings. She's spent considerable time online getting to know the village and its possibilities. The wall to her right is clothed in thornbushes and a trellis of clematis; a great sycamore towers down beyond. She makes sense of the geography. Beyond the wall lies the graveyard at the rear of the old parish church. She's seen pictures: big old Gothic headstones and curlicue inscriptions: spirals of bramble and elderberry; a maze of plastic flowers and broken stones.

She takes a sniff and smells weed. Smells good weed at that. Pungent and expensive and better than she's been able to score in an age.

'Blame it on him, then! Get him out your life. Daddy can't move forward with the will until he knows it wasn't Joy.'

'So you're serving him me?'

'I've got the messages, Deon. All your plans for what you'd get if he did drop dead. I've held on to them because I thought we could make it work but we can't. My daddy's dying in front of my eyes.'

'I wasn't there! I swear! I never touched him. I loved the bloke, you know that.'

Roisin turns at the sound of somebody approaching. Darts towards the steps. She's doing nothing wrong but she'd rather not be caught eavesdropping – not when she wants her husband to survive the next couple of days without any irreparable damage to his fragile soul.

'Brought you a coat,' shouts Big Harry, appearing from behind the rose arbour and tossing her a big wax jacket with a furry hood and a bright orange lining. She snatches it out of the air.

'Don't worry, we've a stack of them,' says Big Harry. He's smoking a huge cigar and water drips from his glasses into his beard and on into his shirtfront. He's been outside for a while.

'Oh, I'm going in, but thanks,' says Roisin, making for the rear door of the hotel. 'Kind of you. And Aector will be worrying.'

'I wouldn't go in that door,' says Big Harry, shaking his head. 'Load of silly Hooray Henrys making a racket. Cleared the place and I wouldn't want to imagine what they'd say if you toddled in soaking wet. Big day for them. One of them's managed to shoot a pure white grouse and they're all trying to work out how to get it back to London to be stuffed without any of the do-gooders at the RSPB cottoning on. I've told them I can take care of it for a grand. I can't, of course, but they'll have forgotten the whole exchange by morning. Forgotten their posh coats and flat caps too. Five-hundred-quid cigars just rolling around on the bar. One silly sod's eating caviar straight from the tin using a folded coaster as a spoon. I've never seen people so excited about shooting a seagull.'

Roisin grins. Slips into the coat. It's warm and silky and smells of earth and heather and flame.

Big Harry sniffs the air. He looks angry, suddenly: a lion

scenting an intruder on their territory. It's weed. Decent stuff, too.

'Over the wall,' explains Roisin, nodding in the direction of the voices. 'Not doing any harm though, are they? Not compared to those rowdy bastards in the bar.'

'It's not that,' growls Big Harry, plucking his cigar from his mouth. He lobs it over the church wall like a grenade. He lets out a growl. 'Deon!' he shouts, suddenly furious. 'Deon, you stay the fuck there, you little shite! You make me run and I'll . . .'

Roisin's amazed by Big Harry's turn of speed. He dashes up the lawn and into the back bar. She stands still for a moment, weighing her options. She can't help herself.

'He's moving pretty fast,' she shouts, a note of apology in her voice. 'I'd get a shift on, whatever . . .'

There's the sound of scrabbling from beyond the wall. A sudden surge of rainfall makes her wince as it hurtles in off the high moors, and then somebody is dropping down through the thorns and the brambles and landing in the bedding plants with a soft oof.

'By Christ, are you all right . . .?'

The figure hauls itself upright. Notices Roisin. Steps forward into the faintest whisper of light. It's a she. A teenager. Pretty and brown-eyed and dark-skinned. She's soaking wet in black hoodie, black jogging trousers, muddy trainers, half on and half off her feet.

'Thanks,' she says, with a hurried, frantic grin. 'Mean it, fam. Thanks . . .'

Then she, too, is running across the grass, disappearing past the row of holiday lets and into the rain-lashed darkness of the caravan. Roisin screws up her face. Wonders who the last person was who called her 'fam'. A moment later she hears Big Harry beyond the wall, bellowing at the retreating figure who made their escape in the opposite direction.

Roisin stands still. Giggles to herself. That was fun.

SIX

Audio transcript, 27.03.23
David Hood, D.O.B 02.04.1954

'I don't mind, not at all, love. At my age, any pretty lass asks you for a few moments of your time you take her up on it – even if they're a copper! Oh, sorry, can't say that, can I? I'll watch it, don't you fret. Happy enough to have a natter, though I've nowt new to tell you since the last time. Still a bloody shame, that's about all there is to it. Always fond of Ishmael, both me and the wife. Everybody liked him. How could you not? I mean, he'd had a past but we all have, haven't we? I'd hate to be my age and not have a few naughty stories to tell. And with Ish, well, he never got to have a normal sort of a life, did he? His dad was Moose Piper, for God's sake. Of course, nobody mentioned that to him the first few times they had a beer with him, but everybody knew and he didn't ever make you feel like a dickhead for bringing it up. Sorry, sorry, that's the language alarm going off, isn't it? But aye, I knew him well enough to call him a friend. Friend rather than friendly, if you'll make the distinction. I'm always friendly, right enough, but there's some I'd call a pal. Wasn't easy those last few months – not since he got ill. Thing with Ish was, well, he kind of made a living out of just being himself. You know how women get to be called scatter-brained, or they're thought of as charming if they're a bit ditzy? Well, that was Ish, really. He wasn't much good at stuff. He was a dabbler. Picked stuff up and played around with it, then got bored and went looking for something else. Have you heard any of the music he made when he was still trying to be a rocker? I mean, bloody hell, I'd rather listen to Ringo Starr's solo stuff. But you always wanted him to do well, that was the thing, whether he was writing poetry or building observatories or starting work on his Tomb of Wonders. I mean, that's the kind of idea that only comes to you when you've smoked enough heroin to kill a blue whale, isn't it? That was his plan right before he got sick – get some lads in, clean out the old mine out the back of his place, open it up to the public. He was going to fill it with all these crystals and geodes and then light it so that it really dazzled. I mean, it wasn't ever going to happen, no matter how much money he had left. Felix and that wife of his kept him on a pretty short leash that way, and I reckon he was grateful to them, though if I were having to check in with my friends every time I wanted to spend a few quid, I reckon I'd be a bit pissed off. No wonder Joy was doing her best to change the arrangement. I mean, he was fifty when he got diagnosed. Fifty! He'd been off the gear for years. He could make his own decisions. Yeah, Felix might be some sort of financial wizard, but Ish was entitled to hold his own purse strings, don't you think? I do, any road. Sorry, sorry, you weren't really wanting all this, were you? Just the night of the fire, yeah? Well, same as I told your young man, me and the wife were coming back from Stanhope. We don't get out often but there's a nice restaurant over that way. Cuban place. Or is it Mexican? Much of a muchness to me, really: just sizzly stuff with cheese and chunky ketchup. But the wife likes it. Must have been not far off ten when we were heading home. She'd had a bottle of the rosé and I'd made do with a bitter shandy – cross my heart. No, I can't be more exact. You'll have the record of the nine-nine-nine call, won't you? So why are you asking? So aye, say nine fifty-five or so. Pouring down with rain, wind rattling across the moors, black as pitch. Awful night for driving. You know I was a fireman, don't you? Sorry, firefighter, that's what they're called nowadays. Aye, twenty-four years before my knee blew out playing football. Saw some bloody horrible things. Learned to read the air, if you'll forgive me sounding all poetic. Sometimes you just get a feeling something awful's happened somewhere, though up on that bit of the moor there's barely a bugger for it to happen to. Happened to Ish this time. I smelled the smoke before I saw it. Must have just wafted on the gale and come in through the air-con. The wife caught a whiff of it too. I said it was maybe the toffs burning the heather the way they do, but it was a mad time to be doing it. And then we saw the smoke. Ish's place is next to the big old chimney. You'll have seen them on the hill there: two big chimneys sticking straight up and then another smaller one next to what looks like a factory of sorts. Aye, Ish's place was next to that, just tucked out the way. And there was smoke coming out of the roof. It was well underway, like. I didn't even think, love. You don't, do you? Just turned the wheel and went down the track. It's all lumpy and bumpy and you get jerked about, but I was going like the clappers in case there was anybody hurt. I know you'll want me to be proper clear on this, but I can't tell you for certain whether I saw another car or whether I didn't. It's so dark and I was proper bouncing around and if I did see a vehicle it wouldn't have registered because there's always some bugger up there with him. So no, I don't know. But once I pulled up, I could tell straight away that the fire was going to win. It had proper taken hold of the roof. My first thought was for the girl. Delilah. Sweetest thing, so clever. Adored her dad. I didn't even think about the French woman. I didn't really know her so she wasn't in my head. I thought of Joy, of course, though the way I've heard it, Joy was off somewhere in one of her strops. She and Ish could proper argue, like. And he'd got himself a bit paranoid towards the end, accusing people of this and that and the other. This is the same guy who's pretty much told everybody he's ever met that he's going to leave them a little something in their will! Was bloody awful to find him there like that. Honestly, I thought he was a statue on his side. He was laid out with his arm in front of him – like Superman. No, like one of those poor buggers at Pompeii. And she was sitting there beside him. Delilah. Her face was glistening. One eye was shut. She'd been in the house when the fire took hold. She was just sitting there, holding his hand. And I swear, that hand looked like it was made of stone. The cement bags had split, see. And when he'd fallen, or slipped, he'd pulled it down on top of himself. So he was just this statue in this garden of sparkling rocks and crystals. It was beautiful and horrible all at the same time. The only thing that mattered then was the girl. I phoned nine-nine-nine, of course, but it always takes an age to get anybody up there.

It just made sense to take her with me. So I did. Took me coat off and wrapped her up. She was mumbling something but she didn't seem like she was in any pain at that moment. Shock'll do that, won't it? So I took her back to the car and took off towards the village. There's a nurse lives in the corner house. Ex-nurse, actually. Joy's living there at the moment, in case you were wondering. I took her straight there and banged on the door like a bailiff. Must have woken half the village, though by that point there were sirens and blue lights and all sorts. I was shaking. Had to go straight outside for a tab. That weird witchy bloke was down at Peter's allotment collecting his clippings. Weird's unkind, actually. I reckon lonely's a better fit. Wife left him and ran off to Spain, the way I heard it. Lives out Nenthead way in some knackered old place, though he's never complained about it with me. He was going to give a talk at the pub, as it happens, but it never happened. I don't think the events lass down there knows her arse from her elbow. They were going to have me in to do a local history talk but it never got off the ground. He was going to talk about Weardale's Witches: Leddy Lister and all that crowd. Bit obsessed on that score, I reckon. Ingle, that's his name. Len? Maybe Len. They'll have his details at the hotel, I shouldn't wonder. Ask Big Harry. But anyway, Ingle gave me a wave, like. He was collecting his odds and ends, same as I'd seen him do before. You ever see a grown man trying to pick up a spider's web from a wet bush? Not an impressive site. He'd been out there a while 'cause his jacket was proper soaked through. One of the hotel's spares, I think, though again, it's Harry you'll be wanting. But that's it, really. Not much else to say. Next thing I knew, Felix was in the main bar sobbing his eyes out, smoke and tears on his face. Ishmael was dead. Lass upstairs too. Delilah never said owt you could make sense of. I think she wanted her mam, but with that set-up it could have been either lass she were talking to. She just said something about the lady; the lady did it. Found out later how lucky she'd been, of course. The fire investigator who did your report, well, he's an old pal of mine. I don't like the way people are reading stuff into his findings, I'll tell you that. I mean, yeah, the fire was started downstairs but that doesn't mean Ish started

it, does it? She lights it in the living room, goes for a nap –
accidents happen, don't they? I heard the fire investigators just
don't want to say one way or another, like. She could just as
easily have knocked over a candle or dropped her tab. How
do we even know he didn't rescue his little girl from the fire
and then slip on his way out? She won't tell, will she? Can't
remember any of it, that's what I was told. I just know it's a
bloody ugly thing to have happened and nobody deserved it.
Can't help thinking that if I'd have been there half an hour
earlier I might have been able to do more. You'll keep us
posted, won't you, love? Really has hit this community proper
hard.'

ENDS

SEVEN

McAvoy's been reading in silence for the last twenty minutes. There's nobody left in the dining room. He has a vague memory of somebody clearing plates and bringing him a drink, but whether he ordered it or said thank you is anybody's guess. He's been in a state of suspended animation ever since he started reading about Ishmael Piper – the words on the page and the pictures in his head taking up the entirety of his consciousness. It takes a real effort of will to raise his head from the shiny screen and reacquaint himself with reality. He blinks a few times, taking bites of the air in a way that makes him look like he's swallowing something that doesn't want to go down. He takes in the brass, and the dying fire, the wrought iron and the gleaming weaponry. Looks down at the brandy that's appeared on the wooden table. Looks across to where Roisin's supposed to be sitting and then glances at his watch. She's been gone an age. Was he supposed to go and find her? Had she popped back and given him instructions that he'd been too distracted to take in? A chill feeling settles inside his chest, a little flurry of snow pitter-pattering down in the place behind his heart; the place he keeps her, and the kids, and the memories of the dead.

He raises the drink. The tumbler is expensive. Cut crystal, perhaps. But it's brandy, not whisky, and he can't help but wonder why a hotel that trades on luxury would serve a spirit in the wrong glass. He takes a sip of soft, warm flame. Feels it slide through him like molten gold.

'. . . couldn't grab the little bugger but if you get your arse down now I reckon you'll be able to spot him . . .'

McAvoy turns towards the main door. Big Harry is looming in the entranceway, blocking out the light, phone to his ear. There are raindrops on his glasses, his hair slicked back, his beard darkened by rain.

'. . . aye well, I said I would. No, I called her but no answer.

Must be away on whatever it is those posh lasses do on their weekends off. The mind boggles. But look, keep your temper or it comes back on all of us. Aye. Aye.'

McAvoy watches as Big Harry ends the call and slips the phone into his trouser pocket. He doesn't speak. Just sits and waits. He can feel a prickle of temper inside himself. He feels like he's been lied to. Feels like he's been manipulated. He has a horrible suspicion that somebody's taking the piss.

'Sorry, sorry,' mutters Harry, jovially, as he makes his way to the fireplace and plays with the burning logs. The poker has a sword handle and a lethal-looking twist tapering off midway down its length. It puts McAvoy in mind of a barb on a fish hook.

'Sounds like you've got a lot on your plate,' says McAvoy, his eyes upon Harry's broad back and round shoulders. 'All's well, is it?'

Harry wipes the raindrops from his beard. Drops himself into a seat at the next table. Gives McAvoy a once-over. 'Your good lady's a treat, isn't she? Doing cartwheels out there. Barefoot. Absolute joy to watch, that one.'

McAvoy manages a smile. 'Still out there, is she? I should probably go and see if she's OK.'

'Right as ninepence,' says Harry. He's still holding the poker. It lies across his knees, giving him the appearance of a medieval knight resting between wars. 'We've got coats and boots and blankets in the cloakroom. Took her a waterproof so she's grand. She was talking to the doves when I left her.'

'She loves animals,' says McAvoy. 'Loves nature. She hasn't been so well though, so I'd best see if she's ready for another drink. Early night, if not.'

'Don't waste your calvados,' says Harry, nodding at the amber liquid. 'Finest in the building, that stuff. Felix was clear. Nowt but the best.'

McAvoy holds the glass in his palm. Takes a sip. He's never really drunk spirits but he can taste the quality on his tongue. 'It's from Felix?'

'Told you he's a pal of mine,' says Harry, with a grin. 'There are flowers in your room for the lady, too. Or there should be, at least. I asked one of the girls to do it. Pink roses, as it goes. How're you enjoying the book?'

McAvoy nods, appreciatively. 'Sounds like an interesting subject. We won't be back up any time soon though.'

'Shame you won't get to meet Ingle, really. He'd give you the lowdown on Ishmael. God knows what he'll be like as a public speaker but he's interesting if you can keep him on track.'

'You mentioned somebody called Leddy Lister, as if I should have heard of them,' says McAvoy, keen to put one nagging worry to bed.

'They reckon she was a witch,' says Harry. 'Of course, if you really want to see who's a witch and who's just a weirdo, you have to rub the sap of an elder tree in your eyes, which doesn't sound like a picnic. Leddy was a shape-shifter, by all accounts. Load of locals saw her as a hare or a rabbit or something – chased her home and kicked her bloody. It's a folk tale but that doesn't mean it wasn't true. Then you've Elizabeth Lee from Edmundbyers. When they buried her, they did it right by the church wall and planted a bloody forest of wild garlic to keep her in her grave. Vicar installed an Eye of God in the stained-glass window to keep an eye on her in her grave. I think Ish's dad even mentioned it in one of his songs. You know he was local, yeah? Even before he bought this big old place in Ruffside. Shotley Bridge was his home turf, which gives you some idea why he wanted to get off his face as soon as life presented the opportunity. From there to London and absolute rock-god status – you'd be forgiven for questioning the stories. Maybe he really did make a pact with the devil. He was certainly fascinated by all that stuff. There's a documentary you can watch. Apparently in the Seventies he was so paranoid about evil forces and devils that he had his own private white witch. Kept him safe with her spells and charms and put a great chunk of fluorspar on a cord around his neck. Cremated with it still around him, so Ishmael said. There's still pink and purple sparkles in the urn. Be worth a fortune to some collector, I shouldn't wonder.'

McAvoy licks his lips. He glances at the poker in Harry's broad, pink hands. 'I've been reading about what happened to your friend,' says McAvoy, quietly. 'Ishmael. Sounds terrible. How's the little girl?'

'Sugarbun?' asks Harry, sitting up a little straighter. He moves his head this way and that, suggesting that he wouldn't like to commit one way or another. 'Burns are getting better. Still barely talking though. Some people say kids are resilient – others that she'll never get over it. I don't even know what I hope. I don't think Ishmael would want her to get over it, to be honest. Adored one another, those two. I can't help but wonder if it might have been better if . . .' He stops himself, shaking the thought away. 'No, she's got such light about her. World's better off with her in it. But whether Ish would want her to have the future she's got now . . . I don't know.'

'I read an article that says he's left quite a large amount of money,' says McAvoy, sipping the brandy again. 'And surely Felix will see to it that she's well looked after.'

Harry takes his glasses off. Wipes them on his front. Replaces them and wrinkles his nose. 'It's all getting a bit bloody nasty, truth be told. It's not just money, though that's always at the centre of stuff, isn't it? Ish inherited a great chunk of his dad's money, but stacks of that went on inheritance tax, so no bugger knows whether he was a secret millionaire or as potless as the rest of us. But whatever he has left, well, it's Felix who's the executor and he's not in the mood to thank Ish for that particular honour – not when every bugger has their own theory on what actually happened. He's entered a caveat – that's the phrase, isn't it? – the thing that blocks any application for probate for six months. Entered it not more than a month ago. He can't stomach the thought of Joy having any money when he's not sure she didn't bump him off.'

'And that's a real possibility?'

Big Harry shrugs. 'We're all capable of owt, ain't we? And they did fight like cat and dog. And he wasn't so well towards the end. But nah, she loved him proper, if you ask me. She might have done Heloise, just for the sheer cheek of slipping into the marital bed, but I won't be saying that out loud, if you follow me. But Felix has his doubts.'

McAvoy keeps his face inscrutable. Acts like a man having a casual chat. 'The police haven't identified any other suspects?'

Harry's whole demeanour drips with scorn. 'Coppers? Round here? No offence, but they couldn't find my arse if they were living in my trousers. I mean, yeah, it might have been an accident, mightn't it? He was poorly, and he was no stranger to self-medicating. But he wouldn't have taken that nasty shit – not with her in the house. Not ever, if you ask me. He'd got himself clean years ago and it was one of the few things he was proud of. But even if he did – even if Joy had made him so bloody miserable he couldn't see any other way . . . why go outside? Middle of a storm like that? I know how it looks, but, well – people who adored him when he was holding court and telling tales and buying drinks, they're the first ones to point the finger. You ask some people around here and Ishmael killed his girlfriend, tried to kill his daughter and then did himself in. Of course, the others will have you believe that he was a victim. Joy found out he was changing his will and did him in before he had the chance.'

McAvoy drains his brandy. Enjoys the burn. 'What does Felix really think?' asks McAvoy, teeth locked together.

Harry rubs his jaw. 'You heard me on the phone to him just then, yeah? He's got us looking out for a lad called Deon. Bit of a rascal from over Consett way. Been sniffing about Felix's daughter for months. Good girl, she is, and good girls have a habit of falling for bad boys, don't you find? We know Ishmael was buying from him and Cliffy – the bloke with the allotment by the churchyard there; he reckons he saw Deon heading up towards Ishmael's place on his little moped the night it all happened. He's told Saville – posh copper who's been bugging everybody these past few months – but the lad just gave it the whole no-comment thing when they had him in.'

'And Felix would like a word with him, would he?' asks McAvoy. 'I'd urge you not to get involved. There's always more going on in an investigation than you might think. Just because nothing seems to be happening, doesn't mean it's not.'

'Aye, but nobody's getting any money yet, are they?' snaps Harry. 'And as for Joy, well – she's doing her nut. She and the little one are bunking down with Beth at the house on the corner, but they've barely a brass farthing to their name, which is a bit of a pisser when you might be about to inherit a few hundred grand, and you're doing your damnedest to get your little girl smiling again.'

McAvoy licks his lips. Breathes in and out, watching the fire. 'Felix is on his way down, is he? Out looking for this Deon chap, I presume?'

'He'll probably send somebody,' shrugs Harry. 'Maybe even a tame copper. His old friend's deputy crime commissioner.'

'She's on the payroll, is she?'

Harry shrugs. 'People with influence tend to assert it without needing to put their hands in their pockets. He's got powerful friends. His mate's been up there this evening, giving him the latest bad news. They're scaling down the investigation – as if it were ever much of one to begin with. He's a good lad is Felix, but these last few months have half killed him. Bit obsessed, I think you'd say. They were more like brothers than friends.'

McAvoy hides his laugh behind his fist. Manages to keep the anger from his face. Brothers? He remembers what Felix thought a brother was for. A stepbrother, at least. Remembers the taunts. The teasing. The casual little jibes. Remembers those first few weeks when Felix welcomed him into the family fold by pinning him down and sitting on his chest, sticking his hand down the back of his own shorts and then smearing his stinking fingers across McAvoy's top lip. He thought it was the best fun imaginable. Told McAvoy he'd cut his ears off in his sleep if he squealed. Felix was sixteen. McAvoy was ten. He's barely had anything to do with him since. Barely had anything to do with Crawford either. But he knows that both men have taken an interest in his career. Moreover, he knows that such men believe in the natural hierarchy of things. And McAvoy, a good few rungs beneath them, is just the sort of pathetically grateful underling who they could manipulate into popping north to provide answers to a question that's eating them up.

'Is Felix going to inherit anything?' asks McAvoy.

'No bugger knows,' shrugs Big Harry. 'Of course, there's nobody within a ten-mile radius who isn't secretly hoping he's left them a few quid, or a guitar, or the shirt his dad wore at

Altamont. Always very good at whispering in people's ears, was Ishmael. Made a lot of promises. Told a lot of people he'd put "a little something" aside for them when his time came. You can imagine, can't you? When people heard he was ill . . . a lot of folk, even decent folk, well, they could be forgiven for wanting to hasten the end, don't you think?'

'Hasten the end?' asks McAvoy. 'You mean commit murder?'

Harry shrugs. 'Not as simple as that, is it? I mean, he wasn't well, was he? I think he knew he was on borrowed time, so to speak. Maybe that's why he agreed to speak to Ingle. I mean, he'd put it off long enough, but . . .'

McAvoy realizes that he's being drawn into something that's none of his business. He decides to pull back while he still can. 'Sorry Harry,' he says, holding up a hand. 'I'm going to see if I can find Roisin. She'll fall asleep under an apple tree if she's half a mind to and we promised the kids we'd call before bedtime.'

Harry opens his mouth to speak. Closes it again. He has the look of a raconteur cut off before the punchline. 'Aye, aye, sorry to have kept yakking. Bill's on the room, yeah? Give me a moment, I'll bring you a jacket. Blowing a gale outside . . .'

McAvoy shakes his head. He's been listening to the sounds drifting through from the bar. The laughter and the roars have drifted into silence. He can hear singing: a single voice, ethereal and fluted and not quite of this world. He knows where she is.

'Ah,' says Harry, suddenly tuning in. 'By Christ, she sounds like she's from Middle Earth.'

McAvoy smiles. 'Elf, not orc, I hope.'

'I'd take her up the Misty Mountains, that much is true,' laughs Harry, extricating himself from the chair. 'Nice chatting with you. I'll send Felix your way if he does show his face.'

McAvoy stands. Straightens his clothes. He takes his phone from the table and slips it into his pocket. He'll listen back to the recording later, once he knows whether his suspicions are correct or the entrenched paranoia of a poor boy growing up in a rich man's house.

It's as he's reaching the door that he notices the movement beyond the glass. It's sudden, as if a shadow has
appeared and disappeared in the blinking of an eye. He
pauses, staring out through his own reflection. There'd been
somebody at the window. Somebody had been loitering by
the glass, pressed up close, huddled in to the great stone
wall. For an instant they'd looked otherworldly: an insinu-
ation of bloated skin, of grey ash. For an instant it had
seemed as though a statue had stepped out of the graveyard
and taken up a position by the window. McAvoy feels the
hairs on his arms rise. Feels a painful pricking sensation at
the nape of his neck and across the pads of his fingers. He
feels as though he has somehow detached himself from
reality – as if he has stepped out of one world and found
himself within its echo.

> *'Oh Lord I wish my child was born*
> *And all my troubles could be gone.*
> *So all you maidens good and true*
> *Never change the old love for the new.'*

The noise of the bar comes back; the glow of the fire; the
warm yellow lights set in the wall. Her words like honey; her
song, like sex.

He steps into the bar. Sees his wife. She's sitting on the
end of the bar like a crooner in an old-fashioned cocktail bar.
She has her eyes closed and she's singing. The half-dozen
men who form a semi-circle around her are utterly transfixed.
Even though she's soaked to the skin in her tiny little dress,
her dainty feet are patterned with grass and leaves and
earth, they're watching her with something close to enchantment. These men, with their gaiters and their tweed and their
moustaches and cigars – they stare at Roisin McAvoy as if
under a spell.

McAvoy stands in the doorway and enjoys her. Drinks her
in. Feels the sheer static energy that seems to crackle around
her. He half expects to see flowers sprout around her.

The spell breaks as soon as he's noticed. One of the men
turns to see who's letting in the draught. They clock the big

man with the scars and the shiny pink face, his shirt straining over his broad chest.

'Watch out boys – the Jocks are invading!'

There's a roar. Half a dozen faces turn to McAvoy, eyes hard, gazes appraising.

And Aector McAvoy, his guts a-churn, his cheeks burning, is ten years old again. Ten, and far from home, and so fucking lonely he could die.

EIGHT

She senses a change in the atmosphere – hears the rustle of tweed upon tweed, the subtle shifting of splendidly upholstered leather shoes moving against the cold grey stone. Her voice echoes back from the curved roof so that it feels as though she is harmonizing with herself. She's cold, suddenly. Cold and wet and wishing she'd ended the song a minute ago, or never started at all.

Through the haze of her damp lashes she sees him, her Aector, standing in the doorway, face crimson and white. She could weep for him. Knows that, for a moment, he's the same little boy that his bitch mother dumped at the gates of the big Gothic-looking school just weeks after telling him she wanted them to be closer, to be together, to be a proper mummy-and-son.

'By God but you're a bruiser! Bare-knuckle bout with a tiger, was it? Glad you're here, as it happens – the Range Rover needs lifting!'

Roisin's voice doesn't falter. She sings from the place behind her heart – the place where love lives.

The sniggers become outright laughs.

'How do you shave your pubes, eh, big lad? Gingerly, I'll bet! Ha! Gingerly!'

'Oh look at that! What a colour! I'm going to start self-identifying as a redhead, Cartwright. I'm transginger!'

Whatever spell the song had woven, it's starting to lose its power. *Oh Aector*, she thinks. *Stay strong. Raise your head, my love. You're a big strong man. You're in love with somebody who loves you back. Stand tall, please.*

'Sorry,' he mumbles. 'Sorry.'

She hadn't intended for him to see her here, sitting on the edge of the bar in the curious, stone-walled crypt. There are heraldic shields on the walls; big iron candle-holders; wooden tables and plush, cushioned chairs. The spirits behind the bar are worth a copper's monthly wages. She'd ignored Harry's warnings and strolled in to reclaim her husband. She found a party in full swing. Walked in to a sea of shiny red faces and high foreheads, floppy quiffs and plus-fours. Two tall, spindly-looking men were drinking brandy from the silver tubing that surrounded their cigars. A shotgun was laid out across the bar. A plumpish, round-faced man in a plum-and-khaki gilet was berating the young man behind the bar for not being able to provide him with whatever information he had so artlessly demanded. The lad looked downright scared. Had looked at Roisin with something like pleading in his eyes. She hadn't been able to turn away. She'd simply served herself as a distraction. Given a theatrical cough, dropped the waxed jacket, and stood there in her cocktail dress, dripping water on the stone floor.

'Evening my lords, I was looking for a gentleman . . .'

They'd treated her like a visitor from an alien world. The shouts had fallen silent; the raucous singing dwindling out to nothing. They'd stared at her with the looks of men entirely unsure whether to treat the newcomer as a visiting maharani, nanny, or a stripper. They'd made room for her at the bar. They'd ordered her a Bellini. They'd asked her whether her accent was County Wexford or Killarney. One of them had told her she looked like a singer from a group his wife used to rather enjoy: three sisters and a brother from somewhere over the water. They'd asked if she could sing. All the Irish could sing, apparently. Gypsy-look about her, that's what they'd muttered. One of them had begun to hum a line from *Carmen*, expecting her not to know the line about love being a Gypsy child and knowing no laws. So she'd obliged. Sung a lullaby and soothed the heads and hearts of half a dozen men, drunk on gunpowder and port, her lilting voice an anti-dote to the bang-bang-bang of the shotguns that had buckled in their hands as they fired wildly at the desperate, flapping birds as they clattered up from the heather and into the red-misted sky.

'Private party, old chap,' comes a voice, crisp above the general din. Roisin watches through her lashes. The man who addresses her husband is a full head and shoulders shorter, but his voice comes with the clipped, officer-class enunciation of those used to giving orders and being obeyed. His head looks misshapen, as if the features have slipped forwards like sausages and bacon on a tilted plate. There's nothing of interest in the top half of his head but his features are crammed into a little triangle where most people would keep a goatee. If his remarkable looks have knocked his confidence, he's not showing it. He looks as though he's bought and sold men like Aector McAvoy most of his life. Looks like he's about to reach into the coins in his pocket and make an offer for everything he owns.

'Let the bugger stay,' shouts another chap, as the titters grow. 'We could use a bouncer in case Max does the old trick with the Cuban. I'd wager our friend here could throw him out the second he reached for his fly.'

'Fancy an arm wrestle, do you? I've got a good right arm . . .'

'We all remember that, Porker!'

The bar erupts in laughter. Roisin stops singing. She notices the chap standing nearest has been subtly filming her on his phone, tilted to capture her grassy feet, bare legs, and whatever might be visible up her skirt.

'Aector, my love,' says Roisin, making sure that her smile of welcome radiates with absolute delight. 'Meet my friends. There's a Porker and a Cartwright. Hugo, I think. And a Max. One of them might be a Farquhar though I might have invented that. Come on in. It's rather Fortnum and Mason in here. I'm doing my best to add a little Lidl.'

McAvoy doesn't respond. He hasn't spoken since he walked in. Hasn't moved. He's just looking at the floor, inert with embarrassment and a desperate wish to be anywhere else. She wants nothing more than to pull him close to her and stroke his hair until the demons in his memory retreat back behind the locked doors. He's told her about his first weeks at prep school. Told her of the agonizing loneliness; the trembling bass-note grief that seemed to vibrate in his very core; the gallons of unshed tears that sloshed about inside him as he dragged himself, heavy-footed, through the polished corridors and frigid air of the big Gothic school that Crawford insisted

would be the happiest time of his life. It wasn't the beatings
that broke him. It was the knowledge that he'd chosen this
path – that he'd failed to be whoever it was his mother had
hoped he might have become in her absence. He'd walked
away from his dad and his brother because they'd all said this
was what was best for him. Loneliness was best for him.
Isolation. Seclusion. And in every letter home he had to act
so pathetically grateful for all of it. He was, as everybody told
him, a lucky boy. An education like this was a privilege. He
was developing character, fortitude, mental toughness. It wasn't
every chap who would foot the bill for a stepson to go to the
finest of prep schools.

'This your chap, is it?' asks a floppy-fringed man to her
left. He smells of the outdoors, beneath the cigar smoke and
the brandy. Smells of heather and feathers and blood.

'My darling husband,' says Roisin, her voice loud. 'Detective
Inspector Aector McAvoy, though he won't thank me for using
his rank. Wife's privilege though, isn't it? To be proud of her
husband and make a show of him?'

'My God, he's a rozzer!'

'Looks more like a robber than a cop. Ha! Hear that one,
Hugo? More robber than cop!'

'Tried to arrest a rhino, did you, old chap?'

'You'd do well to question old Cartwright here. There are
things on his laptop that are downright criminal.'

'Going to do something about these saboteurs, are you, old
boy? Had a beauty in my sights over at Muggleswick. Deserve
a bloody medal for not pulling the trigger . . .'

Roisin slides down from the bar. She makes her way through
the gathering of jostling, laughing men, all smiles and flirty
touches. She can play this game in her sleep. She can diffuse
a riot as easily as she could start one. There's a crash from
behind her. The barman has dropped a glass.

'Pay peanuts, get monkeys,' says the one she's identified as
Cartwright. 'Silly sod couldn't even tell me the provenance
of the olives. Rough as tits, some of these bar staff. Twice as
bad since Brexit.'

He's wearing a blue pullover with a checked shirt underneath; the collar neatly frayed by the grey stubble on his florid

cheeks. He has the air of an unreconstructed bully – the sort who believes that emotional abuse and borderline sexual assault are just good character-building stuff.

'Bit of a prick thing to say, Cartwright,' says Roisin, looking disappointed with him. 'Suffer a flashback, did you? Sudden memory of a slippering on your buttocks, was it? There's people you can talk to, y'know. You don't need to carry all that trauma.' She turns to the barman. His eyes are glassy, his face pale. 'You all right there, matey? Put that on Cartwright's bill, I reckon. And another Bellini for me.'

'Got you there, old boy.'

'That's you told, Cartwright, old chap! Read you like a book!'

Roisin grabs her coat from the back of a bar stool. Reaches her husband. He's staring at the floor.

'Doesn't say much, your chap. Sure he's a copper, are you? Seems an odd pairing. Beauty and the Beast, is it?'

'The policeman and the pikey – sounds like a romance novel!'

Roisin watches McAvoy raise his head. She feels her heart slow down; the skin at her wrists and at the back of her neck begins to prickle, the way it always does when the air temperature drops and the room goes cold and the certainty of violence billows in upon the wind. McAvoy's face is the colour of dry stone. His hands are in fists. He turns to look at the last man to speak. He's head to toe in tweed and has a great shark-fin of a nose, deep-set eyes and curly hair. He's drinking some thick, unctuous claret and there's a little hoofprint smile curving above his wet lips.

'What did you say?'

'By God, it speaks! Thought you'd turned to stone there, old chap. Epidemic, what? First Ishmael, now you . . .'

'Too soon, Hugo, too soon!'

McAvoy's eyes are locked on the one called Hugo; the one who referred to Roisin as a pikey. He withers a little, under the glare.

'I think I must have misheard,' says McAvoy, in what Roisin recognizes as his police-officer voice – the one that's firm, fair and thoroughly reasonable. 'You didn't use a racial slur, did you, sir?'

Hugo scoffs, his laugh utterly contemptuous. 'A racial slur? What the devil do you mean?'

'My wife is Pavee,' says McAvoy. 'Gypsy. Traveller. Romani. These are all terms she's perfectly content with. You used a word that she doesn't like. I'd ask you to apologize.'

The mood in the bar changes. All eyes turn to Hugo. He's so shocked it looks like his eyes are trying to pirouette within their sockets.

'I'll do no such bloody thing! Honestly, can't say anything these days. Wasn't it just a fortnight ago that "gypsy" was banned? Honestly, I can't keep up. You should be bloody grateful we let her join our little shindig, let alone come stomping in here yelling the odds. Who the bloody hell do you think you're talking to? I'll have you know that I'm close personal friends with—'

McAvoy clears the space between them in two swift strides. He steps into Hugo's personal space. He peers down at him, unblinking, noses an inch away from touching.

'I don't care,' says McAvoy, quietly. 'I don't care what you're about to say. You could be best friends with the Home Secretary, whoever that is this week, and it wouldn't make a difference to me. You insulted my wife. That makes this a different situation to any that you're used to. Say you're sorry.'

Roisin looks to the man who had been filming her. He's turned his camera towards the unfolding drama between his shooting chum and the big bruised police officer. Roisin might not know their names, but she's always known men like these. She knows how the world is structured and she knows where people like her fit and where they don't. She knows that her husband would throw away his entire career to defend her honour and she has no doubt that these men, these silly, rich, influential toffs, have the power to take away all that he's worked for. She would love to see her husband finally get the chance to heal his trauma and annihilate the boarding school bullies who still taunt him in his head. But she can't let it happen.

'Aector, my love. The champagne's doing its work. I think it's bedtime for me. Will you be a dear and scratch my itches?'

She says it in her most seductive voice: a dirty Dublin

streetwalker propositioning a soldier on leave. The men in the room respond as she'd known they would: all cheers and back-slaps and rugby-match chants. She slips to her husband's side and slides her dainty fingers over his broken knuckles. He's still staring at Hugo, who has turned his head to glance at his chums and can't seem to return his gaze to McAvoy's.

'Shall we, my love?' She leans up on her tiptoes, pulling him down by his shirt so she can whisper in his ear. 'I need to talk to you. I've found something. Let it go. I don't care.'

She feels the tension bleed out of his body. Steers him back towards her and on towards the door. He glances to the barman. 'The Buttery,' says McAvoy. 'That's our room. That's where I'll be. Don't put up with more than you think you can take.'

Roisin folds her hand into his. Pulls the door open and turns back to the room. 'It's been a pleasure, gentlemen. I hope you all enjoy one another's company the way my husband is about to enjoy mine.'

She leads him from the room. Hears the door bang shut behind her. There's no cheer from the assembled drinkers. She rather likes the idea of them feeling a little foolish; enjoys the idea of them imagining what the rest of the night has in store for them in comparison to what McAvoy is about to enjoy.

They stand together in the cool of the little stone room that connects the bar to the dining room. She looks up at McAvoy and places her palm on his cheek. 'Sorry I left you so long. I got lost.'

McAvoy closes his eyes. 'It was like I was a little boy again. Like being told off by a prefect. I hate them. And I hate myself for hating them.'

Roisin watches her reflection swim on the big brown mirror of his irises. Feels a desperate urge to wrap him up in herself and keep him safe from the things that make his soul cold. 'You don't hate them. You don't hate anybody. You had eight years of being the butt of everybody's jokes, Aector. Eight years of being picked on and ground down and made to feel like the shit on their shoe because you spoke with a Highland accent and didn't know which knife and fork to use and hadn't ever been skiing or visited the South of France. But you came through it, my love. You've made something of yourself. You've got people who love you. Really, truly love you, all the way down to the bone. It bruised you but it didn't break you. And for all their influence, all their money, I reckon that you're here for more than a birthday party. I reckon your darling mother and stepfather and fancy-pants Felix need your help.'

McAvoy uses the heel of his hand to wipe away a tear before it falls. Roisin knows that it is boarding school that taught him not to cry. Boarding school taught him to be a good chap; to hide his pain. It taught him not to be a wet, or a sneak, or a squealer. It taught him that the world most people live in, and the ones behind those grand cloistered walls, were as far apart as the sun and moon. He'd never have become a police officer if not for boarding school. He'd never have chosen a life dedicated to seeking justice for those wronged by cruelty, violence and oppression. She hates how much he suffers in his pursuit of doing the right thing. She knows he doubts himself more and more; doubts that the police service is the same organization that he first joined two decades ago. He's caught killers and locked up bad men and women but he doesn't know whether he's still on the side of the angels. Whether he ever was.

'Ishmael Piper,' says McAvoy, grasping for the name which bobs like a life raft in the churn of bad memories. 'He was Felix's best friend. I've been reading about what happened to him – about the night he died. His daughter. The lady upstairs. It's wrong, Roisin. It all feels wrong. I mean, who knows, right? It's just hearsay and headlines but, I don't know . . .' He stops himself. Presses the bridge of his nose between forefinger and thumb and tries to get his thoughts in order. 'There's some suggestion he was killed but it doesn't look like the investigation is getting anywhere.'

Roisin licks her lips. She angles one leg across the other and rubs at an old scar on her bare leg – a white line that bisects her tanned shin. She's known pain and violence as the result of being a policeman's wife. But she wouldn't sacrifice Aector for a life without fear. 'You're wondering whether Crawford's cooked up this party so you can come and look into it for Felix, aren't you? You don't want to be thinking it, but you're definitely thinking it.'

McAvoy screws up his face. 'Bit arrogant of me to think that, Ro. I mean, why would they think I'd be an asset? The big man on the front desk says he's got a local deputy commissioner in his pocket so, even if Felix was thinking it would be useful to have a tame copper at his disposal – I mean, he'd just offer money, wouldn't he? It's not as if we've ever had any kind of relationship. We've barely had a conversation this millennia! What does he think I could do?'

Roisin pulls on her lower lip. She sometimes wishes she could pick him up and shake him. He's got no idea what he's capable of. Roisin knows. And she's no doubt that, on some level, the influential men in Crawford Darling's circle have identified McAvoy as a very valuable asset.

'I saw your niece,' says Roisin, suddenly. 'She was having an argument with some lad – crying, caterwauling, telling him she was going to have to tell the truth. Then Big Harry went charging after them both. She ran past me but I recognized her. Felix's daughter.'

McAvoy leans back against the cold wall. Shakes his head. He sighs. 'I rather liked the idea that we were just being invited to a birthday party.'

'Maybe we are,' says Roisin, smiling. 'Maybe we are being paranoid and there's no ulterior motive.'

She shivers as the cold, rain-speckled breeze whips in through an open doorway. Puts her hands inside her coat and feels something lumpy in the inside pocket. She rummages through a multitude of fusty, damp little places: an archaeologist searching for evidence of previous inhabitants. She finds two shotgun cartridges and a shiny brown conker. She unzips the inside pocket and the other little one folded almost into the lining. Her fingers close on a big rectangular fold of paper. She pulls it out and holds it to the light. It's a printout of a magazine article: the lettering tiny, the date barely eligible. There's a picture of a woman with dark eyes and white hair and inset, a grainy image of Moose Piper, leaning back with his fingers clawed around the neck of a purple guitar. The headline reads: 'Dilly: The Mysterious Witch Who Saved a Rock Star from His Own Personal Hell'.

McAvoy takes it from her. Unfolds it as delicately as he

can. A small pen slips out from within the folds and he catches
it instinctively. The words 'Tomorrow's Ghosts 2021' are
printed down one side.

He looks at the paper again. Reads the words written in a
neat hand at the top of the blank page. *'Lister. Lee. Jeffreys.
Pressor. Parker.'*

'Mean anything to you?' asks Roisin, looking up. She
wrinkles her nose as a strange, coarse smell rises from
the page. It smells of smoke and animal furs; the unmistakable
ammonia reek of cat-piss and sulphur. She turns to McAvoy.
'I think you're going to have to talk to Felix. And you're definitely going to need to speak to this DI. Big Harry seems to
know plenty but he's too bloody enigmatic by half. And that
prick in the bar – he mentioned Ishmael . . . some joke about
turning to stone.'

McAvoy puts his head back against the wall. Groans, put
upon. 'I didn't even get a pudding.'

Roisin tugs his beard. 'The night's young.'

McAvoy casts around, hoping his eyes might fall upon a
decent excuse. 'It's nothing to do with me. It's an active
investigation. I'm just here for a birthday party.'

Roisin puts her hand on his cheek. 'There's a little girl
whose dad isn't ever coming home again. Imagine if that was
Lilah.'

McAvoy closes his eyes. 'That's all I'm doing, Ro. That's
all I can think about.'

'You've got some time before the party – if there's even
going to be one. It wouldn't be the worst thing in the world
if your mummy's helicopter landed and you'd already found
who killed Felix's best friend. I mean, I know I'd like to see
that . . .'

McAvoy hides his smile behind his hand. 'You looked beautiful in there,' he says, pulling her close. 'Your voice – it's
like something from another world. You had them eating out
of the palm of your hand.'

Roisin giggles. 'Men are so bloody easy to control,' she
says, shaking her head.

'All men?' asks McAvoy, leaning down and kissing the
peaches and champagne and tobacco from her parting mouth.

Roisin smiles around his kiss. 'What was that you said about the palm of your hand . . .?'

'Eating out . . .' begins McAvoy.

Roisin grins. Bites his lower lip. 'Aye, that would be lovely.'

NINE

Dilly: The Mysterious Witch Who Saved a Rock Star from His Own Personal Hell
Book Review, by Nico Hagen

t was the mid-1970s and the world was going to Hell. For many rock stars, that was no bad thing. David Bowie was in his Thin White Duke phase, existing on a diet of coffee and cocaine. He had an altar in his living room. He kept his nail clippings and nostril hair lest they fall into the hands of those obscure and malignant forces trying to take possession of his soul. Music fans have certainly revelled in the results of those fantastical ruminations about Nazis, Manson, cocaine and bodily essences. And those who've delved a little deeper will surely be familiar with the now legendary story of Moose Piper's encounter with something evil while under the influence. Indeed, many of his finest songs are the result of that meeting between rock royalty and this prince of darkness. What fewer people are aware of is the intervention of a more benign spirit. A new book by music journalist Enzo Ingram lifts the lid on the mysterious Dilly: a white witch who, if Moose's recollections are to be believed, saved his immortal soul.

Moose's former roadie, Huck Tantree, tells Ingram: 'Bowie and Moose were pretty tight for a while. They certainly shared a lot of interests. It's no secret that for a while there, Bowie was obsessed with using occult magic to attain success and protect himself from demonic forces. But Moose was off the scale, man. It all stemmed back to where he was from. Shotley Bridge is just on the edge of the Dale – this great wilderness of abandoned mines and the leftover shells of houses. It's a ghost world up there. And he was raised with no shortage of occult overtones. Even the Methodist minister used to keep a spell book next to their bibles. He told me once about this bloke he was taken to see when he was a boy. He had a nasty stye in his eye and the doctor was too far away, so they went to see this bloke who was a Methodist minister of a weekend and a bloody white witch the rest of the time. He took this nut from his pocket and rubbed Moose's eye and, if you'll credit it, he said some kind of old-world incantation and the eye was better by the time he got home.

'Moose never had any doubts about the fact that the modern religions are just a veneer over the older, deeper beliefs. He could talk for hours about the links between Catholicism and paganism. He was well into reincarnation. Witchcraft. Honestly, he had candles burned around the clock, he regularly performed banishing rituals, and he protected his friends by drawing sigils on their hands. But once he got too far into the cocaine, all the worst aspects of his paranoia got hold of him. He lost himself for a while. He felt inclined to go on very bizarre tangents about Aleister Crowley or the Nazis or numerals a lot . . . He was completely wired. Maniacally wired. He could talk for twenty-four hours a day and he was absolutely convinced something evil was trying to reach out to him. We were living in an old manor house in Surrey for a few months there and he was absolutely certain that this painting in the hallway was possessed and that something was coming through and reaching out for him. The record company put me in touch with a woman who'd done a bit of work for Bowie. She was the real deal, proper white witch with the full black velvet dress and emerald eyes. But she was off dealing with her own psychic battles and couldn't help. Moose was proper off his head at this point and I ended up contacting a woman in the north who professed to being Wiccan. And she sent us Dilly. I swear, you wouldn't have thought she was some supernatural powerhouse to look at her. She was just this dumpy housewife from somewhere out in the middle of nowhere near the Border. But she came down so fast you'd have been forgiven for thinking she'd come by broomstick. And she did the business right enough. She had no doubt Moose was right – there was something malignant trying to get to him. She brought him peace and she scared the crap out of me. I swear, she had us reciting all these spells, holding amulets, gripping great chunks of fluorspar. You won't believe it, I know you won't, but the painting burned and bubbled right off that canvas in front of our eyes. It blackened the gold on the frame, I swear. She gave him a big chunk of crystal and told him it would keep him safe then just disappeared and didn't come back. She saved his life, man. Every decent song he wrote in the next twenty-five years – they were all a thank-you to her. The folk stuff he wrote afterwards, that was only because his soul had a bit of peace. He may still have been a bit of a bad lad and he wasn't much of a dad to poor little Ish, but the world got a lot more music out of those bewitched fingers and my mate got to live a life that wasn't all about fear. We did our research, like. This Dilly, whoever she was, she just dropped off the radar. I don't know what I believe but I know I saw something incredibly powerful that night and I reckon she was equal to the devil himself. And he remembered every last word she said to him. You want to look through his albums for evidence of some demonic connection, you have my word, they're there to be found. That's why I don't grieve for him. He's still with us, somewhere, somehow. His son keeps his remains in a big crystal box. Local stones. And he was cremated wearing the necklace so I reckon his mortal remains are pretty well protected from anything beyond the veil. Dilly said it plain and simple. There cannot be a believer in Wicca who can doubt the existence of reincarnation. It is the ground work on which our religion is built. We pay, either in this life or the next for the wrongs we commit. Life on the earth plane is only a school. We work our way up on the astral planes, of which there are seven, by returning over and over until we reach true spiritual enlightenment. So we'll meet again, as the song goes. I just hope he doesn't remember how much money I owe him from last time around . . .'

TEN

Petra can hear Mum and Daddy arguing. They don't shout, the way she's heard some parents do, but they can talk to each other for hours in a way that makes the air in the house seem heavy and greasy and full of unspilled rain. They talk in the kitchen, where they think she can't hear them. They've never taken it upon themselves to track down the breeze that emanates from the ornamental vent near the big Rayburn cooker. If they did, they'd know that their voices are amplified by the walls of a boarded-up chimney and then disseminated through the various extractor vents built in by the original architects. She can hear every bloody word they're saying. Usually she doesn't want to. Most nights she puts her headphones on and listens to a true-crime podcast or a recording of some old prog-rock recommended by Uncle Ish. If the weather outside isn't cooperating, she'll play sound effects – rain on aluminium; the sizzle of hot coal; the crackle and burn of logs on an open bonfire. She finds she concentrates better when her head is full of noise. She needs to drown out the din of voices, within and without.

'. . . can't stand the looks on their faces. They look at me like I've got the keys to the vault. I never asked for any of this.'

'Neither did he, Felix. It's cruel.'

'He made it clear all those years ago – he doesn't want what we have to offer. What choice do we have? He's an asset. You know what Daddy says . . .'

'Oh Daddy-this, Daddy-that. What do you think Ish would say?'

'Ish isn't here, is he? His problems are over. I'm the one still picking up the pieces and he's nowt but worm-food.'

'Don't say that. That's horrible.'

Petra lies back on her pillow. It smells of the outdoors; of her own sweat and damp hair. She hasn't showered since returning from her run. Her feet are steaming in her sodden socks; a stain spreading across her old-lady bedspread where her saturated jogging clothes leave an imprint of her body.

'*Harry says Deon was here again. Here in the village, bold as brass. If I'd just been there, I could have made sense of it all. I could have grabbed him and made him . . .*'

'*Made him what? What is it you really want from all this, deep down? You're not this man. You don't smile any more, Felix. You don't hold me. You don't even look at Petra. You're so angry and I'm so lonely . . .*'

'*Christ, could you make it a bit more about you? My best friend is dead and nobody gives a damn who killed him! Any one of those people who rub my shoulder, who pat my back and tell them how sorry they are . . . any one of them could have knocked him down and watched him die.*'

'*Or it could have been an accident, like Tara says. He was back on the stuff, it's right there in the report. That's what you need to focus on, not roping in this poor man and expecting him to make everything clear for you.*'

'*Poor man? I'd swap places with him in an instant. Harry says his wife's been sitting on the bar singing to a shooting party, showing off all she's got. Made a right show of Cartwright – and herself, for that matter.*'

'*Lower your voice, she'll hear.*'

Petra thinks of Deon. He hadn't looked the way she'd imagined. She'd expected rage. Maybe even disgust. Instead, he looked heartbroken. He looked as though he was going to cry. Deon, her bad-boy. Her bit-of-rough. What was it Daddy had called him? A delinquent. A latch-key kid. A proper ASBO-waiting-to-happen. She hadn't known any of the labels so she'd looked them up. She knows now. Knows what Daddy thinks. Well, Daddy can relax now. It's over. She's finished it. She's properly ended it. There'll be no more messages, no more meeting up for those warm, delicious, sweaty fumbles in the dark. He won't send her pictures of himself pulling silly faces, or eating chips, or playing with his dog. Won't send her Snapchats at two a.m.: spliff between his lips, telling her she's beautiful, just fucking beautiful. She's ended it. Ended it the way she should have done months ago.

'The thought of it – of him with our girl. She still sleeps with a teddy, for God's sake. She idolized Ish, you know that. If she knew what she'd done, however well-intentioned.'

'Oh so you're definite now, are you? A moment ago it could have been any of them – now it's definitely Deon. What about Joy?'

Petra rolls on to her side. Rummages about on her bedside table, trying to locate her phone. She knocks her near-empty beaker of water on to its side and hears the tell-tale thrum-and-drip as a trickle of water runs over the lip and on to the wooden floor. She groans. Makes no move to tidy it up. She's pretty sure she hasn't left any of her paperbacks in harm's way and if one of her old crime novels happens to end up soggy, she's pretty sure she'll find its replacement in one of the charity shops in Hexham. Grandad sends her a book allowance each month. It's their little secret. Daddy wouldn't like it if he knew. Mummy wouldn't care either way.

'. . . can't stop seeing it. Seeing him. It was like Pompeii. He was just stone. Stone and this pool of blood, reaching out. I'll never unsee it.'

'It was an accident, Felix. A horrible, horrible accident.'

She thinks of Deon again – that look on his face as she put her hands on his shoulders and braced herself, keeping him away, not letting his wet lips find hers. She had to be honest. She had to get the words out. *I'm going to tell them what you did, Deon. I haven't any choice.*

He'd looked so confused she'd almost backed out of the whole thing. She'd almost told him she was joking, she didn't mean it, that she would take his secret to the grave. But then big Harry had shouted from the back of the hotel and Deon's face had twisted into a nasty snarl, as if she'd set him up, and he was running through the headstones while she was clambering up the oak tree and slithering her way along the branch, dropping into the courtyard garden like a ninja.

She hadn't recognized the lady at first. Her heart was beating too fast and her head was a fog of adrenaline and doubt. She'd just flashed her a mad grin and hared away across the wet grass. It was only as she vanished down the back alley at the back of the holiday cottages that she made sense of the image that her mind had photographed. Cocktail dress, slashed to the waist. Bare feet. Big silver hooped earrings and dark hair. It was her uncle's wife. What was her name? Something Irish-sounding and hard to pronounce? She's seen photographs of her online: seen snaps of her looking hot and unmumsy with her two kids. Cousins, she supposes, though it's hard to use such a word to describe a relation when you've never met them. She's only met Uncle Aector once, and she wasn't much more than five years old. Daddy was trying to 'build some bridges' or 'mend some fences' or 'extend the olive branch' – any one of a number of clichés that hadn't made much sense. All she remembers is a big, open-faced man with red hair and huge hands who blushed when she asked him if he and her daddy were brothers. He'd sat in their kitchen at the old house. He'd drunk tea and turned down the biscuits that Mummy had ordered in especially. She'd gone a little mad, purchasing Scottish delicacies from the finest delicatessens. Arbroath smokies. Dundee cake. Finest Edinburgh tablet. He'd said no to all of them. He'd been polite enough. Told her he liked the drawings she kept passing under his nose for inspection. But he hadn't spoken much and had looked as though he would have given his right arm to be allowed to leave. She remembers Daddy asking him about his son. About his wife. About work. He'd just been made detective sergeant. He was going to be working with a celebrated detective superintendent whose name Daddy knew. Had it been Doug something? Doug Roper, maybe? She can't remember now. She just recalls feeling vaguely sorry for him and finding it hard to imagine he was a police officer, or that they were part of the same weird, tangled-up family line. She knows all about him now, of course. She's done her research. Uncle Aector got badly hurt not long after he came to visit. He nearly died. Then he joined the new unit at Humberside Police: Serious and Organized, under the command of a boss who looks like a smaller, dumpier and considerably better-endowed version of his wife. He's caught killers. He's been rewarded for bravery. She's even seen grainy footage of him online: some midnight bare-knuckle brawl at a Traveller site on the outskirts of Hull. His name had come up in the comments section. He was, agreed the commentators, a double-hard bastard.

He's here now. He's in their little village. He's a mile down the road, snuggled up with his pretty wife. He thinks he's here for Grandma's birthday party. She doubts the celebrations will even take place. Grandfather might turn up to make sure everything goes the way he's planned, but she'd be amazed if Grandma will be willing to make the flight just for a chance to make merry with a son she washed her hands of years before. She barely acknowledges his existence. Her biography on the company website makes no mention of her first husband or her two children and starts only from the moment she started working for Crawford Darling, OBE. Petra would love to talk to Grandma about that brief window of time when she lived in a whitewashed croft amid the heather and the drizzle and the boundless sky. But Grandma isn't much of a conversationalist. She talks about politics, and science, and money. She's very interested in money, is Grandma.

Petra texts Georgia. She doesn't doubt that she's done the right thing but it's nice to have it confirmed. And she can always rely on Georgia to support her every decision.

You will come with me, won't you? I can't face this without you.

There's barely a moment's pause before the reply comes through.

I promise. Whatever you need, I'm here for you.

He looked so broken. He didn't look like my Deon.

You're being true to yourself though. He has to answer for what he's done. You've done so much for him. It can't go on.

I love him so much.

I know. But if he loved you, he wouldn't have done what he did.

He did it for me. For us.

He did it for money. It was always about money.

I hate money.

I've never had any to hate.

Petra pulls a face as she types out the message. She thinks she seems a little pathetic. A little needy. Deon once told her that he hated needy lasses. He liked lasses who could take

it or leave it. He hated feeling like he owed anybody anything
or that they owed him. That's why he'd never seen anybody
for longer than a fortnight. It was different with her, though.
He couldn't stop thinking about her. He needed to hear from
her every moment of every day. He kept catching himself
smiling just thinking about her. He didn't care about the age
difference, or what anybody else had to say. He'd wait for her
to turn sixteen and then he'd turn his stolen kisses into something that would blow her mind. They could get a place
together. He'd work, if he had to. He'd stop dealing, if she
promised she wouldn't get bored with him and if she could
handle the repercussions. He owed money to bad people, he
said. But if he could get square, if he could find a way, there'd
be nothing to stop them. It could be like a movie, he said. It
could be like one of the films she made him watch on her
phone in his uncle's car, snuggled up under a scratchy blanket
with his slobbery dog between them. If Ishmael hadn't found
them together, things might have gone very differently. Ishmael
might still be here. Mum and Daddy might not be arguing in
the kitchen. But he had found them. He'd knocked on the
window of a car he'd recognized. He was out to score an
ounce – just enough to take the edge off the pain. He'd seen
her. Seen what they were up to. Seen his best friend's daughter
half-dressed in the back of a dealer's car. And he'd made a
decision. He'd keep their secret, if they kept his.

'He'll still be awake – my brother. I could go now. Tell him
the truth. He's a decent sort, he'll understand, and if not, well
– he'll still do the right thing.'

'It doesn't work like that. They have their own jurisdictions.
He's not for sale, Felix.'

'No, so he'll do it because it's the right thing to do. I do
love these saccharine moral types – they're such a bargain.'

'What's happening to you?'

'My best friend was killed!'

Petra rolls off the bed and crosses to her desk. Plonks herself
down in her swivel chair and opens up her laptop. Navigates
her way to the website she's visited so many times over so
many weeks and months. Reads about Ishmael's dad, and the
things he did before he died. She opens her email. There are

another half dozen messages. Just photographs, same as before. Photographs of a figure standing at the roadside, hands in their pockets, watching a cottage on a hillside burn to ash. In one of the shots, a bird is captured in the dark air above, its white wings aflame.

Petra feels her insides turn to ice water. Balls her hands into fists. She knows what she has to do. She knows what he wants. It's a simple transaction – just like all the others that have come before. This has to be the last time. It has to be. Eyes misty with hot tears, she raises her top. Takes the picture. She doesn't know what he can get out of the blurry, badly posed shots, but the days when she doesn't send them, he gets nasty. His threats become more detailed: more visceral, more nasty. So she obliges. Gives him what he wants.

She retreats to her bed. Pulls the covers over herself. Grabs for her headphones and holds them to her ears, music turned up as loud as she can bear. She listens to Ishmael's voice, bleeding out from her phone.

She weeps until sleep washes over her.

Dreams of Uncle Ishmael.

Dreams of the burning girl.

ELEVEN

McAvoy listens to the low thrum of music from the room somewhere to his left. He'd like to be the sort of person who felt comfortable complaining about noise. He'd like to be able to phone reception and tell them that he's trying to sleep and that he doesn't need to be hearing Elkie Bloody Brooks at this time of night, thanks all the same. But he hasn't paid for the room. It's a gift. And he's not at work tomorrow, so can't justifiably moan about having an early start. And it's not even midnight yet. He can't justify being irritated. But he's irritated nevertheless. He fancies that if he were Felix, or any of the Hooray Henrys from the bar, he'd simply click his fingers and all assaults on his delicate synapses would immediately cease. He doesn't like this part of himself. He hates the way he resents hereditary privilege. Hates how he instinctively bristles in the vicinity of landed toffery. More than anything, he hates the fact that for all his carping and regrets, it's the quality of his education – and the doors that his stepfather's money opened – that laid the rose petals at his feet as he picked his path through life. He might never have fitted in, might never have belonged; might have traded it all for a mum who wanted to read him stories and kick a ball around, but he's done pretty damn well out of the deal he made more than thirty years ago. Maybe he really does owe them everything, the way they seem to think. Maybe he should be pretty dashed grateful for the opportunity to provide a service for the family that he's tried so hard not to be a part of.

'You're thinking really fecking loud, my love. Do it quieter.'

McAvoy looks down at Roisin, her hair spilling artfully across the whiteness of the pillow. Her eyes are closed and she's been asleep twice already – waking once to tell him off for eating fudge, and another to apologize for falling asleep before she'd done anything to provide him with sweet dreams.

For all her talk in the corridor, she fell asleep almost as soon
as she'd made herself happy astride her husband's beard. After
fifteen years together, he's used to these minor disappointments
and rather enjoys the feeling of sitting up in the dark, watching
her doze, stroking her shoulders with the backs of his knuckles
and hoping she's sleeping soundly, safely; well.

'Can you hear Elkie Brooks?' whispers McAvoy. 'Should
I ring down? I should ring down. Felix would ring down,
but, I mean, I didn't pay, did I? And they'll know that. So I'll
just seem ungrateful, and . . .'

Roisin rolls away from him. Starts to snore.

McAvoy pulls a face. Rubs his hands over his face. Looks
at the empty plate on the bedside table and wonders whether,
if he concentrates hard enough, he can fill it with replacement
fudge before the morning. He realizes he isn't tired. Realizes
that he's feeling positively itchy underneath his skin. He's
irritated. Pissed off, even. He'd like to pull his clothes and
his boots back on and stamp up the hill to whichever palatial
bloody mansion Felix lives in. He'd like to tell him thanks
but no bloody thanks. Tell him that he should spend some of
his limitless cash on hiring a private investigator, or better yet,
asking his mates at the golf club or the country club or the
bi-weekly yoga-and-tiddlywinks league to be a good sport and
find out who killed his chum.

McAvoy pulls a face, disappointed with himself. He always
seems to struggle with the warring aspects of his character
when he's separated from Trish for any length of time. They've
had little to do with one another for weeks: he recuperating
from his injuries, and she tidying up the mess left by the last
investigation conducted by the Serious and Organized Unit of
Humberside Police. It will be the Major Investigation Team
by the time he gets back. Trish will still be in command but
there'll be a new DCI. McAvoy will be third in command.
He's happy enough with that. He hadn't ever really wanted to
step up from detective sergeant, but Trish had told him that
the only way to keep the unit from being amalgamated
into the main body of CID was to meet a specific staffing
criteria and that meant he had to be officially recognized for
a job he'd already been doing. He hopes there'll be more

paperwork and less time on the front line. It always surprises his colleagues to realize that, in a perfect world, McAvoy would never leave the safety of his own little office cubicle at Clough Road Police Station. Just because he's spent a decade catching gangsters, rapists and serial killers, doesn't mean he gets a kick out of it. He just happens to be rather good at it.

He rolls out of bed and hears the old floorboards squeak beneath his weight. He locates his trousers and hangs them over the back of the plush armchair in front of the vanity mirror. He rummages in the pocket and finds his phone. He makes his way to the bathroom, closing the door fully before switching on the big overhead light. He's trained himself to be a considerate husband and knows from bitter experience that Roisin, if roused from a deep slumber, has a tendency to fling footwear in the direction of the inconsiderate fecker who's turned on the light.

He looks at himself in the unforgiving brightness of the bathroom mirror. Looks at the scars and the fading bruises: the knobbles and twists of surgically repaired tissue and the protuberance of ribs improperly healed. He washes his beard in the sink, largely for something to do. Plays around with the expensive lotions in the basket by the bath, rubbing shampoo, bubble bath, conditioner and hand cream into the dense carpet of his red-grey facial hair. He starts to panic when suds begin to rise. Catches a glimpse of himself, all bubbles and froth, and wonders what kind of a person would ever think him capable of catching criminals. He wouldn't trust himself to get his shoes on the right feet if it weren't for the patient tutelage of the two women in his life. Three now, given Lilah's recent transition from adoring little girl to sarcastic pre-teen. He's cringe, apparently. He's a Boomer. He's too old to get it. None of what she enjoys is aimed at him so there's no point in him even trying to understand what she's laughing at or crying at or posting on social media message boards about.

He succeeds in rinsing the worst of the expensive soaps out of his beard. Towels off and considers himself. His beard is now so fluffy that he looks as though he's smeared his face in glue and then rolled himself in duck-down.

He turns his attention to his phone. Trish has messaged

twice. She's sent a picture of her bare legs, propped up on a
sun lounger and facing a pleasing shingle beach and blue sky.
She's got toddler knees and the varnish on her toenails is
chipped, but he can't help noticing that she's shaved her shins.
He wonders if she's met somebody. Wonders why the thought
of it makes him feel so cold inside. The second is a text, sent
midway into her second bottle of red. Is he missing her? Is
he behaving himself? Has Roisin been arrested for stealing
agricultural machinery from some poor farmer's outbuildings?
She ends the message with two kisses – a sure sign that she's
happy, and pissed.

McAvoy sends her a swift reply. He's OK. Lovely hotel
and the food was good. Feeling a bit lost, but no change
there . . .

He stops himself before he begins to tell her about Ishmael
Piper and his mounting suspicions. She'll tell him to trust his
instincts and do what he's good at. She'll tell him that crime
doesn't respect boundaries and that if that little voice in his
gut is telling him to nose around, then he should damn well
do it and bugger the consequences. She's never asked him
what that little voice actually sounds like. He's glad about
that. It would be embarrassing to tell her that it speaks with
her accent, her intonation, and her repeated finger-jabs to the
chest.

'Ishmael,' he says to himself, looking into his own eyes and
hearing the sigh in his voice. He shakes his head as he realizes
that he has been so wrapped up in his own melancholy that
he hasn't even considered the woman who lost her life in the
house fire. He feels his cheeks start to prickle; the blood
in his hands and feet prickling as if infected with a slow-release
venom. He feels a profound sense of his own inadequacy; the
familiar sting of shame at his own selfishness, his own
egocentrism.

He sits on the edge of the bath, a towel wrapped around
his middle. Tells himself that he's not committing himself to
anything – he's just acquainting himself with some particulars;
just undertaking due diligence. And besides, if he weren't a
police officer, natural human curiosity would compel him to
have a basic rummage around online for the particulars of a

crime that took place just a few months ago within a stone's throw from this plush, comfortable room.

He opens a search engine. Starts to play.

It's an hour and fifteen minutes later that McAvoy emerges from the bathroom. His head's spinning. He feels the jet-lag fog of being exhausted and energized at the same time. He crosses to the sideboard and looks longingly at the kettle. He'd love a cup of tea but the sound of it boiling will wake Roisin. So too the fancy coffee machine. Uses the hot tap to makes himself a thick, treacly hot chocolate that's neither hot, nor particularly chocolatey, but which does at least provide value for money by adhering to his teeth in a film of sugary sweetness that he fancies it will take a hammer and chisel to remove.

He makes fists with his hands. Tosses the phone to the foot of the bed and immediately picks it up again.

'This is what it's come to, is it?' asks Roisin, sitting up. 'You're playing "fetch" with yourself.'

'Sorry,' he whispers, for nobody's benefit. He suddenly realizes that Elkie Brooks has fallen silent. The only sound beyond the thick drapes is the ceaseless thunder of rain upon glass.

'How is she?' asks Roisin, wiping the sleep from her eyes. 'Her Majesty?'

'Trish? Having a ball, I think. Weather looks good.'

'Sent you a bikini pic, did she?' asks Roisin, turning her nose up. 'Please tell me she's not wearing ankle bangles. I bet she's bought a toe ring, hasn't she? And got a henna tattoo . . .'

McAvoy sits down at the foot of the bed. Stares at the wooden floor. Roisin rearranges herself behind him, her teasing falling prematurely short. He feels her arms around him, her cheek against his back. 'We can go,' she whispers, against his skin. 'Say the word, and we go to another hotel, or we park up in a layby and sleep in the car. We don't need to be here. I made you agree to come and I knew that all the muck at the bottom of your brain would get stirred up like bog-water. Seeing you walk into the bar like that – you just froze. It was like you were braced for something – like you were expecting harm, or hurt, or . . .'

McAvoy wraps his fingers around her wrists. Pulls her tighter around him. 'They just make me feel like I'm three inches tall, Ro. They don't even mean it. They've just got this confidence – they're so bloody sure of themselves and their rightness; their own superiority. And I've never had that. At home, back with Dad, I wasn't a good crofter. Duncan was better than me. Even at school I wasn't the best in the class and there were only five of us in my year. And then Mum turns up and she says she wants us to be together and that she's showed some of my letters to her teacher friends and they think I've got something – I don't know, something of worth, and she says it's a great opportunity, and she'll help me, and my head just fills with all of these imaginings of her reading to me and taking me to the theatre and going to museums and all the stuff Duncan and Dad didn't have the money for . . .'

'It's OK,' says Roisin, softly. 'You don't have to.'

'Dad told me to go,' says McAvoy, quietly. 'Not harshly. Not like he wanted shot of me. He really did think I'd be better off with her. So that was that, you know? And then I'm at this big house by the waterside in Rubislaw Den and she's introducing me to this tall Englishman with floppy hair and a tartan coat and he's telling me he's pleased to meet me and he's heard all about me and that he thinks I've got quite the romantic soul. And he tells me I've got a room down the corridor from Felix, who's in his last year at the school whose name I was supposed to be impressed by but which I'd never bloody heard of. I'd been there a month before they even told me I was going away; that they'd pulled strings and got me into Felix's old prep, and they'd have to get me measured for blazers and shirts because I was too big for Felix's old ones . . .' He stops, his shoulders slumping. 'Nobody ever asked me. Nobody ever even told me. It was like they all thought I would know. That I'd work it out for myself. And everybody acted like I was supposed to be grateful, Ro. Acted like I'd be the worst person alive if I didn't spend every waking hour exuding absolute gratitude.'

Roisin moves to his side. Puts her palm on his face and smooths his beard. 'And Felix?'

McAvoy closes his eyes. 'It can't have been easy – me just turning up. I don't think they even knew Mum had been married before. I mean, her and Dad, it was never going to work. She was a bio-scientist on a gap year and she fell for this guy who made her think the world was one way, and then by the second winter she knew it wasn't, and that she wasn't. It was better that she go rather than stay and pretend. And Dad did right. But then she got it into her head that I was this prodigy. It was just a poem, a few lines I wrote to her about how I felt and what the Glen looked like on a cold morning, and she showed it to some friend and the next thing I'm a bloody savant and she wants to help me be all I can be. So yeah, Felix was horrible. But he'd been at boarding school for years and by Christ I know what that does to a person. He was older, and he was at ease with himself. He had good friends and he was into sport and he had that whole easy-going charm that I just can't seem to stand up straight in the face of. He really did seem to like the idea of being a proper big brother. But I spent my first year staying so quiet I was almost mute. I wrote my letters and did my work and did what I was told, and nobody realized that the only reason I didn't open my mouth to ask for anything was because if I did I'd have burst into tears and begged to be taken away. There were so many boys like that, Ro. So many lads who needed to be near sedated so they didn't throw themselves through the dorm windows when their parents dropped them off and drove away. Felix had endured all that and it had made him somebody to be reckoned with, so I did what he suggested and kept my head down and didn't make a fuss.'

He stops, his throat closing up as he thinks back. He'd known what the house master was up to. He didn't know the particulars, but he knew that it was wrong. He knows now, of course. He sat through the public enquiry; listened to testimony from the endless stream of former pupils who gave evidence about what they'd endured at the hands of the master who was supposed to take care of them. McAvoy had never been touched. Never even been beaten. But he'd known what was happening to the others. And he'd done what his big brother had told him. He'd kept his head down. He'd refrained from rocking the boat. He'd been a bloody good chap. He's been making amends for it ever since. Felix didn't go to the enquiry.

Felix thought the whole thing was a witch-hunt against a teacher who'd always been dashed good to him. Been dashed good to his chum Ishmael, too. The boys with the serious money were never at risk. It was the vulnerable. The grateful. The ones nobody would believe. Sons of rock stars and chief executives could just float through life free of the fear of molestation in all its forms.

Roisin holds him closer. Lifts herself up a little and kisses him, softly. 'What on earth is it you smell of?' she asks, smiling.

'I think I might have overdone the lotions,' says McAvoy, wiping his hand under his eyes. 'You should send this place a sample pack of your stuff. I'd get a kick out of knowing all the toffs were washing themselves in potions you cooked up in our kitchen while knocking up shepherd's pie.'

Roisin laughs. Yawns. Stretches. 'Need a wee,' she says, arching her back. 'It's too far. Could you cup your hands?'

'Stop it,' smiles McAvoy. 'Jesus, would you listen to the rain?'

He steps away from the bed and crosses to the window. He pulls back the drapes. He can see his own reflection: shirtless, red-faced, wrapped in a towel that barely reaches his knees. He suddenly needs to feel the cold air on his face. He reaches forward and slides open the sash window. There's a glorious gust of rain-salted wind, his damp hair lifting from his forehead and his beard twisting into crop circles as the brisk, heather-scented darkness plays with his face. He screws up his eyes. Looks out across the square; out across the little gravel-carpeted marketplace, hemmed by old cottages; old stones and hanging baskets; a gleaming black anvil and a witch's willow-bristled broomstick leant in the arc of a half-open door.

He blinks again. The door's open but there's no light beyond. It's the house at the far end of the row: the corner plot. It's as dark as the others: no lights behind the closed curtains. The front door shouldn't be ajar like that. Not in this weather. Not at night. Not if he's got his bearings right and that's the place where Ishmael's widow and child are seeking refuge.

Something moves in the periphery of his vision. It's a flicker of white; as if steam is emerging from a vent and forming a shape on the twirling wind.

He jerks his head right. It's there again. Small. Slim. Fragile.

It's a little girl in a white nightdress, soaked to the skin. She's standing by the market cross, barely visible in the pitch darkness. She's staring up the glistening road that leads out of the village and up on to the moors. She's staring in the direction of the blackened shell of her old home.

'There's a girl,' says McAvoy, turning back to Roisin. 'A little girl . . .'

He ducks his head back out of the window. He doesn't want to shout; doesn't want to startle her, but even at this time of night there could be cars, and it's bitterly cold. She needs to be at home. She needs to be looked after.

'Hey,' he half-whispers, half-yells across the square. 'Hey, are you . . .?'

She turns, slowly, as if stupefied. Her actions are rubbery, her manner somehow drunken. She raises her face in the direction of the unexpected sound. The wind whips at her nightdress – pulls her hair back from her face.

McAvoy has to stop himself from reacting physically. He wants to look away; to jerk back – to not have to see what the flame has done to one half of her face. He thinks of wormholes at low tide. He can't help himself: his imagination floods with memories; so many twisted worm-casts in the soft, grainy sand. The devastation covers all of the right-hand side of her face: puckered pink skin shiny around the dark, sticky mass of her eye-socket.

McAvoy swallows. Something hot and cold and painful rises in his chest. He thinks of Lilah and her soft, smiling cheeks. Feels tears fill his eyes. Feels his hands grip the windowsill. Feels a knuckle crack.

'Wait there,' he shouts, his voice almost lost on the swirling rain. 'Please, just wait . . .'

She turns away. Dismisses him as if he'd never spoken She looks back towards the village: past the entrance to the hotel, and the dark mound hulk of the church; the graveyard; her daddy's unquiet grave.

Begins to move across the gravel, her bare feet making no imprint on the sodden, sharp stones.

'Ro, there's a little girl! Ro . . . she's on her own . . . Roisin!'

McAvoy begins tugging on his shirt. Yanks on his trousers. Tugs on a boot. Leans back out of the window to tell her, again, that she just needs to wait.

Stares at nothing but cold, dark air.

TWELVE

McAvoy feels the rain pummel his exposed skin as he yanks open the big front door and clatters out into the cold fury of the dark night air. He tries to get his arm into his shirt. Stamps his left foot into his boot and feels the sting in his still-healing ribs.

'Mr McAvoy? Mr McAvoy, sir?'

Had it been Big Harry who'd shouted his name as he'd thudded through the soft orange light of reception. He hadn't so much as paused.

There's an anguished creak from overhead: the huge metal pub sign swinging on the wind. The sound is of sailing ships; of old trapdoors in abandoned castles.

Shit, what was the girl's name? He can't shout for her unless he can dredge it up from the recesses of his mind. He lets out a low growl and begins to jog up the silent road, looking up at the swollen bellies of the storm clouds as a billion raindrops fall through the streetlamps like tiny spears. He darts between a silver Range Rover and a sleek, long-nosed sports car. There's a long white house over the silent crossroads, its red front door framed by an arbor decorated with unseasonal white roses. There's an autumn wreath on the front door and a jaunty skeleton stuck to the downstairs window, trapped between the white-painted shutters and the rain-jewelled glass. Ahead, a row of terraced properties, huddling together in the face of the driving rain. The old school across the way there, set back behind a great moat of shingle and stone. A tea room now. A steep road diagonally across the way, leading up to a vicarage, set behind a screen of trees. A little cottage, shrouded in absolute darkness; the shape of a fat cat slinking in and out of the differing shades of dark, and . . .

McAvoy stifles a shiver as he reaches the church. It's built from the old stone of the abbey: the same stone that forms the building blocks of the rest of the village. Dead leaves fall from the branches of the thrashing trees, obscuring the thick, dark windows. He glances up, just as the moon emerges from between two curtains of cloud. It looks like an angry eye; a yellow iris half hooded: accusatory, challenging.

'Delilah.' The name rises unbidden. 'Delilah.'

He makes his way down the wet path. The trees throw a mad, mazy pattern on to the sodden grass, bisecting old Gothic tombstones, slicing down ancient table-slab graves. He winces as a tangle of brambles catch at the sleeve of his shirt. He fumbles in his pocket and grabs his phone. Half slips as he tries to get the damn torch to light up. Angles the thin beam of yellow light, swishing it back and forth, illuminating moss-covered graves, illegible inscriptions, memoriams to rectors and gentlemen, curates, headmasters, doctors and landowners. He hurries on, down the little footpath at the side of the church. Smaller gravestones here. Blackberry bushes and twists of timber; great tangles of wildflowers and long grass. He peers through the rain. Catches the faintest glimpse of white.

'Delilah!'

He hurries forward, planting his feet firmly, blinking the rain from his eyes. The graves are newer here, the tombstones shiny, the lettering easier to read. He ducks under a mass of sharp branches, past a little brick outbuilding. Under the low branch of the overhanging tree. He stops sharply. Comes to a dead halt. The little girl is curled up on a little hump of earth. She lies the way Lilah lies when she climbs into her parents' bed at night: one hand under her cheek, knees drawn up, elbows tucked in to her waist. Her scarred features are pressed to the ground so from where he stands there is no sign of the damage done by the flames. She looks beautiful. Looks peaceful, as she lies upon her daddy's grave, making a mattress of earth and bone. Beneath her, the grass has yet to heal; the sods neatly bisected by a gravedigger's spade. The plot is the furthest from the church, at the far end of a line of newer graves. The light catches in the iridescent folds of cellophane that clothe a bunch of dead stems.

'Delilah,' he says, gently. 'My name's Aector. Are you OK?'

There's no reply. If she hears him, she doesn't raise her head.

McAvoy moves closer. The rain is hitting him so hard it feels as if the gale has been salted with teeth. He crouches down, his nostrils filling with the scents of turned earth, of wet grass; of wet clothes and medicated shampoo.

'Delilah,' he says, again. He wishes he had a coat he could lay over her. His shirt is clinging to his skin, transparent around his muscles and scars. *What now?* He thinks. Christ, I should have waited for Roisin.

'This is your special place, is it?' asks McAvoy. 'It's cosy. We all need a special place, don't we? Somewhere we feel safe to be ourselves? Would you mind if I shared yours?'

She raises her head for a moment. She regards him coolly: a cat considering a new toy. Wrinkles her nose. 'You are soaked to the skin,' she remarks, disappointed in him. She makes a face, as if surprised by her own voice. 'Fine then,' she concedes. 'But stick to your side.'

McAvoy's joints crack as he lays himself down on the wet grass. He tucks himself in against a gravestone, three or four feet away from where Delilah lies. He alters his posture to mirror hers. Lies there, among the dead, and thinks of his bed at home: the way he and Lilah would lie forehead to forehead, breathing one another in, when she was small. He feels his heart clench; feels a desperate desire to hold his child. For a moment it seems as though the cold is climbing up into him, as if something is leeching out of the bone-filled dirt and seeping into his own living tissue. He grits his teeth. Forces himself to give Delilah his full attention.

'Bit of a horrid night for sleeping out,' he says, quietly. 'You must be tough, are you? I'm not. I'm a big softie. I feel the cold.'

Delilah looks at him again. Looks at his bulk; the sheer mass of his bovine skull; the great mound of shoulder. 'Daddy felt the cold when he got poorly. Some days he wore three shirts. I had to help him with his buttons. I'm good at buttons.'

McAvoy fights the urge to put out a hand. She's so delicate. So fragile. He wants to shield her from the rain with his body.

'Does Mummy know that you come here sometimes?' asks McAvoy, conversationally. Above, two birds flap and fight in a tangle of blackened branches and dying leaves. 'Would you like to maybe come and get a blanket? Or an umbrella?'

'Mummy doesn't like me coming here,' says Delilah, making a face, as if Mummies were an inconvenience that one simply had to endure. 'She says it's morbid. Is that the right word? Morbid?'

'I know that word,' says McAvoy. 'What is it about this place that's so special for you, then? Is it that big tree? I like that branch. You could make a good tyre-swing from that branch.'

'Daddy made tyre-swings,' she says, eyes bright at the memory. 'Daddy did loads of stuff that Mummy told him off for, but they were always the best fun. He made me a bow and arrow. I don't have it any more. I don't have anything, really. There was a fire.' She blinks her good eye. Slowly, she raises her head so McAvoy can see the ruined skin and sight-less eye that she had pressed to the wet grass. 'I got hurt. I'm going to have an eye made of glass, or something a bit like glass. I can't have it yet though. I still need more operations. I hate operations. They make your brain foggy.'

'You were in a fire?' asks McAvoy, in the voice he uses when Lilah tells him about something that he's meant to find amazing. 'Goodness, that must have been scary.'

She nods, pressing her face into the grass. 'It was. Mummy Number Two was asleep upstairs. She died. Mummy Number One says she didn't feel the fire on her – the smoke put her to sleep like the stuff they give you in hospitals so she didn't feel any pain. I suppose that's good. Or better. She wouldn't have liked to feel the fire. She burned herself once making a casserole and made such a fuss.' She smiles suddenly, as a memory falls like a dead leaf. 'She used to make these amazing dinners with wine in them. Wine and onions and weird sausages. She even made something out of tripe and it was actually nice. Can you imagine eating tripe and not wanting to be sick? She was a brilliant singer and she played all these different instruments. She was teaching me the harmonium. Have you heard of the harmonium?'

'She sounds amazing. I'd love to hear you play.'

She scowls at him. 'The stupid fire ate up all the instruments.

You should go and see our house. It's just all black stumps, like the other old ruins on the moor. They won't even fix it, I think. We're staying with a friend for a while, until things are OK, or whatever Mummy thinks is OK. It's all up to Uncle Felix, really. They're arguing about money and stuff. Daddy hates it.'

McAvoy watches as Delilah raises her hand and strokes the wet grass as if she were lying with her head on her father's chest. 'He was already poorly when he died. He told me he wouldn't be around to walk me down the aisle. I mean, like, yuk – I'm seven! But he'd been poorly. He was getting worse. That's why he and Mummy were always arguing. He'd get ideas in his head and you couldn't shake them. He got cross more than he used to. The man who came to see us, the one with the fox-tooth – he made Daddy so angry it actually scared me, and I was never scared of Daddy, and . . .'

'Oh Christ, you are going to fucking kill me off, do you know that?'

McAvoy and Delilah raise their heads in unison. Stamping between the graves, her face set in a rictus glare of absolute fury, is a woman that McAvoy knows instantly to be Mummy Number One. *Joy*, thoroughly unconfined. She's mid-forties and red-haired, fine features set in an oval face, plumping a little around the neck and cheeks. She's wearing baggy pyjamas under a thick patchwork coat. Men's pyjamas: a paisley pattern on bobbly white cotton.

'This is Mummy Number One,' hisses Delilah. 'Sorry Daddy – I've got to go.'

McAvoy starts pulling himself to his feet, trying to find the eight words to explain the position in which they have been discovered.

'My name's Aector, I'm a police officer . . . I saw the girl on her own, in the street, I was worried . . .'

She reaches down and grabs Delilah by the hand. Hauls her up, even as she's crouching down. She ignores McAvoy and stares into her daughter's face, her hands on her cheeks, the one unlined and perfect, the other scarred beyond recognition.

'Delilah, you can't. You just can't. Do you know how scared I was? Do you?'

Her voice cracks as she talks, the anger breaking across her relief like a stick across a knee. 'Sorry Mummy. He was lonely. He was sad.'

McAvoy plucks at the material of his shirt. Pushes his wet hair back from his face. He doesn't want to be here any more. Doesn't want to hear this conversation. He's no right. He's no place here, among this much sadness, this much grief.

'You can't say things like that,' she says, her hands on her daughter's shoulders. 'Oh God, you're frozen. They're going to take you off me! I can't . . . I can't do this . . .'

She slips out of her coat. It's a huge thing and looks as if it's made of squares of old carpet. She wraps it around her daughter and starts rubbing at her arms – her pyjamas quickly soaking through. She turns her head to McAvoy, eyes glassy with tears. Rain sprays from her lips as she tries to hold back the sobs that threaten to spill out of her like blood.

'I know who you are,' she stutters, eyes on McAvoy's. 'I know what you're here for. I've told her, I've told him – it wasn't me. I don't care about money. I don't care about the instruments or whatever phantom bloody story he had to tell when he was off his head at the end. I just want what she needs to get well, and it doesn't matter how many tame fucking coppers he sends to interrogate me or my little girl – I've nothing new to say.'

McAvoy swallows her words down: coins dropping into a slot. He shakes his head. 'I'm Aector,' he says, again. 'I don't understand.'

'That's quite the fucking boast,' spits Joy, leading Delilah away from the grave by the sleeve of her coat. 'You're the best money can buy, are you? He'd have been better off with Her fucking Majesty, and she's a chocolate teapot.'

'You're funny,' laughs Delilah, beside her. 'Daddy says you're always funniest when you're cross.'

She ducks under the brambles, tugging her daughter along. McAvoy follows, wet leaves slapping at his face.

'Best money can buy?' he repeats, trying to keep up. 'Best what? I'm here for my mother's birthday party. I saw your little girl from my hotel window and was worried. Which effing Majesty?'

'Don't give me that,' she spits, waving one arm in his direction while stamping past the outbuilding, leading like a dog. 'Felix made it quite clear. Doesn't matter what that horse-faced, toffee-knickered, snotty-nosed bitch-bag tells him, it's not enough. We've got nothing, you tell him that, yes? We did nothing. But he won't do the right thing, no, no – not while he's got all that anger and guilt inside him. Has to use it as a stick to beat me with, just because I've never been afraid to say what I think, and . . .'

McAvoy wants to step in front of her like a traffic officer. Wants to force her to stop moving and make some sense. But she's pushing on towards the rear of the church, throwing her words back over her shoulder.

'He was back on the stuff! That's it! He was in too much pain and his head was a mess and he reached out for something he knew, just like he'd always done. And he died for it. Died for a silly mistake, just like poor batty Heloise. It was horrible. But we're still here, and I'm the one having to try and give our daughter a life, but Felix has to have his moment, doesn't he? Has to wield the power like the big "I am"! And we're relying on the kindness of strangers just to have a roof over our heads! You ask all the questions you bloody want, but I'm not playing ball, you understand, and if you try and talk to sugarbun again, I swear I'll call the real police, not his horsey fucking playmate, you hear me?'

McAvoy stands still, inert from the sheer force of her anger. She drags her daughter down the path beside the church. McAvoy stays rooted to the spot, trying to make some sense of the words she'd hurled like rocks. Horsey playmate? Toffee-knickered bitch-bag? He shivers, suddenly chilled to the bone. He glances back in the direction of Ishmael's grave. It feels as though the chill of the earth has bled into his marrow – as if something unfamiliar, something uncanny, is slowly chilling him from the inside out.

'No,' he mutters. 'No, you've got it wrong . . . wait, just a moment, I need to . . .'

A shape looms out of the darkness. Red-faced, wide-eyed. Big Harry stumbles out of the gloom like the prow of a ship. He's wearing an old-fashioned nightshirt beneath a biker jacket, his feet stuffed in unlaced boots, glasses askew on his nose.

'Thank fuck!'

McAvoy steps back, heart thudding. He glances down at Big Harry's shiny shins. Wonders, for an instant, if everybody in this insane little village wanders around in their nightclothes.

'You'll help, won't you?' asks Harry. 'I'm not going up on my own and it'll take half an hour for the useless plods to get here from Bishop Auckland. You have to, don't you . . . I mean, it's your job, and we can take the Landy, if you hang on . . . there's a spare coat on the back seat . . .'

McAvoy puts his hands up. He's getting a bit pissed off, truth be told. He's tired of people speaking in riddles and thinking that he knows what the hell they're talking about.

'I'll do what?' he asks. 'Bishop Auckland? Just take a breath. What's happening?'

Big Harry does as instructed. He visibly calms himself down. Takes a breath. Makes himself clear.

'Ish's place, or what's left of it. I've got security sensors up there. Felix too. But Felix isn't waking up, and I bloody guarantee you, that little weasel's trying to finish what he started. And if not, that other prick will be rooting around looking for the entrance to Narnia or Middle Earth or whatever he thinks is hidden away, and—'

'No,' says McAvoy, in his most official police officer voice. 'No, just stop there. You're telling me there are intruders at Ishmael Piper's property?'

'At what's left of it,' says Harry. 'We've had a dozen of the buggers since he died. Dunno if it's buried treasure or souvenirs they're after, but they won't be told. Knocked down walls and videoed themselves in one of his tunnels last time out. Me and Ned saw them off, but Ned's out at Ponteland with the missus and I don't like to ask Cliffy, he's in his eighties, and then I saw you from the road getting your bollocks rinsed by the wicked witch, and I thought . . .'

McAvoy screws up his face. Shakes his head. Two minutes away is a warm bed. A hot drink. The warm and tender kisses of his loving wife. There is nothing that he would like more than to tell Harry it's none of his business, and to wait for the real police. But Harry knows these people. Harry can translate some of what Joy bellowed at him. Harry can tell him whether his suspicions are correct. And he can't help himself. He wants to see where Ishmael Piper lived, and died.

'Fine,' mutters McAvoy, waving him forward. They can't walk down the church side by side, they're too broad. So McAvoy follows, grumbling to himself.

'I appreciate it,' says Harry, over his shoulder. 'Gave you what for, did she? She's doing a good impression of the grieving widow, I tell you that for free. Of course, if she didn't do it, she's entitled to feel as angry as she looks, which is a thing-ummy, isn't it? Catch-22 . . .'

McAvoy doesn't speak. Just glances down at his phone, and starts recording. He knows to his bones that this is going to be a very long night.

THIRTEEN

ngle feels the tiredness in his arms. Feels it across his back and at the base of his neck. His hands are numb. For three days he has been administering pain, an agent of righteousness: an implement of good locked in righteous battle against a force of demonic psychic energy. And still she fights him. Still she refuses to acquiesce.

He looks upon her, upon what is left. It takes him a moment to focus. The cluster of warts upon his brow adds a lumpy canopy to his vision. The other eye is cloudy, a ying-yang symbol painted in crimson and ivory, like a pearl dipped in blood. The room is thick with smoke. The fireplace is blocked up now and the curling white plumes billow back into the small, low-ceilinged space. The room smells of burned flesh and mildew. It smells of singed feathers. It smells of blood.

She's waking up again. He has begun to recognize her mannerisms. She always wriggles and writhes before her eyelids flutter open and she tries, so desperately, to fix her gaze upon him. There is always a moment before memory returns: an instant of glorious incomprehension, before she places herself. Then the fear comes. Fear becoming terror. And then the rage. Rage as she fights him. Kicks and spits and bites and writhes and tearing the skin from her wrists and ankles as the rope gnaws at her pale, blood-speckled flesh.

He sits in his chair. Watches. She is tied to four iron stakes, each hammered into the soggy wooden floorboards. Her head points north, as the Book dictates. He reaches out with his own bare foot. Touches his grimy big toe against the soft whiteness of her calf. She flinches. Stiffens.

He wonders whether she will try to speak. She has a leather pouch inside her mouth, filled with his totems: feathers, stones, crystal, coin. The skull of a mouse, killed when she shapeshifted into her feline form, has been denuded of flesh and placed at the centre of the bag, wrapped in red thread. He wishes he had something more arcane to bind her mouth than the gaffer tape he has resorted to. But the Book offered nothing and he'd had to make do as best he could. The alternative was listening to her screeches, her pleas, her threats and lies.

'Today,' he says, as he watches her strain against the bonds. 'Today you will reveal yourself, witch. Today you will break.'

She starts to mumble and whine, to screech against the gag. It's an ugly sound. He picks up the hand mirror from the little table at his side. Considers his own reflection. There has been no change. His face still weeps. He is still a mess of sores and running wounds. He feels a sudden rush of anger. Has he not suffered enough? Has he not endured more than any man could stand? Has he not undergone the agonies of the true believer? And yet the wounds persist. The voices, too. He is still a victim of these unholy persecutions. The witch will not cease in tormenting him, and until she releases him from the dark enchantment he will remain a prisoner here, trapped within the walls as surely as the entity in the mirror remains imprisoned behind the glass.

She mumbles again. He can almost define a meaning. He knows what her voice sounds like unencumbered by the charms. He has had to release the gag during the pricking or else she would not be able to tell him the names of those she has enchanted; those she has harmed; which beasts and demons she has suckled and lain with. He has searched every part of her in his effort to discern the teat where she feeds the devil. The two moles upon her lower back bled as soon as he ran them through with the pin. He knows from his research that the true devil teats should not bleed. And so he continued to probe. Only when he cut off her hair with the sheep shears did he find the little withered oddity on her crown. When he touched his pin to its gnarled surface, she did not cry out. It did not bleed. And he had known himself to be doing good and noble work.

He looks at the fire. The irons are heating in the coal, the tip glowing ice-white and vermilion. He fancies she will speak before the dawn. She will condemn herself, as so many of her kind. She will beg for a mercy she has never shown. Then he will build the pyre. And she will burn.

He winces as her telephone rings. It is one of her alarms – the one set to remind her to take one of her vitamin pills. She has many such alarms: for wakefulness, for exercise, for meetings. Her possessions are bundled in a pile by the door to the kitchen, in amongst a towering pile of mildewed, leathery books. For all that he is an adherent to the old ways, he is no stranger to modern advancements. He has familiarized himself with the contents of her phone. He had not been surprised to find so much detail about himself tucked away in the document file and in the little voice recorder, but it had still felt damnably odd to see his life reduced to a series of staccato paragraphs and a flurry of rushed, half-incomprehensible utterances.

He crosses to the pile of clothes and picks up the phone. The battery has almost gone. He has left the home screen unlocked so as not to have to go through the tiresome process of pressing her middle finger to the screen each time he wishes to pry. He feels well acquainted with her, now. She is a Katherine, not a Kate. Her middle name is Faye. She has 113 friends on Facebook and twice that number on her professional profile. She takes pictures of pretty clouds. She takes pictures of horses. She takes pictures of herself, sometimes smiling, sometimes ferocious in her glare. She plays word games on her phone. She visits websites about equine matters; house prices; cricket. She has a subscription to the *Daily Telegraph* but visits the *Evening Chronicle* website every day. She has a subscription to the gym at Slaley Hall. She has visited websites about complex legal matters pertaining to wills and legacies. She has visited sites linked to the rules concerning music royalties and guardianship clauses. She has visited the defunct website of a freelance financial consultant. She has read newspaper articles on Moose Piper. Upon his son.

He strokes his thumb over the screen, leaving an imprint of pus and blood on the prancing pony photograph that fills the screen. He activates her voice memo. Listens, again, to her last memorandum. It is dated three days ago, and was recorded a little under two hours before she knocked upon his door.

'. . . triple check CCTV at LCH . . . 1984 Mercedes S-class registered to one Diana Nightingale, née Stempel, residing in

Cuevas Al Jatib, Badajoz, Andalusia since June of last year
. . . vehicle previously registered at one Baelfire Bastle, outside
village of Garrigill, near Alston. Property registered to one
Leonard Nightingale, ex-partner of Stempel and occasional
visitor to Ishmael Piper's residence . . . note that Nightingale
is referred to as Ingle in witness statements . . . also referenced
in witness statements as customer of protective charms crafted
by Heloise . . . HOLMES check reveals incidents of violence
in youth . . . time spent in a facility, incarcerated in Bomana
Prison, Port Moresby, Papua New Guinea . . . ask Felix about
connection . . . also follow-up on information from Companies
House re. Felicia Holdings and insolvency . . . will call upon
arrival, sending now . . . signal's bloody awful . . . I'll try
again when I'm back in civilization . . .'

He marvels at her as she writhes against the bonds. He
glances again at the mirror. Sees *her*, trapped beneath the
glass. For a moment she looks straight at him, straight through
him, the way she did in those first few months; the way she
did when he first began to feel the extent of her power. For a
moment he remembers. Diana had still been at his side, then.
Diana, with her motherly hips and knowing smile and her kind
words and hands. This was to be their new beginning. They
had enough money to live on. They had secured the little house
for next to nothing. He was excited about the work that lay
ahead of him. He knew himself to be a hard worker, a diligent
craftsman. He had years of work ahead of him: a glorious
future, indulging in what he liked best – ripping out timbers
and knocking down walls; transforming the gloomy little property into a light and airy home. Diana kept herself busy planting
vegetables, crops, sewing seeds. She bought chickens and
delighted herself with how good she was at taking care of
them: even building a coop and fencing them off from the
predators that roamed the stony, heather-draped wilderness at
the far end of the boundary line. She bought goats and learned
to milk them. She learned to keep bees. She started pickling
their produce, making wines and decoctions. She cured his
smoker's cough with a rosehip and elderberry syrup. Perhaps
things might have continued in good fortune were it not for
the chance comment made at the farmers' market in Hexham

as she settled in to her new pitch and began to thrill to the idea of selling her wares in perpetuity. It was little more than chit-chat: a way of passing the time of day with a customer as she bagged up her honey, her home-made sauerkraut and range-baked potato scones. The customer was on her first visit back to the area since she was a girl. She'd been intrigued by the village mentioned in Diana's sign. Some seventy years had passed since she'd thought of the little village near Alston as her home, but she had vivid memories of playing in the old mineshafts and abandoned buildings between Alston and Garrigill. She and her friends would tease each other, challenge one another, see how close they could bring themselves to get to the eerie old bastle on the hill. They'd called it the witch's cottage. Had a bad energy, so they said. A child had died there, so they said. A woman had been burned in her own fireplace by a group of villagers convinced she had bewitched their cattle. Another had been hanged, drawn and quartered for her role in the procurement of body parts: supplying the hearts, kidneys, eyes and fingers of children for a coven of moon-worshipping heathens. Diana had taken little notice. She'd told her husband only because she knew him to have a passing interest in matters occult: a hangover from his days in the Merchant Navy, travelling to distant lands and immersing himself in the peculiarities of other places, other ways. She did not know what she unleashed. She did not know what those words brought into their home. He began to see things. Hear things. Feel an encroaching, gathering darkness. The crops began to wither; the plants die. One of the goats found their way into the abandoned mineshaft in the next valley and was unable to find its way out: its death a rhapsody of mournful, frenzied bleating which screeched up and out of the labyrin-thine darkness beneath the moor. Diana began to talk to him differently. His thoughts grew dark. And then the growths began to sprout upon his flesh: warts and sores, moles and verrucas, spreading out across his face and neck, down on to his shoulders. The skin upon his fingertips split like sausages; the webbing between his toes cracking, splitting, weeping. She began to look upon him with revulsion, even as the woman who had begun to appear in the mirror behind him looked

upon him with hunger; desire. He began to look into the stories
she had relayed to him. Began to search for the truth about
the cottage that had terrified generations of locals and which
had sat empty and malevolent for a decade before he and
Diana had decided it could represent their bright new dawn.
He found little evidence that it had ever been home to any
witches rounded up during the persecution of the seventeenth
century. No local historians or elderly residents could provide
satisfactory answers about those who had come before: offering
only vague words of warning that he would do well to look
forward, not back, and that any bad energy soaked into the
fabric of the place would have long since dissipated: not least
thanks to Diana's joyful, colourful ministrations.

Then he found the book. Found the great chunky tome,
wrapped in greasy hide and tucked beneath a flagstone
between the parlour and kitchen. It was accompanied by a
green bottle, sloshing with some frothy liquid and the chink-
chink of bent pins. He had unwrapped it like a gift from the
heavens. Had read the succession of names on the flyleaf,
written in a multitude of hands and all stained to the same dull
brown hue. The most recent was dated 1965. The name written
alongside it was Adela Lavender. It was a name he knew. It
was a name he had seen upon the deeds when he made the
purchase of Baelfire Bastle. Long dead, now. Spent her last
years in a nursing home in Corbridge. Died childless. Never
married. Left her money to a charity for cats and the upkeep
of the little church in Garrigill. He would have left things at
that if not for the curious name she had bracketed next to
her own. It read *Dilly*. He couldn't put the book back. Nor
could he resist uncorking the stoppered bottle and inhaling
its metallic, ammonia reek. The book was called *Tractatis
di Nigromancia*. It smelled of meat. Each time he licked his
swollen fingers and turned the pages, he felt as if he were
at communion, taking the body of the host upon his unworthy
tongue. It did not take long for him to see the text for what
it was: a grimoire, a magical textbook, containing prayers,
invocations, exorcisms and conjurations: page upon page of
text and diagrams, overwritten in places, annotated in others
by a multitude of hands.

Soon after he made the connection between Adela Lavender and Ishmael Piper.

Not long after that, Diana left. She was afraid of him, she said. Afraid of his moods; of the look upon his face when he talked to the darkness as if it might reply. He needed more than she could give him. He had to start helping himself: taking his medicine, talking to the people who wanted to make it all better. He didn't care. He had a new companion now. He had been chosen. He was special. Only when he failed her did she unleash her wrath. He knows he is not permitted to fail her again. He must make the witch speak. He must force her to unbind him; to lift her curse; to allow the dark energy in these ancient walls to dissipate like an oily tide.

He takes the hot iron from the coals.

Sets about his work with the sincerity of the true Believer.

Smells her burning flesh, and knows himself Blessed.

FOURTEEN

It's warm inside the Land Rover. Warm and cosy, with its comforting fug of male air: jalfrezi and shandy, Marlboro Lights and the lingering whisper of damp dog. The heater's been on for a good while. There's steam on the inside of the glass. Harry's been sitting here for longer than he implied.

'That should fit you,' declares Harry, shuffling his bulk around in the driving seat and reaching into the back to grab a dusty coat from a mound of fabrics on the back seat. He hands McAvoy a red cord jacket with a soft white fur lining: something between Santa Claus and Wolverine. It's not exactly to McAvoy's taste, but it's a double XL and looks a damn sight more appealing than the sodden shirt that currently clings to his skin in some unsettling parody of a Pirelli calendar photoshoot. He starts struggling his arm into the sleeve. Shivers and tries not to show it.

'Here, hang on,' says Harry, his accent becoming more pronounced. 'There are some beer towels.' He rummages in the back seat again. McAvoy takes the proffered cloths gratefully and wipes his face, scrubbing at his hair. He can feel the dirty water oozing out of his trousers, bleeding into the cracked leather of the upholstery.

'Sorted?' asks Harry, watching him carefully. 'There's a drink back there, if you're parched.'

McAvoy shakes his head. 'Come on then,' he mutters, and waves a hand in the direction of the empty road ahead. 'Let's have a look.'

Harry gives a tight smile of thanks. 'I knew you'd be up for it. I mean, it's the job, isn't it? More of a calling than just a way to pay the bills, isn't it? Like the priesthood, or being a footballer, or something. Can't be easy, like – knowing the right thing to do. I always think I'm doing the right thing but then you wake up or sober up or your temper comes down from the stratosphere and you realize that you weren't really

you when you made the decision, so does that mean you're
to blame? I mean, if you're not yourself, does that mean
you're mad? And if you're mad, that must mean you're not
criminally responsible, eh? I mean, my little wife, she listens
to all these podcasts and reads the crime magazines and stuff
and it's weird the way these psychos are like rock stars. I
mean, we remember them but not their victims, don't we?
Makes you think, dunnit . . .?'

McAvoy squints through the mess of rain and dirt on the
windscreen, wincing as the wiper screeches across the glass.
A blue light flashes past to his left. There's a social club, the
entrance to a little play park, and then it's just trees and fields
and darkness, the Land Rover hugging a low boundary wall
as it powers out of the village and into the wilds beyond the
bridge.

'Lived there for a bit,' says Harry, conversationally. He nods
in the direction of a big old tavern, faceless and black, hugging
the lip of the curving road. 'Staff house for the hotel.
God, the parties. There's nobody under the age of fifty who
hasn't woken up in the bath there. Your brother's up yonder, in
the old chapel. He'll be on his way up, I shouldn't wonder.
Spent a fortune on that place. Doesn't really like inviting the
locals in – you can see the poor sod wincing whenever one of
his mates forgets a coaster, y'know. He's social, but that bit
apart, if you get me. Weird dynamic sometimes, in a village
like this. You'll have millionaires drinking alongside blokes who
can't afford to put a tenner's worth of fuel in their car to get
themselves to work. Some weird bedfellows, right enough . . .'

McAvoy can't face much more in the way of local history.
He's cold and wet and more than a little baffled and he's
already feeling the familiar creep of regret. He's made a poor
decision. He's jumped in with both feet. He's going to make
a prick of himself again, he can tell.

'Bugger, that's nigh-on a reservoir up ahead, innit?'

McAvoy makes a face as he runs Harry's thick local accent
through the software in his head. He follows Harry's gaze.
The road becomes a river a little further ahead. There's a
colossal stretch of fast-flowing, frothing water churning across
the carriageway.

'I'd give it a bash in the Fiesta but if the Landy packs up then I'm in the shit. We'll gan Townfield way . . .'

McAvoy jerks back in his seat as the vehicle swings right, sending a colossal wave of water into the flood ahead and accelerating up a steep side road past a rising bank of trees. Little farm cottages flash past through the dark bars of sodden tree-trunks.

McAvoy waits until there's a relatively clear stretch of road before he turns in his seat and looks at the side of Harry's enormous head. He asks the question without preamble, nothing but gentle curiosity in his soft, low voice. 'Joy seemed to think I was here on Felix's behalf, Harry. Had the distinct idea that I was – what was the phrase? – on the payroll, that was it. Don't suppose you'd know anything about that, would you? I mean, I'm here for a birthday party. Seems an odd conclusion to jump to.'

Harry keeps his eyes on the road. 'Lovely church that,' he says, nodding in the direction of a great chunk of nothingness hiding behind the rain. 'There's a bloke I know who's writing a book on some of the old myths and legends from round here. Knows his stuff. I could introduce you, if you're inter-ested. Got his number in my phone . . .'

McAvoy works his jaw in a circle. There's an audible crack as hinge and bracket realign themselves. He feels the pressure diminish at his temples, even as the pain in his neck and shoulders begins its familiar throbbing scream for his attentions.

'She seems a lovely girl,' says McAvoy, still staring at Harry. 'Delilah, yes? Has she done that before? Gone to lie down with her dad?'

Harry makes a face. 'Was that what she was doing? Fuck, half the locals think she's up there digging him up and the others say she's there to make sure he's six feet under. Poor lass. By the time she's old enough to tell people what really happened, I doubt she'll remember what's true and what's a – whaddycallit? – a projection; an invention. I mean, I heard that there's no such thing as a real memory. We just make up narratives and convince ourselves that's what really happened.'

McAvoy lets the silence stretch out. He peers up through

the glass as the wiper momentarily scrapes away the raindrops and falling leaves. The clouds roll and roil like molten lead.

'So Felix hasn't told people that I'm looking into the death of his friend?' asks McAvoy, and he allows a little irritation to bleed into his voice. 'He hasn't let Joy think that even though the local police haven't got anywhere, he's got a tame detective in the bank – somebody who's going to shake the tree and see what falls out? Nothing like that, no?'

Harry glances across at him as the thick, chunky wheels of the Land Rover rattle over a cattle grid. The sound of the raindrops on the bonnet and glass becomes something closer to gunfire. Behind his dirty, rain-streaked glasses, his eyes are jittery and fast, scanning the road ahead, the mirrors, the back seat. Harry's nervous.

'You do know that I'm barely anything to the Darling clan, don't you? I'm not one of them. Never was. Don't want to be. The idea that we're brothers is absurd. We've barely had half a dozen conversations these past thirty years. His dad married my mother. That's the end of it. I'm not some private detective or armchair sleuth that's going to get suckered in to some crazy murder mystery. I'm a detective inspector with Humberside Police and I'm having a few days off. Now, please, tell me what he's told people.'

Harry fiddles with the heater. Glances in the mirror again. He sags a little, even as his knuckles grow whiter around the wheel. 'He's not getting over Ishmael,' he says, as quietly as he can above the thunder of the rain. 'He can't let it be an accident. He's convinced himself somebody did this to him – somebody who wanted his money, or someone who just didn't like him and how he lived and how much privilege and luxury he'd spaffed up the bloody wall. He was a charming sod, y'know. Charmer, when he laid it on. He'd have you laughing one moment then breaking your heart with some bit of poetry that bubbled up out of him like water from a spring. Remembered a good turn, too. Knew how to square his ledger. You did him a good turn, he'd do one for you, no matter what. Couldn't stand an unsettled debt. Man of his word and I'll not hear anybody say anything to the contrary. You could go six months without seeing him but if he popped into your local he'd know whether it was him or you who'd bought the last round. That's why people have no trouble believing his promises. He'd always tell people he liked, or who did him a service – don't you worry, there'll be something set aside for you when I'm gone. Just pub talk, mostly, isn't it? But when the person who's sayin' it is the only son of one of the biggest rock stars of his age? When you don't know how much he's got but you're pretty damn sure it must be a tidy sum? At a time when people are choosing between feeding the bairns or putting the heating on? People's minds might start to turn dark. He got ill, see – he knew he wouldn't be here for ever. He made his arrangements. Made them with Felix and his solicitor. Everything would be going to Joy, and Heloise, and then to Delilah. A good chunk of it was going to be shared about between the people who he'd cared about. Is that a fiver or fifty grand? Is that a teaspoon or his dad's old Stratocaster? And then he has an accident? Happens to fall down and bang his head and skewer himself and pull down half a bag of cement on top of himself? Happens to start a fire along the way? You tell me, in a village like this, who wouldn't be gossiping? Who wouldn't be asking questions? Did he do it himself? Was it Joy? Was it some husband? Some dealer? Or was it one of his so-called mates from the village, hastening along the inevitable to find out whether they were going to be a few grand better off before the winter sets in?'

McAvoy doesn't ask any questions. He lets Harry talk. He's warming through a little, though the lingering cold that had seeped into his marrow as he lay upon the fresh grave has not totally disappeared. He feels oddly violated; perversely colonized, as if an intruder has rummaged around inside his home and left without locking the doors.

'Felix is executor of the will. It should have all been cleared up as soon as Tara told him there was zero chance of building a case against anybody or even proving that it was anything other than an accident. But he's convinced himself that one of us killed his mate. Well, not me, I mean, we're pretty tight. But there's half a dozen different people in the village who are expecting to hear they've been left a few bob, as Ishmael promised.'

'Including you?' asks McAvoy, pointedly.

'Aye, including me. But unless it's six figures, it'll do nowt but pay off half the bailiffs who are after me for council tax and parking fines and unpaid energy bills. It's nowt to me. I'd have liked some of his fluorspar boxes, but he flogged them off long since and they weren't worth much to begin with. Grandad was a miner, see? Worked alongside Ish's grandad, up yonder. For all that he's a rock star's son, he's a lead miner's grandson and that's more important to me than what's in his bank account. And I don't believe none of those silly rumours about voices and rituals. I'm just trying to do right by my mate.'

'Which one?' asks McAvoy. 'Ishmael or Felix?'

'Same thing,' shrugs Harry. 'Thick as thieves. More like brothers than friends, them two . . .' he stumbles over his words as he realizes who he's talking to. 'I mean, I've no doubt you and him could have been close, if circumstances were different, like. Everybody knows that Ish had his wild years. It was Felix who got him clean, sorted him out, brought him home – gave up the London life to be close enough to him to keep him on the straight and narrow. They lived in each other's pockets. Felix is just trying to do the right thing. He might have dropped your name here and there – just a subtle little snippet of conversation to say you were popping up for a catch-up, maybe celebrate with the family. Your name just bubbled up, and in this day and age? Any bugger is going to Google, aren't they? And then people talk.'

McAvoy rubs his hand across his jaw. Up ahead, a ramrod-straight chimney is rising above the rugged slopes of heather-clad moorland. It pokes into a sky the colour of crushed damsons, pulverized sloes.

'House is next to the pumping station,' says Harry, as he rolls the vehicle to a halt. He makes a face, squinting through the glass. 'Balls, I can't see Felix. Can't see owt else either.' He fishes his phone from his pocket and finds the security app that had alerted him to intruders. 'Here,' he says, and replays the footage that had been pinged on to his phone. McAvoy narrows his eyes. There's a static camera pointing at a sagging outbuilding and a tangle of fire-damaged timbers. The video moves jerkily, like stop-motion animation. But there's no mistaking the figures that pass into shot. A big, bulky mass.

Two more, moments later; just a glare of white flesh and bright eyes, high collars, low hats.

'And you've called the police?' asks McAvoy.

'Aye, good luck with that. Unless you've got Tara on speed-dial and your name has a hyphen, there's no chance. I do have her in my phone, like. She can be a snotty cow but she's a laugh when she's had a pink gin.'

McAvoy knows that he should stay in the vehicle. He doesn't want to step out into the rain and poke around in the ruins of a dead man's life. He doesn't want to go looking for intruders in the cold and the dark.

'I've got a crowbar in the back,' says Harry, who seems to be having the same conversation with himself. 'Or we could just knock it all on the head, eh? Pop back in the morning. Silly idea, now I think about it. And if Felix is so bloody concerned, he can do it himself, eh?' Harry starts fiddling with the gearstick, looking in the mirror again.

McAvoy puts his hands in the pockets of the borrowed coat. He can feel old receipts and sweety wrappers. 'You loaned Roisin a coat earlier on, Harry,' he says, making no move to get out of the car. 'We found some paper in the pocket. A map, you might say. I'd like to ask you if they mean anything to you. I'd like to ask Felix too. To be honest, I'd like to—'

McAvoy doesn't get a chance to finish the sentence. He sees movement by the window at the exact moment that the glass shatters and the butt of a shotgun cracks into the place where his jaw attaches itself to his skull. For a moment there's the sensation of cold, and the billow of needle-sharp rain, and then there's crystals of glass in his hair and in his cheek and his head is ringing as if there are church bells in his skull.

He looks to his left just as his attacker spins the gun.

The barrel pokes through the broken glass – rain plinking off the metal with a sound like plucked piano wire.

'No, don't . . .'

McAvoy isn't sure whether it's he who speaks, or the big man beside him.

The click of the trigger is as loud as breaking bone.

And then it's just noise and smoke and the great explosive blast of shot and powder and heat.

FIFTEEN

McAvoy knows that pain is coming. He can't quite work out where he hurts, or whether he's facing up or down, but there's a low, dull throb somewhere just out of reach of his consciousness. It's coming, he knows that. But here, now, he's somewhere between dream and wakefulness, almost numb.

'Fuck, it's like shifting a wardrobe . . .'

The words are muffled, hanging somewhere nearby. He thinks of written letters: speech bubbles in a graphic novel.

'There. That bit. Tie it on . . .'

'Fuck, he's got hands like bloody lobsters.'

'Don't piss in my ear – I had the other one.'

'You had the trolley.'

McAvoy feels as though his true self is floating just outside the outline of his physical form: as if the part of him that's truly him has been dislocated: a straw refracted through water. He probes gently at his consciousness: a burglar trying windows and doors.

'You got the bits?'

'I'm drying off, you prick.'

'Have you, though?'

'Of course I bloody have.'

McAvoy starts to come to. The pain is gentle at first, almost tender: just a prickling, like a dead limb coming back to life. There's a thudding in his head; a sense that the world has been muffled with layers of thick, damp cloth.

'You going to? Really?'

'It's the job.'

'But it's a bit, y'know . . . bit extreme.'

'Situation's extreme. And it'll work. Trust me.'

McAvoy hears a soft moaning from somewhere to his left. He raises his head instinctively, trying to follow the sound. There's a sudden roaring pain at the base of his skull; a flash

of bright white in his vision. He feels as though his head's in
a vice. He can suddenly feel every individual dart of pain.
There's a clamminess on his cheek, thick wetness in his ear;
his skin feels tight across his cheek and temple. He can taste
blood. Blood and dirt and burnt paper.

'Give him a drink, eh? Don't let him see a mirror.'

'Big Harry's got burns. His beard's burned off down to the
skin, man.'

'He wasn't meant to be there. Silly bollocks.'

'He won't want to see this. I don't want to see this . . .'

McAvoy lets out a low growl as the pain continues to hammer
at his nerve endings. What had happened? They'd been in the
car . . . him and Harry . . . there'd been a disturbance and
they were going to check out Ishmael's abandoned home . . .
there'd been a bang, and glass, and then the blast of a shotgun
right beside his ear and his world had become all smoke and
flame and . . .

McAvoy tries to centre himself; to work out whether he's
on his knees or his arse; whether he's blindfolded or simply
blind. *On your belly*, he tells himself. *You're lying on your
belly with your hands stretched out above your head.* He's
bound at the wrists, anchored to something hard and unyielding.
He's on hard, wet ground. He can smell oil. Dirt. Grease.

'Do your thing.'

McAvoy hears the ugly ripping sound of gaffer tape being
torn from the roll. His head is yanked upwards: a fist in his
hair, and then the tape is wound roughly around his head.
There's a moment, no more than that, when he glimpses his
surroundings. It's a small, low-roofed space. Dark, but illumin-
ated with the cones of light from one or two torches. There's
machinery in the shadows: the rusting hulks of equipment long
since discarded. Harry's sitting up against a brick wall, eyes
closed, half his beard burned off and his face glistening with
pink sores. He must have taken the worst of the shotgun blast,
though if it had been loaded with tungsten rather than bismuth,
he'd have lost more than his beard – his head would be smeared
all over the inside of the Land Rover.

McAvoy feels cold fear flood him; every cell in his body
suddenly alive with fevered imaginings. He hears his breathing

start to quicken – ragged breaths panted through blood-stained, fire-scorched lips.

'Calm down, big lad. Do what we tell you and there's no need for your night to get worse.'

McAvoy jerks and writhes: a marlin trying to dislodge a buried hook. He feels plastic bindings slice into the skin at his wrists. Yanks harder, desperately trying to snap whatever is anchoring him to the ground.

'None of that, big lad,' comes a voice, close to his ear. 'Don't be letting yourself down. We'd heard you could handle yourself. Don't be acting the fanny, eh?'

A boot thuds into McAvoy's ribs on his other side: all the breath whooshing out of his body. The pain is like white flame: a blade lancing into his guts. He feels a rib splinter and tries to curl himself into a ball; to wind himself around the throbbing agony of the impact.

'Top right corner, that,' comes a second voice. 'Stuart Pearce penalty, that, I reckon. Rob Lee, mebbe, just outside the box. Remember that Ginola volley when he was playing for Spurs?'

'Never mind him,' says the other speaker. He's somewhere by McAvoy's right ear – the one that isn't humming with pain. 'Talks a lot. Has to keep his lips flapping or he loses the hole where the food's supposed to go.'

'Funny fucker. Funny.'

'Heart's in the right place, though. And he's keen. Can't put a price on youthful ambition, can you? That proper exuberance you get when your balls are still big and bouncy. I'm not exactly geriatric but I do hanker after those days.'

'What is it I've got? Exuberance? Is that right?'

'Aye, that's the word. Well done you. You'll have a better vocabulary by the time you're my age, I guarantee it. Good chance to expand your horizons, prison. Make sure you're nice to the librarians – that's the thing the decent lads tell you on your first day inside. Good advice, that.'

'Not much of a reader, me. My mind drifts.'

'There's pills for that. Pills for everything, if you know who to ask.'

McAvoy holds himself completely still, letting the voices ping-pong back and forth across his prone form. He realizes he's still wearing the cord jacket. Still damp underneath. A tooth feels loose in his gum. He can smell burning hair.

'I've learned a few things inside, over the years,' comes the voice, chatty – the words arriving in a faint cloud of fruity sweets and lager, mouth so close to McAvoy's ear that he feels the touch of his lower lip against his cheek. 'It's like university for some of us, and there's no tuition fees. Always makes me laugh the way coppers think that locking us up is the best thing to do – as if we'll come out and buy a suit and tie and get a job as a village GP instead. Last time I did a stretch I learned how to make a tattoo gun out of an old radio and a biro nib. I mean, that's ingenuity, innit? Can show you, if you like. Can put a tag on you – let you know you've been here – make sure you remember what we have to say.'

McAvoy rubs his tongue around the inside of his mouth. Swallows painfully. 'What do you want,' he asks, his mouth against the damp stone. 'I don't know what you . . .'

'One fucking job,' comes the voice, cutting him off. 'One fucking job and you can't even do that. Go on, lad – do what you're itching to . . .'

McAvoy hears himself cry out as the boot thuds into his ribs again. His ribs, already bruised to the bone, already kicked out of place, feel like they have all been broken clean in two by the force of the impact. McAvoy tastes blood. Feels as though his bones are being rearranged inside his skin.

'Get his belt, soft lad. Go on, let the darkness see the moon.'

McAvoy feels rough hands at his waist. Struggles, pain stabbing into his guts, as hands grasp at his waist, yanking at the buckle of his belt, tugging at his damp trousers. Fear rises like a scream.

'Don't go getting yourself excited, big lad,' comes the voice. 'We'll be getting friendly, but not in the way you're worrying about. Not my type, if I'm honest. I like the Eastern Europeans. The blousy, dolly-bird sort: scowls and platinum hair and little skirts and puffer coats and whatnot. You just don't get me going in that way. Sorry.'

McAvoy squirms and thrashes. Feels himself cringing, helpless, icy fear puncturing every fragment of his being as he feels his boxer shorts being tugged down. Lies still, shame burning his cheeks, vulnerable and terrified beyond comprehension.

'I think you've got his attention, laddo,' comes the voice, still oh-so reasonable. 'Reckon he's going to listen to what we have to say, don't you? But just in case, slap it on his bare arse, let him feel what we're working with.'

McAvoy cries out as something cold and hard is slapped against his exposed flesh.

'And t'other little toy, if you would.'

Something sharp and metallic is dragged across the small of his back. He feels it graze his flesh. Feels a sudden wetness as blood wells up.

'We've got a pipe, and a length of barbed wire,' comes the voice. 'You're not going to like what happens next but, if nothing else, you're going to have a really interesting entry for your diary. Woke up, poked my nose in, got shot in the face with rock say, had a pipe shoved up my arse and was left for dead in a burning building. It's got teeth, an entry like that. You'll probably always mark the anniversary.'

McAvoy can't force himself into silence. He'll do whatever they want. He'll tell them whatever they ask. But they're not making any demands of him. He strains his ears, desperate to hear the sound of approaching sirens; of Roisin, out on the hillside, shouting his name. All he can hear is the rain and the wind and the faint banging of an open door.

'It was a cell-mate told me about this,' comes the voice again. 'The gypsies do this if you come across as the hard man. I heard about a lad in Lincolnshire who had the old Gypos on his land. He brought in a massive great tractor and tipped half a dozen caravans and sprayed the others with pig shit. Thought he was being a proper Billy Big-Bollocks. They came back later that night. Bent him over and rammed a pipe up his arse. Then they pushed a length of barbed wire through it – the other end tied to his wrists. Then they pulled the pipe out. Left him there with a length of barbed wire in his guts and the only way it was coming out was if he yanked it out. They set fire to his house just to speed up his thinking. Ingenious, innit? I mean, I for one am very intrigued to see whether you're the sort who'd rather burn to death or unravel your guts and crawl for help. These are the kind of questions that I can ponder for ages.'

McAvoy grinds his teeth together. The restraints are biting into his wrists. He begins to strain against them, tugging his arms back towards himself, trying not to let either man see what he's doing.

'We'll film it, of course. When you're proud of your work, you want to share it. It'll be a bit of a calling card for us – a nice bit of PR and marketing. Stick a video like that up on the right websites and you'll get all manner of people tickling you up and asking if you'll take on a little job for them. We've all got a person or two that we want to see hog-tied and bleeding, don't we? It's more of a growth area than you'd think.'

'Can I do it now? Can I?'

'Patience, lad. He needs to know, doesn't he? Needs to know what he's done to get himself into this little pickle. He deserves that much, surely.'

'You're telling him? Fuck, I wouldn't tell him.'

'That's because you're a spiteful bastard, lad. Truth is, big man, there's nowt to tell. This is a favour, see. Favour that comes with a price tag, but a favour nonetheless. You've upset somebody, somehow, and they'd like you to be out of the picture for a while. Not dead, not if it could be helped, but certainly not sticking your nose in.'

'Could we maybe take his nose? They didn't say we couldn't.'

'Some things are implied, son. Your mate over there – he was supposed to just drive off and leave you. Silly bollocks was still sitting in the car, wasn't he? Going to see more than he bargained for if he opens his eyes. Now, get the pipe. Let's get on with it . . .'

'Lie still, you prick! Lie fucking still.'

McAvoy feels the bonds break. Blood floods into his hands. He rolls on to his side, lashing out wildly, his fists clubs. He hits something. Lashes out with his legs: a toddler on their back, thrashing wildly. He claws at the tape around his face. Feels something smash against his shin. Feels weight on his back, an arm at his throat.

He drags the tape free, one eye glaring out madly. One of

his attackers is on his knees, blood dribbling out of his nose and mouth. He's older than he sounded: slight, with a paunch that hangs almost to the floor. The torchlight illuminates a bald head ringed with lank, nicotine-stained hair.

'Get him! Get him, Dad!'

McAvoy pushes backwards and slams against a wall. He feels something break in the midriff of the man on his back. The pressure at his neck goes slack and McAvoy grabs his arm and hauls him over his shoulder and slams him down on the back of the older man.

McAvoy spins around wildly. The room is little bigger than a garage: brick-built, with old timber beams and a slate roof. There's a bench along one side: an old vice set into its length at one end: shelves filled with glass jars and soggy wooden boxes disappear into the darkness where the torchlight peters out.

'Stay down,' spits McAvoy, as the younger man tries to get to his feet. 'Stay fucking down.' He tries to pull his trousers up. Tries to get some feeling into his fingers. Glances back to where Harry is gradually starting to stir; twitching as the pain of his injuries invades his sleep.

'You're dead! You're so dead!'

McAvoy spins back to where the younger man is pulling himself up. Stands there, panting. He's not much more than a teenager. Shaved head and a chunky gold necklace; football shirt under a puffer jacket. He's plump; all puffy fat disguised as gym-muscle. Sweat pours down his face. He's holding the pipe in his hands. He swings it wildly, recklessly. McAvoy jerks back, avoiding the blow. Takes the second one on his forearm and cries out in pain. McAvoy throws a right hand. Misses. Swings it again and catches him with his elbow: a wild backswing. Watches it slam into the younger man's jaw and pitch him backwards. He stumbles forward and grabs McAvoy by the head, his hands either side of his skull. Lets go for a moment, and slaps his great flipper-like hands against his ears, one after the other. His ears ring; his skull slapping against the inside of his head. Every circuit in his brain shuts down at once and he drops to the floor in a great puddle of splayed limbs.

'That'll do, cunt,' hisses the older man, on his knees. He's wrapping barbed wire around his fist. He glances towards the bench. The shotgun lies across it like a street-sign.

'Don't do it,' wheezes McAvoy. 'Just don't . . .'

He makes a lunge for the gun. McAvoy hurls himself towards the bench and thuds into the back of the older man. He takes a punch to the gut. Another to the chest. He feels the barbs puncturing his skin. His arms feel rubbery, feel useless. He swings his head: makes a wrecking ball of his huge skull. There's a sickening crack as his forehead slams into the other man's cranium. He staggers back, hearing bells and steam trains. Watches as the older man slips to the floor like a bag of butchered meat.

McAvoy drops to his knees. Puts his face in his hands. His fingers, barely functioning, rub feebly at the glass that peppers his face. He smears the heel of his hand at the blood that leaks from his ear. He tries to stand up and finds that he can't quite work out up and down. His eardrum's perforated. He feels sick. Feels as if he's just stepped off the waltzers. He manages to drag himself towards Harry. He's sitting against the wall, eyes wide, face pink where his beard's burned away.

'McAvoy?' he asks, eyes wide. 'There was a gun . . . am I shot . . . fuck, I didn't mean, I swear, I didn't . . .'

McAvoy manages to pat him on the forearm with his useless hand. 'Felix?' he asks, raspily. 'Felix told you to bring me here?'

Harry tucks his arms into his sides as the pain grips him. 'Not for this. I swear, he said there'd been a break-in . . . said you might help . . .'

'But they said you weren't meant to be here – said you had to drop me off and scarper.'

Harry looks at the two unconscious men. Looks at McAvoy, face bloodied, eyes wide. 'Who are they?' he asks, dropping his voice. He looks around, suddenly frantic. 'Where are we?'

'Phone,' says McAvoy, putting out his hand. 'Now.'

Harry fumbles in his pockets. Drags out his phone, the screen smashed across the middle. The photograph on the lock-screen shows a happy, well-upholstered couple: Harry on his wedding day, tweed and a Teddy-boy quiff, marrying a smiling, curvy girl – the cat who's got the cream.

'Open it,' says McAvoy, and waits as Harry keys in the code. McAvoy wriggles his fingers. Paws at the different icons on the screen. Goes through Harry's messages. There's nothing new – the message from Felix reads as Harry claims it had.

'They'll just have been making shit up – scoring points, fucking around – I swear, if I was into all this nasty shit, I'd have a lot less debts . . . I'm everybody's mate, I don't argue . . . this is nowt to do with me.'

McAvoy pats his pockets. He feels the outline of his phone. Squeezes it free like a bar of soap in a wet palm. He fumbles with it. Glances at the screen. It's still recording. He's got every word they said. For all their big talk, they were too amateur to check his pockets.

McAvoy turns at the sound of groaning from the far end of the building. The younger man is starting to stir. McAvoy limps over to where he lies and goes through his pockets. He has a badly forged student card in the inside pocket of his coat. It's in the name of Deon Harrison. McAvoy rummages in the pockets of his jeans. There's a roll of notes wrapped in an elastic band and a vaping machine. The key to the Land Rover is in his inside pocket. His phone is in his back pocket, inside a case that shows a picture of Bob Marley and a cannabis leaf. McAvoy slides it from the case. The pass-code is written in marker pen on the inside of the plastic. There's also a strip of photobooth pictures: Deon, leering and grinning, arms draped over a slim, dark-eyed girl with high cheekbones and smooth, honey-gold skin. He recognizes her as Petra: as Felix's daughter.

'You want me to call the police?' asks Harry, his voice quavering. 'Fuck, do you know how long it took to grow this beard? I use oils and everything? I don't think I can hear out of this ear. That's Deon, isn't it? Little shit. He deals, yeah? Tried to grab him earlier on in the church but he was too slippery. Who's the older bloke? Fuck, is that barbed wire? What did I miss when I was out? God, my head hurts . . .'

McAvoy crosses to the older man. He's groggy, eyes swimming in his head. Blood runs from his mouth, his nose. One eye is milky, blood-smeared.

'Who told you to do this?' demands McAvoy, forcing his face into the man's wandering vision. 'Who sent you these pictures? What do they want?'

The older man's eyes roll back. McAvoy remembers the impact of their heads. He wonders if the older man's skull is fractured. Whether his brain is swelling. Whether he'll live.

'Ambulance,' says McAvoy putting out a hand to grab the workbench and hauling himself upright. 'No police. You found them here. Head injury – suspected fractured skull.'

Harry starts to haul himself up but his feet give out from under him. 'You sound like you're leaving me here. Where am I telling them I am?'

McAvoy takes Deon by the hood of his jacket and hauls him upright. He drags him towards the door and kicks it open. The little building fills with rain and wind; the scents of diesel and honey. McAvoy peers outside, squinting into the distance. He can see the shimmer of the Land Rover's bonnet; can hear the thunder of rain on its surface.

'We're where we're meant to be,' growls McAvoy. 'Ishmael's house. Get them here before he dies, yeah. And if you're lying, if you've set me up . . .'

'I didn't, I swear . . .'

McAvoy holds his gaze. Harry looks away first.

'Where are you taking Deon?' he asks, at last.

McAvoy reaches down and picks up the shotgun. Hauls the semi-conscious young man out and into the cold night air.

'Felix,' growls McAvoy. 'I think it's time for a reunion, don't you?'

SIXTEEN

Roisin dreams.

She's only partway asleep, restless and agitated in the purgatory between consciousness and its older, dark sister. She feels as though she's bobbing in dark water, rising and sinking, grasping for wakefulness, trying to clutch the light. She knows she's in the posh bed, in the posh hotel, in the strange little medieval village where she and her husband have been invited, or summoned, or brought. But behind her eyelids she is slipping, descending: spiralling down into a place of locked doors and long corridors, where ugly things slither and grasp and whisper her name. It has been a long time since Roisin was troubled by such sensations. Things happened to her in her youth that left her afraid to close her eyes. But these past years she has felt safe and loved, cocooned from harm by Aector's embrace. She's suffered for loving him, suffered at the hands of those who would see him broken, but she has always known that she would rather face the shadows holding Aector's hand than the true darkness that floods in when they are apart. Here, now, she feels like a child again, her hands grabbing at the bedsheets, whimpering as she twitches, jerks; tears running out of her screwed-up eyes to puddle in her ears and pool upon the soft white pillow.

Inside the dream, she stands a dozen paces from a burning house. The flames are cartoonish, childlike: a collage of red and gold leaves stuck upon the black hulk of an old, once-pretty home. There are birds pecking at black grass. Somewhere nearby she can see a white cat with mismatched eyes. It's horribly thin: not much more than fur stretched over a skeleton. It looks as though it has dug itself free from a long-closed tomb. It's staring past the house, mewling pitifully. She finds herself moving forward: gliding over wet earth; the heat of the flames seeming to scorch her skin, to singe her hair. She tries to turn away. Rolls over in the bed and lets out a cry as she feels the flames upon her back.

Suddenly she feels ice cold. She's standing up to her waist in freezing black water. She's in a deep, dark place: not enough air, something hideous and squelchy between her toes. She puts her hands out. Feels slimed, crumbling brick. Her heart thuds in her chest; a bass-drum pedal slamming against her ribcage. She can't breathe. It's as if some grotesque, viscous tuber were worming its way into her mouth, into her nostrils, into her ears. She tastes metal. Tastes earth. Feels the sleek wet fur of some screeching beast slap at her cheek. Her eyes open like a door being kicked. She knows she's awake and yet the sensation lingers. An image hovers there, a stencil outline superimposed on to the soft yellow air above the bed. It's a statue of a man, lying upon his side: a depiction of pure and perfect anguish, face contorted in pain, in grief. As she stares, its stone eyes creak open. Blood pours down petrified cheeks, dripping down, into her mouth, splashing on to her breasts and belly, puddling in her ears . . .

She jerks upright, hands in front of her face. Breathes deep. Clutches the black Madonna that hangs at her neck. She glances at the empty pillow at her side. He's not back.

Roisin rubs at her arms. She's goosepimpled. Soaked to the skin. She expects the dream to fade but it remains at the forefront of her consciousness; a picture so vivid that the colours seem wet. She picks up Aector's pillow and holds it, seeking his scent. She finds none. He's barely even lain down since they arrived. She remembers him shouting something about a girl in the graveyard – some mad panic that required his instant attention. She'd barely acknowledged it. He's spent the majority of their life together dashing off to deal with some emergency or another and she has never felt the urge to grumble at him for putting the well-being of others before his own. She knows what kind of person that would make her.

She glances at the clock on the bedside table. It's 3.04 a.m. She's heard it called The Devil's Hour: a time when the gap between this world and the next is at its thinnest. It's Samhain in a day or so: another diminishing of the veil. It's the end of the harvest: the dawning of winter. In another age, it was a washes her face with cold water, wraps a towel around and returns to the bedroom, finding her cigarettes and in her handbag and crossing to the window. She slides n and sits on the sill, feeling the cold, dark air as it swirls the room, hurling fat raindrops against her skin. She lights Breathes the smoke deep into her lungs. Feels herself calm wn a little. She flips open her phone. There are missed lls from home. Voicemails too. She listens to the panicky essage from Sophia. Lilah's had a night-terror. She woke creaming, wouldn't be calmed. She's in bed with her brother now, sleeping soundly. She shouldn't have called but she didn't know what to do.

Roisin feels her heart swell as she pictures her son holding her daughter; her hair in his face, her little-girl breath in his nose. He'll be awake, she knows that. His arm will be dead beneath her weight, but he won't move lest he disturb her: won't roll away lest he pitch her back into the nightmare.

There's a missed call from a number she vaguely recognizes but which isn't linked to any named contact. A text message too, written in the formal, awkward style of an older user, complete with correct spelling and grammar.

> Good evening Roisin. This is Crawford Darling OBE. We are having a few logistical difficulties and shan't be making our arrival until the morrow at the earliest. I'd advise that you seek out Felix for a better precis of events and the possible repercussions. Pass on my apologies to your husband. I'm sure he shall find something to keep himself occupied. I do hope that the room is satisfactory. Please do add whatever you wish to the tab. Mightily obliged for all that Aector is doing for the family. Cheap at twice the price! Sincerely, CD.

She curls her lip. She has no doubt she will hate Crawford in person as much as she hates him in theory; though, if she's honest, it's Aector's mother for whom she reserves most of her ire. What kind of a prick writes to somebody's wife and insists they get their husband in line? She doubts he's already written to Aector. He'd have told her. Roisin doesn't believe for a

time of ritual and power. Among ~
always been recognized as someboo~
got more than a little otherworldlines~
stands herbs and plants; their uses a~
flashes of the future: pictures in clouds, in
of iridescent colour on top of still water. S~
only owns her husband's heart because sh~
Knows too that her children are the result o~
deep magic for which there will one day com~
and McAvoy don't talk about such matters. Th~
their realities as best as they can: their couplings a~
tion between worlds that should never have collid~
joke about it, of course. They laugh that in centuries g~
she would have been burned at the stake. She slaps him
fully with her rough, tiny hands, and tells him that all the wo~
in her family have known, as if by sense alone, which cr~
and plants and flowers can make a man well; can strike hin~
down; can rouse him from the deepest sleep; can cure aches
and pains; raise their ardour, choke their throats . . .

'Where are you?' she whispers, sucking her lip. 'Who are
you saving now?'

She shivers; the sweat turning cold upon her skin. There's
the ghost of a headache at her temples; a patch of sore skin
across her shoulder-blades, as if she's fallen asleep on her
front inside the sun-bed, the way she used to when Lilah was
small. She groans and hauls herself out of bed, dropping down
to the floor from the high mattress like a child exiting a bunk
bed. She makes her way to the bathroom. Turns on the light
and looks at herself in the mirror.

Sees.

He's behind her: face stone, eyes seeping blood; face locked
in a mask of agony, of loss. He's at once a statue and a living
thing. She spins around, fear rising like bile . . .

She's alone. Alone in the cool, brightly lit bathroom. There's
nobody behind her. No bleeding statue. She glances back at
the mirror. Her back is bright red: sunburnt; crimson in places,
as if she has been held against flames.

'Bollocks,' she mutters, shaking her head. 'Nah, feck it.
Bollocks to this.'

moment that his mum will be pleased to see her son at her celebrations. She's never made any attempt to be a part of his life. She came to see him in hospital when he was on life support but she'd seemed ludicrously out of place: sitting at his bedside reading a book on some botanical artist and scarcely even looking in the direction of the bed. She'd engineered things so that she didn't cross Roisin's path. She bumped into Trish Pharaoh, Roisin knows that. God, how she'd have loved to be a fly on the wall for that particular meeting of minds.

'Missing you,' she says aloud, as she types the words into a text message and sends them to Aector. 'Stay safe.'

She calls up a search engine. Blows smoke out of the window and lets the rain slap her face. Types Ishmael Piper's name into her phone and looks into the face of the man who slithered into her dreams. He's handsome: a lot better looking than the contorted gargoyle who had leered at her in the clutch of her nightmare. He's got eyes like Aector's: deep and full of thoughts unspoken, words unsaid. His gold tooth winks out from a soft, slightly mocking smile. There's a red scarf at his throat: a scruffy beard and tousled, curly hair. There's the look of a Romani about him.

She scrolls down. Finds his father. She recognizes him from some documentary Aector watched one Christmas. Songwriter in The Place: one of the true legends of rock-and-roll. She clicks the first link and the band's most famous song bleeds out of the speaker. It's 'Secrets Far Below', a truly iconic five-chord, guitar-led track – familiar from so many movies and adverts, always accompanying some montage of death: of rural ruination; industrial decay. *Am. Em. C. F. G7.* Repeat, until your fingers bleed. She listens to the lyrics and realizes she's never really taken them in before. Realizes she likes them; the melancholia, the homesickness and whimsy; the mournful yearning for the comforting darkness of a home where the fire has long since burned out.

In the darkness; the cavern's mouth
Say goodbye to the alien south;
The north begins beneath bitch-black seas
Kiss the Wear, the Tyne, the Tees

Dropping pebbles into the black
Belly-slither, pulling back
Cauldron snout, the fluorite glisten
Jeffrey's Rake, the demon listens

You let your fires burn out
You let them fires burn low
My chimneys, just mid-fingers now
Hiding secrets far below . . .

She tosses her cigarette out of the window and slams it shut behind her. Skim-reads an obituary. Pulls up another article at random. Digests the same details. Skips forward a couple of pages on the search engine and finds another story about his will.

Roisin thinks upon the collection of items in the pocket of the coat that Harry had handed to her when she was outside enjoying the rain. The garment is hanging on the back of the door. Aector had put the folded paper in the bedside table. She opens the drawer and retrieves the pages. She unfolds them and holds them up to the light. She can make out the faint indentation of words written in a neat hand.

'"Jeffrey's Rake",' she reads, and plays the song again. 'Precisely how off-your-tits were you when you wrote this?'

She finds the album cover on Wikipedia. Reads through the track listings and the basic details about the writing of the album, considered one of the truly great concept records of the age.

She sees a name she recognizes as she scrolls down the page. Sees a link to a separate article about the prevalence of witchcraft in Seventies rock-and-roll. She clicks on another link: a tribute piece to Moose Piper, written by an American music journalist. It's gushing: whimsical and enigmatic. There are comments below the line. One commentator, LNightingale59 has gone on at length.

Fascinating! And almost entirely accurate. I've got what you might call a very personal connection to this incredible story. Wish I could tell you everything but it's one of those secrets that will choose its own moment to be revealed. Dilly may have left this astral plane but she still guides from beyond the veil. She kept things ordered – kept the balance. There were always people like her in Moose's corner of the world – people who kept the bad things from breaking through. Do you never wonder why so many terrible things are happening now? Doesn't the world just feel worse? Lick your finger and hold it up and you'll feel the evil in the air. What if the Witchfinders were right, eh? I'm sure Moose was making us ask that question in the album track 'Leddy Lister's Grave'. What do you think?

There are no replies.

Roisin types the name into Google.

She wishes Aector were beside her, behind her, reading over her shoulder, putting the pieces together as she hands them to him. She wonders if she ever really believed they'd been invited to a birthday party. She doesn't think she did. Something had told her that she should encourage him to head north, and it was more than just the promise of a nice hotel. She suddenly understands why Felix has gone to such lengths to secure the help of an experienced, decorated detective. It's more than just a feeling: it's the cast-iron certainty that Ishmael Piper is a link in a chain – that somehow, the worst is yet to come.

She looks up. Sees her reflection in the glass.

Sees *him*: all stone and blood and pain.

This time she doesn't jerk away. She holds the bloodied gaze.

'He'll help you rest,' she whispers. 'He'll make it right.'

SEVENTEEN

't's too pissing tight, you ginger . . . you . . . Jock! You
pig-bastard Jock!'

'That's terribly racist, Deon.'

'Fuck off. I can't feel my hands.'

'I can't feel your hands either.'

There was a time when McAvoy would have known precisely
how many laws he was breaking by gaffer-taping one of his
attackers to the headrest of a stolen Land Rover. He used to
be encyclopedic in his knowledge of even the most minor
infringement of the rules. After twenty years as a police officer,
he's come to realize that his current course of action should
just be filed under the larger heading of 'totally illegal', and
that none of the minor sub-clauses, addendums and codicils
would make much difference to the overall picture. He's pretty
sure he'll be able to make a case for extenuating circumstances
playing a role in his decision-making, but he's used that excuse
so often in the past decade that he's beginning to fear that
he's become a maverick almost by default.

'Can you even see? You're dead, man. Fucking dead.'

McAvoy glances across at Deon, spitting bile and blood and
venom in the passenger seat, hands taped behind his head with
almost a whole roll of gaffer tape. McAvoy had done his best
to make him as comfortable as he could – even cutting his
hand as he tried to brush the smashed glass from the upholstery. He's had no thanks for it. Deon is barking like a caged
dog, threatening dire retribution for daring to treat him like
some sort of fucking mug.

'Do you know who I am?' snarls Deon, blood on his teeth.
'Do you know who I'm with?'

'You're with me, Deon. And as for who you are . . .?'

'Yeah, prick?'

'I think you are in a great deal of trouble.'

McAvoy glares through the dirty windscreen. The rain has

slackened its assault on the earth but the wind continues to blow in angry squalls: the branches of the trees thrashing madly in a maelstrom of dead leaves. McAvoy has the headlights on full beam but he can barely make out where the road disappears into the muddy lagoons at the side of the road. Big, plump, muttony sheep keep emerging out of the darkness to stare at the oncoming car – forever puzzled by the anachronistic intruder on their mile upon mile of grass and heather and night.

'Stop, yeah?' pleads Deon, his voice suddenly taking on a more wheedling timbre. 'Pull over, eh? We can talk about it. Mixed messages and stuff, yeah? You know stuff, I know stuff . . . she won't understand . . . won't get it . . .'

McAvoy's ears are still ringing, his ribs a familiar cold throb of agony. His hands feel useless, fingers numb as they make fists around the wheel; blood on his knuckles, flesh missing from his wrists. He feels sick: adrenaline wearing off. He can feel himself trembling inside his clothes. He needs something sugary. Needs to rest. Needs Roisin.

'We didn't do it, did we,' simpers Deon. 'We were only going to scare you. I mean, mate, come on, yeah? We wouldn't have done it, man, I swear.'

McAvoy takes his eyes off the road to throw a hard stare in Deon's direction. They both know the young man is lying.

'All right, yeah, but fuck, I'm desperate, man. You're going to set me up. That horsey fucking bitch, she's going to say it's all me, that I did it, and I didn't man, I fucking didn't . . .'

McAvoy stamps on the brake. Deon pitches forward, the gaffer taping biting into his skin. He yells in pain. McAvoy turns in the seat, hazard lights flashing in the darkness like a beacon.

'Didn't do what, Deon,' he says, jaw locked at the hinge. 'Didn't kill Ishmael Piper?' He lets himself shrug – an unfamiliar gesture that makes him feel like a louche French waiter. 'Fine, then. Where can I drop you off?'

Deon narrows his eyes: forehead wrinkling, sweat and blood greasing his cheek. He looks as much confused as angry. 'Don't be a prick,' he mutters, as if the use of profanity is a familiar straw he can reach for. 'Is my dad all right? Did you kill him? If you fucking killed him I will fucking . . .'

McAvoy shakes his head, features contorted in a look of genuine distress. 'Could you possibly stop swearing at me, Deon? Stop shouting and threatening me and generally making so much bloody noise? I've got a perforated eardrum. You have too, I shouldn't wonder. Why not just talk to me like a person, eh?'

'You're not a person,' hisses Deon. 'You're a copper. A bent copper. And you're fitting me up, I know it, and if you want . . .'

McAvoy holds up a hand. Closes his eyes. Starts to count to ten and makes it as far as one.

'I'm a bent copper?' he says, looking genuinely hurt. 'What's that supposed to mean?'

'We all know who you are,' grunts Deon, in a shower of spit. 'You're the brother of Felix Fancy-Bollocks. You're here to do what Saville can't, that horsey fucki—'

'I keep hearing about this horsey so-and-so,' says McAvoy wiping the back of his hand across his cheek. 'Saville? That's the detective inspector, yes?'

'Like you don't know!'

McAvoy moves closer to Deon, who pushes himself back in his seat as if bracing for a blow to the face. McAvoy realizes that – for all his bluster and bravado – he's genuinely frightened of him; that he really believes what he's saying. He thinks McAvoy's dangerous – thinks he's corrupt to the core. The realization hurts. He softens his tone a little. Reminds himself that this is a boy; a teenager. From what McAvoy has seen so far, his dad isn't much of a role model. He tries to loom less large.

'Deon, I promise you, none of what you're saying makes the slightest bit of sense to me. Whatever you think you know about me, you're wrong.'

'Bullshit.'

'DI Saville,' says McAvoy, musing on the name. 'You've provided a statement?'

'No-commented all the way,' sneers Deon, pleased with himself. 'Never got a word else out of me.'

'So you've been asked about your movements on the night that Ishmael Piper and his partner Heloise died, yes?'

'She could have asked me my eye colour and I wouldn't have answered.'

'So where were you?'

Deon looks at him like he's insane. 'Yeah, like I'd tell you. You're probably recording me right now.'

McAvoy shakes his head, overcome with a sudden despair about the future of the planet. Occasionally, spending time with young people makes him feel considerably less guilty about climate change and rising sea levels. He pulls his phone from his pocket and puts it on the dashboard, face down.

'There,' he says. 'Happy?'

'I'm saying nowt.'

'But if you don't tell the police where you were that night, you'll remain a suspect, Deon.'

'Suspect in what, eh? There's no crime, is there? Saville can't make sense of it. It's an accident, innit? Ish fell . . . skewered himself in the fucking rain . . . the witch were upstairs playing with her candles and crystals and was too pissed to put the fire out before it ate her skirt.'

'The witch?' asks McAvoy. 'Heloise?'

'Nowt but trouble,' sneers Deon. 'Joy and Ish were happy before she came along – all starry-eyed and barefoot and looking at him like she wanted him for dinner. Moved herself in, bold as you like. Mummy Number One and Mummy Number Two? All the pricks in the village reckon he had it made – two lasses at his beck and call. Weren't like that. He had twice the problems, y'know? Twice the nagging, twice the headaches. He just let her stay because he didn't have the heart to kick her out. It was Joy who tried to make it all work. You imagine that? Imagine loving somebody so much you'll let them have another wife in the family home? Let them be another mummy to your little girl? It's fucking disgusting.'

McAvoy sucks his cheek, wondering whether Deon's revulsion is real. 'How did you get to know Ishmael?' he asks, keeping his questions conversational, lest Deon remember he's being interviewed by a serving police officer.

'You know that already,' says Deon, and the fight seems to be slipping from his voice. He looks younger, suddenly. Looks like he's about ready to cry. 'That's why you're here.'

McAvoy recalls what Roisin told him just a few hours ago; back when he thought he might still be in Weardale for a birthday party. The voices in the graveyard; the girl who dropped down from the tree.

'You're in a relationship with Petra,' he says.

Deon shrugs. 'Dunno what we fucking are.'

'She's fourteen, Deon. How old are you?'

Deon's expression hardens. 'Never did owt illegal. Never. I wouldn't. She's special, man. We're waiting. Or, I dunno, we were . . .'

McAvoy watches as tears fill Deon's eyes. He growls at himself, furious at his own weakness. Snot bobbles pop redly in his nose.

'You love her, yes?'

'Love each other. She didn't want to end it. That's her dad. That's Saville. That's people like you.'

'Bent coppers, you mean?' asks McAvoy, quietly. 'Who told you I'm a bent copper, Deon? Who mentioned my name to you at all?'

'She did,' snivels Deon. 'Saville. After I gave it the old no-comment. After the article saying it looked like it was all going to be tied up with a neat bow and recorded as accidental death – that it was all going forward to the coroner. She came and found me, didn't she? Made a right arsehole of me in front of my mates. Took me for one of her "little strolls" and told me that it was now or never – that this was my last chance to save my life. Felix had this brother. Copper. Murder police. Some Jock name. Stupid first name. Petra had already told me about him . . . about you, I mean. Said you had nowt to do with one another, not really, but Felix had always said that you would come running if he ever called. You owed him. And Felix didn't believe I had nowt to do with Ishmael dying. He thought it was me. Me or Joy. Or one of the grasping bastards who were counting the days until they could get a few quid out of the poor bastard.'

'You believed this?' asks McAvoy, biting his cheek.

'Made sense, didn't it? All the coppers I've dealt with are bent bastards anyway.'

'And DI Saville implied I would stitch you up?'

'Stitch me up or cut me up,' he says, tears flowing freely. 'I'm not a coward, man. I do shit most people can't do. But then Petra said the same thing, man. Told me you were coming to get answers – to help her dad sleep easy; to make up his mind whether to keep fighting against what's in the will. She came to give me fair warning last night. Told me it was over between us and that she was going to have to do the right thing – to tell you everything, her big scary uncle who would snap me over their knee if I didn't confess.'

McAvoy glances at the road. The rain is starting to come down hard again; hitting the bonnet like pellets from a shotgun. 'So you went and asked your dad to help scare me off,' he says, as the sequence of events starts to take shape in his head. 'How did you get Felix to text Harry?'

'It's not hard. Easy enough to clone a phone. Figured it would be useful to have a rich man's digits.'

'And Harry?'

'Harry's all right, man,' says Deon, with a shrug. 'Wants to be everybody's mate, I suppose. Talks more than he should, maybe. Came chasing after me last night when Petra was telling me all about you. Didn't know what to do when he caught up with me, like – not with a shotgun under my fucking jacket and a screwdriver in my hand. He said that if I tried to hurt him there'd be coppers at my throat inside five seconds. Said there was a big bastard detective inspector staying in The fucking Buttery – would be down in a flash if he shouted. Made sense, didn't it? Confirmed what Petra said. So I scared the big prick, didn't I? I told him that if he didn't get you up to Ishmael's old place before the morning, I'd be climbing in through the window to kill his dog and stick his wife and write his name in her blood all over his bedroom wall. Might be a big lad but he's not a fighter, is he? And he loves that lass of his.'

McAvoy sits back in his seat, taking it in. He realizes that there's a little life coming back to his fingertips; that he can hear more clearly. He considers DI Saville. Compares her to the decent detectives he's worked with over the years. He's heard Pharaoh make all sorts of fanciful nonsense in order to persuade a suspect or a witness to open up. She might have just heard about Felix's detective stepbrother and decided to use the name as a hand grenade: an explosion that would shake some truths from the lips of her prime suspect in what could yet be a double murder.

'Where were you?' he asks, quietly. 'Really. If you want me to believe you didn't kill Ishmael and Heloise, you really do need to tell me where you were.'

Deon's features twist. He starts to cry properly. 'Ingle,' he says, at last. 'Ask Ingle.'

McAvoy feels his patience start to fray. He's on the verge of demanding a better answer when he makes the connection. 'Ingle,' he repeats. 'The witchcraft expert? Friend of Ishmael's?'

'Not proud of it, am I? Ish was good to me, man. Gave me and Petra somewhere to be together. Made a decent moonshine. Talked to me like I was a visitor instead of a nuisance. I didn't want to do it, did I? But Ingle said that was the price, y'know? Ish wouldn't give him what he wanted so he had to get it somehow. And I was the fucking "somehow".'

McAvoy moves closer to Deon. He reaches behind him and with his rapidly waking fingertips, yanks the gaffer-tape apart. Deon falls forward in his seat, shaking his hands, rubbing his wrists, glaring at McAvoy as if he's insane.

'What did you steal?' he asks, quietly.

'Not steal,' protests Deon, wiping his eyes. 'Just a borrow, man. I'd have took it back. I had the run of the place, same as every bugger. Miles from anywhere and people would just wander in and out like they owned the place. Anybody could have took it . . .'

'Took what, Deon?'

He looks down, unable to meet McAvoy's eyes. 'The urn, man. His dad's ashes. Nobody even looked at it – just sitting there with all the sparkly shit. I'd have took them back, I swear. It was just for this thing he was doing – Ish and Heloise, they were into all that witchy shit, weren't they? Ingle was her mate, not Ishmael's. Ish didn't like him, didn't trust him, though he didn't mind paying over the odds for the best gear on the market. But Ish was getting funny at the end, y'know? His illness, it was making him paranoid. He thought Joy was trying to kill him. He had Heloise drawing fucking pentagrams and lighting candles – he was convinced that whatever was under the house was starting to climb out; to come for him – to claim what it was owed . . .'

McAvoy feels cold across his back; tingling beneath his skin, as if every cell in his body has been asleep and is beginning to wake. 'To claim what it was owed?'

'That was what he said to Petra. His dad was into all that shit, wasn't he? The big rock star. We watched a documentary on him, me and Petra – all the occult bullshit, Golden Dawn and Thelema and the big black stain in the swimming pool where the demon tried to rise up . . . you grow up with all that shit in your head, you're bound to start seeing stuff that's not there – especially when you're off your nut on Spice and your body's riddled with Huntington's . . .'

McAvoy shakes his head. Breathes out, slowly. 'And you haven't said any of this to Saville?'

'I haven't said owt to anybody.'

'Petra?'

'She'd hate me, man.'

'Did Ingle pay you to take the ashes?'

Deon closes his eyes. 'Weren't that simple. It was a trade, that was all. He wanted something, I wanted something.'

McAvoy uses his most patient, understanding voice. 'What did you want, Deon?'

For an instant, the young man looks as though he's going to refuse to speak. Then he sags, almost relieved to be unburdening himself of the secret that has wound around his guts like so many worm-eaten roots.

'Peace of mind,' he says, blinking back tears and tapping his knuckle against the centre of his head. 'He was going to close the doors, man. He was going to make the monsters sleep.'

EIGHTEEN

Petra sits at the centre of a great nest of paper. From above, she looks like a bumblebee alighting on a daisy. She's wrapped in her big yellow dressing gown, huddled into its sumptuous folds. It smells of bergamot and sunshine. Mum might be a tedious, piss-weak waste of space, but she's still damn good at the laundry.

Big whoop, Mum, mutters Petra, inside her head. *Way to smash the patriarchy. Laundry, and packed lunches, hoovering and paying the bills. So fucking what? Do you want a medal? You're still a joke. Still a loser . . .*

A sob escapes her lips. She bites it back. Refuses to feel bad for hating her mum. Hates herself for her momentary weakness.

She glances at the clock on her phone. It's nearly four a.m. She snatched a couple of hours of fitful sleep before waking, sweat-wreathed and frightened; the wisps of nightmare skulking away into the corners of the bedroom to gather their strength before the next assault. She's trying to calm herself now. She's taking comfort in childish things. Mrs Faye, the pastoral officer at school, told her to be kinder to herself. Told her that she doesn't need to hold herself to such a high standard all the time – that not all the world's problems are hers to solve. She likes Mrs Faye. She's tall and willowy and her hair is massive. She's got kind eyes and cat-hair on her tights, and she wears weird little wrist supports that she's decorated with doodles, nail varnish and diamanté studs. Mrs Faye doesn't have to deal with people like Petra very often. Most of her day is spent chasing down the delinquents and chavs who only come to school to causes trouble, start fights, and smash up the toilets. Petra's one of the good girls. She's being tipped for top grades across the board when she takes her GCSEs in a little over eighteen months. She's sporty. Arty. She does her homework and belongs to clubs. She went to the new debating society just because she felt sorry for the teacher who had started it with such high hopes and who began to look despondent after four weeks sitting on their own in the assembly hall. But the teachers have been worrying. She seems tearful. Seems really anxious. She handed in a piece of home-work with an apology letter, explaining to her teacher that she knew it was a dreadful piece of work and wanted to give her word that it wasn't going to be the start of a pattern. The rumours didn't help, of course. It didn't take long for staff to start hearing the stories about good, sweet, bookish Petra having a dalliance with some young offender from Summerhill in Consett. Mum dropped her in it, too. Got in touch with the senior leadership team and warned them that Petra might be a little teary for a while as her godfather had died and it was hitting them all very hard. Mrs Faye took her out of German for a little chat in one of the nicer rooms in the Inclusion unit by the Pastoral Office. She'd brought tissues, and a hot choc-olate, and rustled up a packet of posh biscuits. She'd put her head on side, like a bird listening for a worm. Asked her, like two old friends, how she was doing.

Petra didn't let herself down. She cried as much as the moment required. She spoke a little about Ishmael. Spoke a bit about Mum and Dad and the nasty atmosphere in the house. She told her that she was beginning to worry about the future; about which direction to take in life – whether to go the academic route or allow herself to explore the things she enjoys, like poetry and music and art. She'd picked her nails and chewed her lip and given Mrs Faye plenty to jot down in her pad. She'd told her that Deon was just somebody she'd been talking to – that he was a boy and her friend but not her boyfriend. She was too young for all that, she said. She wasn't ready. And if she was, she would do things responsibly. Mrs Faye hadn't offered much advice. It had boiled down to 'try not to worry' and 'try to distract yourself'.

Petra's trying to follow Mrs Faye's advice. She's got her art box out from under the bed. She's creating. Crafting. She's using crinkle-edged scissors to snip out little petals from sheafs of patterned card: gluing them into the centre of a big rectangle of black card. She's got glitter and felt pens, ribbons and wool, crepe paper and old sweetie wrappers. She's got magazines and old newspapers; their pages yellowing, their smell fusty and oddly comforting. She's trying to calm herself – to slow her heart; to keep the doors locked inside her head.

She tunes herself in to the pleasing snip of the blades against the card. Listens to the trees thrashing in the grounds; the shriek of the wind down the chimneys; the slither and rasp of the rain and grit against the glass. Tries not to think about him. Tries not to think about any of them.

Her phone pings. She looks down and realizes that her eyes are hazy, her vision glassy. She's weeping, silently, as if her eyes are trying to find relief without alerting any other part of their host.

It's Georgia, oh so eager, oh so desperate to please.

Saw you were active. You OK?

Petra can't think of what to say in reply. Of course she's not OK. She keeps seeing Deon, with the confusion and sorrow etched so deep into his features that it seemed as if they had been carved there with a blade.

Don't give yourself too hard a time. You had to do it. What choice did you have? You're not a bad person.

Petra laughs, snottily: a high, mad sound that she instantly bites back. Mum's a light sleeper, if she sleeps at all. Dad sleeps on the sofa, or flops into unconsciousness in his office chair, waking up with aching muscles, creaky joints; grey skin and bags under his eyes so deep they look like segments of gone-off orange.

Will you do it after your grandad arrives? It'll kill the mood if you do it before.

Petra turns the phone over so the messages are pressed into the carpet. She can't face replying. She already knows what has to happen next. When the sun comes up, she'll talk to Dad. She'll be his little girl; big eyes and quivering lip and trying oh-so-hard not to fall to pieces. She'll be shame-faced; guilt and regret radiating from every pore. And she'll finally tell him the truth, the way she's rehearsed.

'Daddy . . . I don't know how to say this . . . I just can't, just can't . . . I can't stand to see you tearing yourself to bits over Uncle Ish. I know what happened, Dad. Deon told me. He confessed . . .'

He did, too. Ish had been dead a month and Petra hadn't been able to slip away to see him for more than a quick 'love you' or a stolen kiss. But she'd arranged a 'run' with Georgia, ever the dutiful friend. She got a full half-hour with him. He was waiting in the graveyard, same as always; his kisses all tobacco and Red Bull and the greenish, mushroomy funk of weed. He'd greeted her with tender words and eager hands but it hadn't taken long for his mood to change. Where had she been? Why'd she been ignoring him? Didn't she know what he'd done for her? Didn't she realize how much he'd need her? He was coming apart. The stuff in his head was taking over; the rancid ooze of memory bubbling and popping like hot mud. He'd worked so hard to silence them, to shut them up, to become a person that was worthy of her, to be worthy of love, and a future, and a break from the past. And she'd just left him hanging. Made a mug of him. Mugged him off like he was nothing, like some no-mark prick. Didn't she realize what it was doing to him? She knew about his mum, and what she did to him, and what her boyfriend did when he was small. She knew that he couldn't stand to be ignored, to be neglected, to be abandoned. That's what they'd all done to him, over and over. He thought she was different but she was just the fucking same. And he'd damned himself for her. He'd sent himself to Hell for her. He'd stood in front of a burning building and watched her godfather turn to stone. He'd listened to a little girl's screams. And he'd done it all so that they'd have a chance. Ish had promised him he'd come into money when he died – that he'd leave him something that would allow him to stop dealing, stop fighting – to become somebody worthy of Petra's heart. He hadn't wanted Heloise to die. He hadn't wanted Delilah to get hurt. All he'd needed was for Ishmael to succumb to his worsening illness. A fall. A little accident. It was a kindness, really. He could have hung on for months and years, getting worse, losing his mind, withering and diminishing – dying in increments. He'd spared him that. A little push in the back, that was all. And she'd known, deep down. She'd known that he was thinking

*about it. Why else would Ishmael have told him that he'd
written him into his will? Why else would he have told him
that he saw the decency inside him; that he believed in
him – that he wanted to give him and Petra a chance. He was
all but daring him to do it.*

Petra knows her dad will shout and rage and sob. He'll
demand to know why she hadn't told him this before.
He'll tell her she has to give a statement to Tara, to the police.
And she'll refuse. She owes Deon one kindness. He despises
Saville. Despises all the coppers at Bishop Auckland CID.
She'll give her statement to Uncle Aector. She's read all about
him. He seems a good man. He'll understand. He won't let
Deon get hurt. He'll see things done properly. That's why she
wanted him here. That's why she persuaded Grandad to invite
him to Grandma's birthday party.

The phone buzzes again. She ignores it. She's nothing to
say. Georgia has known the truth from the moment Ishmael's
body was found in the smoke-wreathed shadow of his house:
a fallen statue amid the glitter and sparkle of fluorite, copper
and lead. If anybody asks her, she'll back up everything Petra
has said. Deon admitted what he'd done, and she'd kept
his secret until she couldn't keep it any more. Even if he tells
them he has an alibi, it won't hold up. Ingle's integrity is for
sale to the highest bidder.

There's a creak of shifting floorboards outside her door; the
liquid shadow of a figure beneath the outline of the door.

'Petra?'

It's Mum, her voice weak and reedy. Petra feels her guts
clench. Hates her. Hates her and pities her and wishes she
were dead, or different, or better, or someone else.

'I'm sleeping,' she spits, voice dripping disdain. 'Go away.'

'Please, Petty. Do you want a hot chocolate? Or a warm
milk? I can tuck you in? Snuggle up, if you want . . .'

'I'm sleeping!'

'Please, Petra. I miss you . . .'

Petra feels her throat closing up. For a brief moment she
imagines letting Mum climb into bed beside her. Imagines
resting her head in the crook of her arm – falling asleep as
her hair is gently stroked; as their breathing finds a harmony;

as they slip into safe and comfortable sleep, the way she did before; the way she did when everything made sense and Ishmael was alive; wasn't even sick; hadn't fallen for that witchy slut, with her accent and her crystals and candles and tits.

'Go away!'

Mum doesn't move for a moment. Petra can picture her; face up against the door, fat cheeks squished against the wood, palm against the grain, pitiful and desperate and yearning for people to be nice to her the way they used to be; the way Uncle Ishmael said she deserved to be treated; the way Dad looked at her in their wedding photos.

There's another creak. Then slow, sad footsteps disappearing down the corridor.

Petra cuts out another petal. Sticks it to the big decorative emblem in the centre of the page.

Slides up the arm of her dressing gown without even noticing. Takes the blade of the scissors. Draws another line across the maze of thin white lines on her bicep. Blood wells.

'Please,' she begs, talking to the crimson weal. 'Please take the pain with you. Please make it stop.'

A single drop of blood runs down the length of her arm. It hangs for a moment at the heel of her hand then falls, a perfect ruby bead.

She sits back. Looks at the totality of her work. Nods: a quiet affirmation: pleased with the result. Lies down where she is, curled up amid the paper and ribbons and sparkle.

Makes a pillow of the great decorative pentagram she has patterned with ash and bone and blood.

Sleeps.

And the shadows flood in like oil.

NINETEEN

The witch makes her confession a little after midnight. It comes amid sobs and threats and prayers: spat out in a bubble of blood and spit and bile.

'Yes!' she screeches, as the 's' is elongated, serpentine: a hiss from the back of her throat. 'Yes . . . I confess, I confess!'

Ingle shudders. Feels the golden glow of the righteous flood him like sunlight through stained glass. He is exhausted. His bones ache, his fingers are bloodied and numb. There have been moments when he has doubted himself; moments when he has longed to cut her loose and wrap her in a blanket; to bathe her wounds in ointments and oils and to call for the help of those with the skill to reset her mangled joints and stitch up her lesions. But he has remained strong; remained defiant; committed to his righteous path. The woman in the mirror has ensured that his resolve has not faltered. She has provided him with the food, the water, the nourishment to continue with his sacred duty. Now he has his reward.

'Their names,' he says, and his voice is little more than a croak. 'Your imps. The others in your coven. Tell me their names and you may rest.'

Her face is slack. She drools into the carpet that covers the bare floor. Tears run from her eyes to puddle in the tattered nest of hair that he snipped from her head upon the third day. He has burned great handfuls of her auburn tresses upon the fire. He saw truths within the smoke: saw names within the twists of greasy smoke.

'Ishmael,' she whispers, barely audible. 'Ishmael Piper.'

Ingle makes a face. He's disappointed in her. He shakes his head. Picks up the pincers from the bloodied floor and waves them in front of her face. She flinches, pushing herself into the floor as if trying to worm back into the earth; to return to the Hell where she was spawned.

'Heloise,' she stammers, as if the name might give her strength.

Ingle drops the pincers. He doesn't want to do this any more. He shakes his head. He feels something close to compassion for the witch. He could not have endured the suffering to which she has been subjected. To have maintained her innocence in the face of such pain – her allegiance to Lucifer must truly be written in blood.

'Ishmael Piper was no witch,' says Ingle, softly. 'Not his charlatan lover.'

She blinks rapidly, blood in her eyes. She manages to focus one eye upon him. Licks her parched, peeling lips. For a moment she looks again like the woman who knocked at his door. She looks able, looks strong.

'You killed them both,' she whispers. 'Killed him in front of his little girl. Burned her to death in her bed.'

Ingle recoils from the accusation as if from a blow. He knows with absolute certainty that her words are being drawn straight from the well of Satan. To accuse him of such things is to put a lance through his very soul.

'Ishmael Piper was my friend,' rasps Ingle. 'I grieve for him as I would a brother.'

'No,' she mutters, fury replacing the fear in her eyes. 'No, you drugged him. You soaked his cigarette papers in Spice. Weakened him. Led him outside and smashed his head in with a crystal . . .'

'Lies!' he spits, pushing himself away from her and snatching up the hand mirror. 'All lies.'

'You drugged her. Heloise. Set fire to their house to cover up what you did . . .'

'Why?' he stammers, staring at his own reflection. Beneath the speckles of wet blood, he fancies the wounds upon his face are less livid; the growth above his eyelid much reduced. He scans the glass for the woman: for Dilly. He fears her wrath more than he fears the witch bound and bloodied upon his floor. If she were to hear such accusations; if she were to believe these foul words . . . he knows her fury to be boundless.

'Why?' he stammers. 'Why would I hurt somebody who showed me friendship?'

The sound that erupts from her throat is almost laughter; a

bitter, gurgling chuckle that echoes off the old stone walls, an eerie echo of the ceaseless rain that pummels the thick, dark windows.

'Because you're fucking insane!' she bellows, her blood popping in her open mouth. 'Your wife knows it. She told me all of it – about your illness, your fucking obsession. You convinced yourself you were being haunted by the spirit of a dead witch; the same witch who helped Ishmael's dad defeat his demons when he was strung out on coke and pills and madness . . .'

'No,' stutters Ingle, shaking his head, wildly. 'No, don't say her name . . . no!'

'You wanted the charm that she gave his father; the same charm that Ishmael kept in the urn – right there in his dad's ashes. You needed it to convince yourself you were safe. But he wouldn't give you it, would he? Wouldn't sell it. Wouldn't share. So you killed him.'

Ingle cannot speak. He pictures the boy; the eager-to-please little thug who turned up from time to time to sit on Ishmael's sofa and smoke his cigarettes and kiss his goddaughter. He remembers the look of pure and perfect hope upon his simple, pockmarked face. He'd retrieved the urn as instructed. He'd stolen from the one man who'd ever shown him kindness. Ingle had promised him that in exchange for this one small indiscretion, he would remove the darkness and the demons from his psyche. He'd believed him. Perhaps Ingle had believed it too.

'I didn't know how quickly the darkness would claim him,' sobs Ingle, into the mirror. 'I would have returned the amulet, I swear. I just needed peace; just a moment's respite; a chance to sleep, to breathe . . .'

'You killed him for his father's fucking necklace!' spits the witch. 'Killed her because she saw. You'd have killed the little girl if you hadn't been disturbed . . .'

He scratches at his scalp; long, thick nails digging weals into his scabrous skin. For a moment he is once again upon that darkened, storm-lashed hillside. He is watching the car pull up. He is huddled inside the mouth of the mine, sodden and shivering, watching the man run to the petrifying body of

Ishmael Piper: a statue amid the sparkling stones. And then he is running into the house, ducking into the smoke and flame.

'No,' he says, again. 'No, I killed nobody.' His face twists as he glimpses the woman in the periphery of his vision; the baleful eye turned upon him. He feels her presence pressing against him like cold metal; the air in the room suddenly icy cold. He feels his thoughts twist like smoke. Feels his nature change and darken.

'You nearly fooled me, witch,' he says, teeth locked together. 'Your lying tongue whispered bile and honey in my ear but I shall not falter. I will not believe your lies. You will not name your conspirators? You will not name those who cursed me; who inflicted these plagues upon me? Then I have no choice. Only the flames will rid me of your evil.'

'You're insane,' she sobs, tugging, desperately, against the rope. 'I'm a fucking police officer! They'll find me. They'll lock you up for ever. They'll lock you up in a little room with only your fucking insanity for company. Let me go! Let me go and I can still help you!'

He stuffs the gag back into her mouth. Stands and stretches. He feels the strength returning to his limbs. Feels powerful. He picks up the old spell book and presses his palm to the cover. Opens it at random and pores over the crabbed, spidery text. It is a spell to confer invisibility. All it requires is the liver of a child.

He places the book back down upon the pile of paperwork at the fireside. From the arm of the rotting chair, he picks up the sleek black object that it so pains him to use. He despises modernity. And yet he is not unskilled in its use. With bleeding fingers, he opens the laptop. He looks again upon the photograph imprinted upon the screen: himself and his wife, smiling, arms around one another: sunlight at their backs as they look upon the pretty, white-painted cottage where they are to pursue their dreams and find their peace.

He opens his email. Finds the message from the girl. He zooms in on the picture. Searches her flesh for imperfections. Looks for the teats that will betray her if bewitched. He breathes out, relieved. He does not wish her harm. It would pain him to consign one so dutiful, so biddable, to the flames.

He gives his attention back to the trussed, broken creature upon his floor. Sighs, as one who has grown tired of a game they once enjoyed. He had hoped she would share the names of her co-conspirators; the other dark forces that suckle imps and familiars at their teats and work their dark magic upon good and righteous men. But in the absence of co-operation, he has no choice but to commit her to the fire.

Ingle steps over her and picks his way through the mounds of old books, of bottles and crystals, oil lamps and battered tin. He makes his way down the long, galley kitchen: a single meaty candle guttering on a china saucer, casting flickering flames upon the avalanche of dirty pots, grimy pans and half-empty food containers: flies rising from the mounds of filth and bones as if the darkness were pixilating into so many hovering points.

He clatters out of the rear door and makes his way, barefoot, across the hard, wet ground. Sharp stones pierce his feet. Mud splashes at his bare ankles. The rain is coming down like so many tiny spears, but he does not raise his hands to protect his exposed face from the onslaught. He makes his way towards the little building tucked away beyond the chicken coop. It's humped and tumbledown and the inside is black as burnt bread, but it will serve his purpose. It's a lime kiln. Inside, he's built a pyre. It's not as tall as he would like, but the logs are dry, stacked around a central strut of aged oak. If the wind and the rain conspire to extinguish the flames, he fancies the jerry can of old petrol will do God's work just as well.

He runs his hands over the bundle of kindling. Feels a shudder pass through him. Had she truly meant what she said? Did people truly believe that he could have killed Ishmael? Ishmael understood him. Ishmael was kind to him. And his little girl was so clever, so sweet. The French woman may have sold him lies but he did not wish death upon her. He grieved for Ishmael, even as he sifted through his father's ashes and plucked the protective charm from the little mound of burnt flesh and pulverized bone.

He raises his hand to his throat. He can feel the power of the crystal as he rolls it in his palm. He knows he must atone for taking the protective charm. Ishmael and Heloise were dead within hours of its removal from the family home. But to suggest he killed them? That he started the fire? He hopes she did not make that suggestion when she contacted his wife? She already believes the worst of him. She never understood. She never saw the woman in the mirror. She never felt the power of the entity that had left an imprint of raw psychic energy upon the old stones of the bastle. She was not suitable for the task that he was chosen for. It was him whom Dilly had picked out for a noble, divine purpose. She would teach him the ways of her kind. She would teach him how to identify those witches bent upon harm. She would protect him, even as his face bled and his tumours grew and his insides turned to blood and sour meat.

He looks up at the moon. Gives a nod as he crosses himself. He is not sure whether he is now Christian, or pagan. He does not know for sure whether he serves witchcraft or is its nemesis. Such things are beyond his comprehension. He finds it best not to think about it. Better to take comfort in activity. Better to get on with the task he has set himself.

Better to build the fire.

And watch the witch burn.

TWENTY

The outbuilding is empty. Harry's gone. There's blood on the floor: darker patches on the damp, muddy brick – a mandala of scuttled claw-prints where the rats have slunk in, slaked their thirst, and disappeared back into the darkness.

'I didn't hear an ambulance,' growls Deon, looking over McAvoy's shoulder. 'Where's he fucking gone?'

McAvoy chews his cheek. Curses himself. He shouldn't have left. Shouldn't have come back, neither – no matter the burning question he needed to put to Deon's dad. Should be doing things properly, the way he would have done when he still truly believed that there was a right way to be a police officer, rather than just different gradations of wrong.

He shines the light of the torch into the recesses of the barn, as if Big Harry and Deon's father might be hiding behind the piles of brick and the sacks of cement. He chews the inside of his cheek. Checks the time on his phone. He left Harry fifty minutes ago. Deon's dad was loopy from the blows to the ears – his equilibrium sure to be off kilter for hours to come. He couldn't possibly have overpowered the bigger man. Could he have taken it upon himself to set off towards the village? It's a couple of miles at least – quicker across the moors, but he was dressed in shirtsleeves and Crocs. The rain was coming down with a biblical fury and the darkness thick as paint. No, Harry had called somebody. He'd ignored McAvoy's instructions, and he'd rung somebody to come and pick him up. Deon's dad, too.

'Takes an age for an ambulance to get to places like these,' muses McAvoy, putting his hand on the crumbling doorframe for support as a wave of dizziness washes through him. 'He'll know somebody local, I shouldn't wonder. I should have suggested it to him. Good thinking, Harry.'

Deon raises his T-shirt and rubs at his face. McAvoy gets

a glimpse of his pale, fleshy belly. There's a tattoo of an elven creature inked around his belly button: a leering imp, deep-set eyes and a crown of berries and leaves. Deon sees him looking.

'Green Man,' says Deon. 'Mate did it for me. I reckon he's got a bit of a squint but it covers up the lines, yeah.'

Deon says it matter-of-factly, as if they're pals now and shouldn't feel any unease at sharing secrets. McAvoy almost wishes Deon hadn't confided in him. The boy has endured true suffering – gone through so many types of pain and trauma and violence. The white lines on his stomach were put there by one of his dad's other sons. Darren was older. Bigger. Stronger. He was dangerously unhinged. Deon was nine years old when he left his mother's care to move in with his dad. And Dad already had a houseful of children – two of his own, and three daughters belonging to the Eastern European woman he was shacking up with in between prison stints. Darren made it clear that Deon wasn't welcome. Mean words became insults. Taunts became threats. Threats became violence and a cease-less campaign of abuse. For close to eighteen months, Darren made it his business to torture Deon daily. At first, he did it in ways that wouldn't show: twisting the cartilage in his ears until they popped; whipping the soles of his feet with lengths of flex; pulling his fingers out of joint and then pushing them back in at the wrong angles. Deon learned to take it. Learned to endure. To speak up was to invite social services to come and split up the family; it was to give the police, and proba-tion services, the ammunition to put Dad away. It was when Darren started to cut him that Deon found the strength to ask for help. His brother had taken to carving concentric circles on his stomach with the blade of a scalpel – an inch or two each day; a spreading ribble of agony that cobwebbed out from his belly-button. So he did what the teachers and the telly had told him to do. He told somebody in authority. He told a desk sergeant at Consett Police Station. Her name was Tara. And she didn't give a shit. As soon as she heard his surname, she lost any interest in him. He was from a bad seed. Bad blood ran through him. She didn't care if he'd been scrap-ping with his brother and she certainly wasn't going to send any officers to talk to him. She sent him on his way. And the next time she arrested his dad, she told him about his son, Deon, who was too much of a pussy to fight his own battles and even tried to grass up one of his big brothers. Dad told Darren. And Darren nearly killed him. Darren died while off his face on Spice, taking a tumble off the viaduct and pancaking into the footpath far below. It brought Deon's time of torment to an end. But the memories faded more slowly than the scars. He suffered with shaking hands; with stomach problems; mood swings, insomnia. When he did sleep it was peopled with grinning ghouls and vengeful beasts. He saw no future other than the one Dad had already picked out for him – moving illegal substances from one place to another; recruiting lads like himself to move packages of powder and pills across county lines. He was good at it, in his way. Thorough and efficient. Dad said he had a talent. He could have seen himself sticking with it as a career path if he hadn't met Petra. If he hadn't met Ishmael. If he hadn't met Ingle, and the witch.

'I thought we were seeing the posh prick,' grumbles Deon.

'Felix can wait,' says McAvoy, swinging the torchlight up to where the bottles gleam down from high, dusty shelves. He peers at the neat, handwritten labels. They're instructions: where to place the bottle for maximum efficacy, which phase of the lunar cycle best serves the spell. There's an incantation: a plea to the Goddess Diana. McAvoy snaps off some pictures, determining to ask Roisin if they mean anything.

'Felix is a cunt,' says Deon, spitting on the floor.

McAvoy decides that the bad language can be tolerated just this once. 'Care to elaborate?'

'Treats Petra like she's five, man,' he says, leaning back against the workbench where, an hour ago, he was prepared to cause irreversible harm to the big police officer who he now talks to like a friend. 'She's so clever, y'know? Like, beautiful, yeah, but she's got this way of thinking – her mind, it's like a firework in a phone box. You know when you look into somebody's eyes and it's like looking off the top of a really high bridge, and you feel all woozy and drunk but you sort of want to jump in just to see what it would be like. That's Petra, man. And he can't see it. Keeps her locked up. She's like a bird in a cage. She was always going to fall for someone like me, wasn't she? I mean, stands to reason. All posh kids rebel in the end. But I'm not just this loser, I swear. I'm changing everything about myself for her. I've never lived this well, man. I've never been this fucking . . . I dunno . . . wholesome . . .'

McAvoy wants to give the lad's arm a reassuring squeeze. He recognizes the agonized lament of a man suffering the tortures of pure and perfect love. He has to remind himself that the girl for whom he is changing his life is not quite fifteen.

'Romeo and Juliet, man,' says Deon, as if reading his thoughts. 'She wasn't even thirteen. And anyway, like I say, we haven't. We won't. I had to promise Ish before he'd let us see each other at his place.' He nods up the valley, to the burned-out skeleton of Ishmael Piper's rain-sodden, soot-blackened home. 'I mean, I know we had him to rights and everything, but I knew he'd have come clean to Felix if he'd thought we were shagging. He loved him, y'know? Loved Felix like, well, not like a brother, 'cause brothers are cunts, but loved him like a brother in a film or a book or something. Loved him like Holmes loves Watson, or something. And I swear, those few months being part of his life at the villa? Best months of my life, mate. Sitting in his living room, listening to him play the guitar and tell stories about his dad; all these yarns about Bowie and Bolan and people I hadn't heard of then but who I'm proper into now . . . the people who'd just show up and drink his hooch and smoke a tab and crack on with him about this and that and t'other. He was so friendly. Man. And so full of mad ideas – things he'd half started, things that he'd never see through. It was him that got me into all the occult shit. He had all these books that had belonged to his dad; all these old recordings of Crowley and Gardner; this grainy audio of gatherings and black masses and summoning spells. He'd listen to it like it was music.'

McAvoy glances again at the glass bottles. Something in the depths of his memory is reaching upwards, trying to grab for his attention. He reaches out and plucks a green, bulbous container from the shelf. It's dark green and covered in dust. As he moves to put it back, he hears the sound of something sloshing around inside its base. He shines the light of his torch at the contents. Rusty nails rise up from a mulch of dirty water and rancid meat.

'She sold them,' says Deon, conversationally. 'Princess Paris. Eyeful Tower, that's what Petra's mum called her. Reckoned that whatever magic she'd worked on Ishmael, it involved letting him see up her skirt and down her top whenever he looked at her. Poor bastard never had a chance, did he?'

McAvoy glances at his phone. There's barely any battery left. He needs to call Roisin. Needs to call Trish. Needs to get permission from somebody more senior, more confident, more sane than himself. He needs somebody to make sense of things for him or, at least, to give him a safe space in which he can make sense of them for himself.

'You mean Heloise,' he says, cautiously.

'Who the fuck else?' snorts Deon, giving him a look that suggests he's beginning to worry that McAvoy is thick as mince. 'Mademoiselle Witchy-tits. Joy had plenty of names for her. Petra too. If Delilah hadn't warmed to her the way she did, then I reckon Joy would have thrown her out on her ear, but Ish was starting to need more looking after and Joy had her own thing going on and couldn't be home when she wanted so . . .' he shrugs, marvelling at a pragmatism of which he knows himself to be incapable, 'she said she could move in. Said she'd share him. She could be his carer. She could help with Delilah. She could do her share of this and that. I dunno if Ish was up to getting his end away but I know they shared a bed three nights a week. I dunno if anybody was happy about it, but it was how it was. Joy even told Delilah to just think of the weird French witch as her Mummy Number Two.'

'You keep mentioning her being a witch,' says McAvoy.

Deon snatches the bottle from his hand. 'She sold these, man. Sold all sorts of weird witchy shit. Some of it online, some through the post – other people would come to the door. It was funny, man. Petra and me would laugh about it, piss ourselves over the fact that some people were so fucked up they'd come and buy spells and curses and enchantments. I got it, when I thought about it, like. I mean, the stuff I sell, it's no different, is it? You need reassurance, or escape, or just a bit of hope in the dark. Still, I dunno how desperate I'd need to be before I went and bought a bottle of piss and nails off a French lass with hairy pits . . .'

'This is a witch bottle,' says McAvoy, slowly. He's read about them. Knows that to a certain type of person, they're more valuable than gold. For centuries, such objects served as talismans, mystical objects designed to ward off evil spirits and protect the owner from malignant forces. Sometimes glass, sometimes pot, the bottle might contain nail clippings, iron nails, hair, thorns; all selected to conjure a physical charm for protection – provided that some bodily secretion, be it urine or semen or blood, was trapped and stoppered alongside the charms. The urine attracted the witch into the bottle, where she became trapped on the sharp pins. In the seventeenth century, during the most virulent of the witch-hunts, there were few families who did not seek out such a charm in a bid to keep evil from their home and hearth.

'No, it's a really good-quality chardonnay,' scoffs Deon. The action seems to pain him. He rubs his hand over the outline of his jaw. 'Ingle came to buy one, see. And when he realized who Ish was . . . well, I mean, to a man like him, you could see the wheels turning right in front of you. Petra didn't like him, so I didn't like him. Ish was nice enough to him until he started getting in his face, telling him to name his price; telling him he'd pay whatever it cost; do whatever he wanted, go to hell and back if he'd just let him take a sprinkle.'

McAvoy hears the rain start to fall again; to thunder on the old roof a couple of feet above his head. He can feel the pieces sliding around inside the puzzle-box in his head.

'He wanted Moose Piper's ashes,' says McAvoy.

'Not all of them, man. Just enough for . . . well, for whatever the fuck. I mean, Ish wasn't well, and he was smoking more gear, but he wasn't so far off his tits that he'd let some stranger make him an offer for his dad's ashes. I mean, who does that? Heloise made some money out of it, like. Served him up a little mound of ash in a little clay pot and told him it was the real thing. He was going to pay cash.'

'It wasn't his remains?'

'Cooked a hare in one of the old kilns Ish had snapped up for his crystal garden. Cooked it down to cinders. Stunk like she was roasting dog-shit.'

'She told you this?' asks McAvoy.

Deon shrugs. 'Ish wouldn't have Ingle back in the house and Heloise was a bit of a princess and couldn't be arsed to put herself out. She and me, well, I don't think we liked each other but she knew I didn't mind doing an unpleasant job for a few quid. So I took him what he'd paid for. You should see his place, man. Creepy as shit, right out in the arse end of nowhere.'

'I thought this was the arse end of nowhere,' mutters McAvoy.

'You haven't been further down the valley then?' laughs Deon. 'Fuck, man. Little old place by a river, took me forever to find. Looked like it was half abandoned, and he didn't let me pass the front door, which was mental, given it was half hanging off and the place didn't look like there was owt worth stealing. So I gave him what he'd asked for. He took it like I was handing him God's knob, I swear. Then he took the top off and his face changed. Honestly, I swear to you – sounds so weird saying it but it was like looking at a cloud, y'know, and one minute it's just a cloud and the next it's some great leering goblin coming to eat your face. He looked different. Scared the shit out of me. And I don't like getting scared. My mask slipped a bit, like. I sort of went to pieces – all that stuff with Darren, and Dad, and that bitch Tara . . . next thing I was blubbing and snottering and I couldn't stand upright and my nose was full of all these smells, these horrible smells, like bad egg and shotgun cartridges . . .'

'You told him about your bad dreams,' says McAvoy.

Deon shrugs again. 'I'd only ever told Petra. Lost my temper with her one day and she said it was ugly. Said she couldn't love somebody who could lose control like that. I kept myself together for her but it was never going to last, was it? One bad joint or one bad night's sleep and I'd be waking up with blood on my belly and voices in me head. And he said he could make it better, like. Said he could help.'

'So you took the ashes,' says McAvoy, his voice free of accusation.

'It can't have been Ingle, if that's what you're thinking,' says Deon, splashing the liquid in the bottle. 'The night Ish died, Ingle was meeting up with me.'

'Where?' asks McAvoy.

'Halfway between his place and mine. Hotel in the village.'

McAvoy thinks of the big medieval building, with its vaulted ceiling and flagged floors, its shields and swords and suits of armour. Thinks of Roisin. Thinks of Delilah, and the way she lay down upon her father's grave.

'That's five minutes from here,' says McAvoy, quietly. 'He could have taken the ashes and then gone back to Ishmael's house. He could have lured him outside, smacked him over the head and then set fire to the house as punishment for Heloise trying to deceive him.'

Deon shakes his head. 'He stayed at the hotel overnight,' he explains. 'Tara might be a bastard but she's not a crap copper. Joy gave her Ingle's name, along with plenty others who might have had it in for Ishmael. Mine was on it, but I don't bear a grudge. And Harry's told half the village about the CCTV. Petra told me. Ingle didn't leave the hotel. Had his evening meal, couple of drinks in the bar, went to his room. Car stayed in the car park all night. The stuff with the ashes – it had nowt to do with Ish dying.'

McAvoy takes the witch bottle from the young man's hands.

'It's bollocks, man. Or it's not. Either way, it means something to somebody.'

'Ingle's house,' says McAvoy, painfully aware that he's going to do something stupid, dangerous, and entirely ill-advised. 'You remember the way?'

Deon grins. There's blood in his teeth. 'You're going to see him? Fuck yeah. Bastard owes me what I paid for.'

'He hasn't honoured his side of the bargain?' asks McAvoy.

Deon glares. Taps his forehead with his knuckle. 'I can hear him. Can hear Darren. Every second of every day, he's in here, telling me what he's going to do to me – yelling at me he knows what I truly am; knows all my dirty little secrets. Ingle was supposed to take it away.'

'There are people you can talk to, Deon,' says McAvoy, gently. 'There are people who can help.'

Deon shakes his head. 'Petra's the only person who's ever helped. And Petra's fucked me over. All the lies she's going to tell . . .'

McAvoy waits for him to say more. Watches as he snatches tears away, as he hocks up snot and spits, foully, on the floor. 'It's worse now,' says Deon, quietly. 'It was bad before, but . . . what's that song? I'm hearing a lyric, easier being poor if you haven't seen riches. I had some happiness. I had something that made me feel good all the way through. That house, those people; her hand in mine. And now? It's no wonder Darren's laughing.'

'You can really hear him?' asks McAvoy. 'A proper voice. All the time?'

Deon holds McAvoy's gaze. Looks away. 'Sometimes, all he does is scream. It's so loud I can't hear what people say to me. Sometimes he says things before I do – his voice comes out of my mouth.'

'I'm so sorry for what you've been through, Deon.'

Deon considers it. Chews on it. Takes the words inside. He manages a tired smile. 'Darren fucking hates you,' he says, with a hint of apology.

McAvoy mirrors his smile. 'Tell Darren that I'll probably get over it. And that if Ingle can help you, I'll make sure he does what you've paid him to do. I'll help you rest easy.'

'And then what?'

McAvoy considers it. Sighs, as he thinks of what he faces before the dawn. 'And then I'll arrest him for double murder.'

Audio transcript, 27.05.23
Diana Nightingale, D.O.B 22.01.1959

'Oh sod it, I hate these machines. Saville, isn't it? Not an easy name for a copper, I shouldn't wonder, but I won't make jokes. Oh sorry, it's Diana. Di. Nightingale, as was. You called? About my other half? Sorry it took me an age. Had a bit to digest and the signal isn't so good. So, well, mebbe's I'll just speak, eh? And if you need owt more, just say the word. It's not easy, this. I'm in a place called Badajoz and it's all sunshine and white walls. I'm getting cold all over again thinking about that bastard place out Garrigill way. Bleakest time of my life, though he'll not accept that, I shouldn't wonder. The thing with Lenny is . . . well, it's his imagination, I suppose. I mean, he lives in his head. Some people have a think about stuff – he drowns in it all. What's the word? Introspection? Aye, there's a place for it, isn't there? But he goes into his own skull and he stays there. He has these conversations with himself, you can tell. He has these full debates with you but you're not a part of it and then suddenly, after an hour of not talking, he just blurts out a question and you don't know what he's talking about and feel daft for asking. The cottage was his idea more than mine. If you asked him he'd tell you we had this shared dream of a little patch of paradise in the middle of nowhere, growing our own crops and chopping logs and painting lovely watercolours out on the moors. I mean, it's a lovely picture, isn't it? But I'm the practical one, the level-headed one, and I promise you, I'd never done more than say it sounded all right, but would probably be bloody horrible in winter, and that were enough for him to get the ball rolling. Next thing he's driving me up into the middle of nowhere out Alston way and showing me this little rundown building like it was everything I'd ever dreamed of. I swear, I thought he was showing me the garage and that the real house would be just over the next hill. But no, that was it. It was a bright sunny day when we went to see it and I'll admit I started getting all the good feelings, y'know? Like, it had this kind of music to it – like the air had good energy, like a song in a major key or something. And he had all these ideas. It was interesting, of course – the limekilns out the back and the trees growing out of these half-covered sinkholes and the skeletons of all the old mining equipment just lying out there among the heather. And he seemed so enthusiastic. So happy. He could be giddy like that sometimes. Giddy or absolutely catatonic, that seemed to be the only two gears he had. So I went along with it and wore the right smile and got stuck in. I even did some horticulture classes so I knew when to plant the right stuff and what to do with it when I'd hauled it out of the ground. I'd been a country girl when I was small so I knew a bit about keeping chickens so that was no trouble. The goats were a bloody nightmare but they had character so I didn't moan. And I think we were happy. I mean, what's happy, eh? But that first summer, I think we made more good memories than bad. It was when winter set in that things took a turn. All the lovely positive things you see when the sun shines – they bugger right off once the wind whips in. You try finding a reason to be cheerful when the rain's hammering down and the sky's got all the colour sucked out of it and your bones ache from the damp. I mean, it wasn't fit for habitation, not really. But that's why we got it for a song, I suppose. Lenny did a deal with the farmer who owned it. Said he'd do it up, make it shipshape. Rent was next to nothing as a result. Of course, I'm a nosy sod and can't leave well alone. I had to ask who'd lived there before, where they'd gone, what they'd been like. Wish I'd never started prying, really. I mean, I'm not bothered which god people pray to. Honest, I couldn't care less if you hail Buddha or Orin or just hang up a Live, Laugh, Love poster and tell people you're a creature of light. But there's something about the pagans isn't there? Like, I can't help thinking they know something the rest of us don't. They don't fanny about with all the wishy-washy shit. It's a religion that's all about roots

and earth and . . . I dunno, it just seems sort of more feasible
than the others. Like, it makes sense to me that you could pull
a rabbit's guts out and be able to read the future in them.
That's kind of natural, I think. And the spells, the incantations
– they're practical, aren't they? The herbal stuff actually works.
We all think we're being proper modern when we pop an
Ibuprofen but we don't know what's in them, do we? Makes
sense to me that there's a herb or a root or a seed that'll fix
your problems. But once Lenny knew – Christ, it did for him.
Had to keep digging in, didn't he? Drove himself mad, there's
no other way to put it. Honestly, he just lost himself in all of
the occult stuff. I didn't even know he'd got an interest in any
of that lot. I know he saw some odd things when he was
overseas and there was some funny business when he was in
bother in Papua New Guinea, years before we met, but
the way he started digging in to the history of the valley; the
stories of the old witches, the burning time. I think he forgot
I was there. And it wasn't making him happy. Scared, more
than anything. It was like living with a farmer in the seventeenth century. Everything that went wrong, it was down to
witchcraft. We were cursed. When the chickens died, it was
black magic. When the goat went off and lost itself down the
mine – it was an enchantment. And of course, once he found
the witch bottle, that was it. By the time I left, I genuinely
felt like the other woman – like he was having an affair with
the ghost of an old woman. The house was just full of books
and printouts and pamphlets – every bit of paper he could find
about. She'd been a bit of a celebrity when she was younger,
as far as he bothered to explain it to me. Helped some rock
stars defeat their demons when they were coked up. And when
he found out that Ishmael Piper lived not ten miles away, there
was no way he wasn't going to find a way to make friends
with the poor sod. First time he went and knocked on his door
he was welcomed in. Glass of something home-made, nice
chat by the fire – always people coming in, going out. Then
he met that French lady, of course. Not much more than a
well-meaning hippy, that one, but she was doing her best to
come across as being a bit other-worldly and Lenny fell for
it. It wasn't much more than a racket, really: selling charms,

potions. She made those witch bottles I was telling you about. A protection. Old magic, and if she knew what she was doing then I'm a monkey's uncle. All I know is that he was getting more and more frightened, disappearing inside himself more and more. When I left, I wouldn't be surprised if it took him a month to notice. I've got friends in Spain and they let me have their holiday let for a few months so I'm doing OK, really. I feel like the cold from that place went right into my bones and it's taking a lot of sun and sangria to get it out of me. I'm trying to put that little part of the world in my rear-view mirror. I swear, I didn't know about what happened to that poor Ishmael and his lass until I got your phone call. I'm sure you'll be thinking the worse of Lenny now I've told you all this stuff, but all I can do is tell you the truth, I suppose. And yeah, he might just be capable of doing what I reckon you're accusing him of. He did bad things when he was young, I know that. There was always violence in him. A bit bonkers – that's how he laughed it off when we first met and he was telling me about his mam and his dad and this long line of people who'd had schizophrenia, or spent time being looked after at one point or another. I just shrugged it off. We all have our demons, don't we? But with Lenny, I reckon I got it wrong. I reckon the demon has Lenny, not the other way around. I reckon there's a good bit to him that keeps the badness in check. But whatever he saw in that house, whatever it was that got inside his head when he found that book and read all about Dilly – the Lenny I knew is long gone. That poor girl, eh? You will tell me how it all works out, won't you? And promise me you won't go up there on your own . . .'

ENDS

TWENTY-ONE

Roisin can't get the massage machine to work. She's got it draped around her shoulders like a bionic fur but the various rollers within its leathery embrace are refusing to budge no matter how many times she presses the button. Her headache is getting worse. She can feel lumps and twists of gristle and tension in her shoulder blades and at the base of her skull. She needs Aector's big, strong, tender hands. She has spent much of the last year battling flu-like symptoms: fatigued, foggy-headed, barely able to lift her arms. The last few weeks she has felt her old self again and has thrown herself into the challenge of making up for lost time. But she drank too much last night and has only snatched a few hours of troubled, feverish sleep. She's hurting all the way down to her bones. Worrying too, now. Really worrying, the way she does when she stops being a modern woman and allows herself to think with the deep, uncanny sense memory of so many generations of her people; of the women touched by magic.

'Come on, you fecker,' she grumbles, unplugging the massager and trying a different socket. It still doesn't work. Her fingers are tingling. There's a growling ache in her jaw and temples.

From outside comes the shush and slurp and slap of tyres on the drowned road. She glances at the bedside clock. It's 4.20 a.m. He's been gone too long now. She snatches up her phone from the foot of the bed and checks for missed calls or new messages. Nothing from Aector. Nothing from home.

Roisin throws the massager down on the bed. She sits down on the hard wood floor, her back against the wall. Closes her eyes. She once tried to explain to Aector how it felt to let her deeper consciousness take over; to flood her synapses with the ancient, more pagan part of herself. She hadn't been able to find the words. To be able to see beyond; to feel that which could not be rationally felt – it was a sensation which defied description. She might just as well have been trying to describe how it feels to fall asleep. The best she could come up with was a clumsy analogy about an old transistor radio: the subtle turning of the dial and wiggling of the antennae until the static became something bordering on the recognizable.

She breathes in, deep and slow. Holds it. Breathes out. She wishes she had her cards. Wishes she had her crystal, on its leather thong: something she could dangle over a map and feel the peculiar energies pull its shimmering quartz towards the spot where her missing man might be. She concentrates on thoughts of him, on the feel of him, on the memory of his nearness. She fills her mind with a flicker-pad of shimmering recollections – his smile, his eyes, his blush; the look on his face when she tells him she loves him and he softly, bashfully, provides an echo to her words.

For a moment it feels as if she is moving. Part of herself seems to drift, to stumble, as if dreaming of falling. She feels cold. There's pain in her stomach, in the bones of her hips. She gasps as she experiences the spear-thrust of hot, sharp pain in her middle ribs.

'Aector . . .' she breathes.

And now she is spiralling away. Her sense of otherness is snatched upon the wind, torn away from the familiar, pummelled and redirected by a force stronger than her own. She experiences a great wave of sickness. Her fingers and toes tingle, her temples throb. Beads of sweat stand out on her forehead, upon her back, beneath her arms. She reaches out in her mind and feels something push back. There's a darkness there; a force malignant and powerful. Something is calling her, directing her, buffeting her like a paper boat upon a foaming river of some other, mightier power. She tries to open her eyes. Tries to pull away. She feels true fear. Her nostrils fill with the stench of bog-water, of old, damp stone. She tastes blood. For a second she tastes something sweet; dolorous, heady: a perfume all lilies and candied sweets. She feels drunk on it. Feels high. She shivers, suddenly ice-cold. She feels her own chill breath misting in front of her face, cooling her cheeks, beading the droplets of sweat across her brow. The feeling inside her is suddenly true dread: the total certainty that

something is beside her, behind her, inside her – that something
terrible, some force of ecstatic pain and malignancy, is creeping
nearer: its hunger ravenous, its pain eternal. She feels fire upon
her legs. Smells her own burning flesh.

The knock at the door is gunfire. She jerks upright, as if
yanked by puppet strings. There's a moment of emptiness, a
silent screech of psychic separation, and then she is bent over,
hands on her knees, heart pounding. She wants to throw up.
Her skin still tingles with the memory of the flames. She
glances down and sees that somehow her feet are planted in
a spreading pool of dirty water; dead leaves and moss-slime
smeared across her soul.

'Mrs McAvoy. Mrs McAvoy, it's urgent.'

Roisin breathes out, slow and ragged. Glances to the door.
The voice is female and unfamiliar. She grabs a towel from
the foot of the bed and wraps it around herself. Wipes her
face dry with the palms of her hands. She opens the door
cautiously, part of her afraid that some ugly force will spill
into the room like a maelstrom of whirling bats.

The woman in the hallway looks far from demonic. She's
plump to the point of outright roundness but her face is pleasant
and friendly: bright eyes and ready smile. Her hair is pulled
back in a tight ponytail and she's wearing a colossal T-shirt
with leggings and UGG boots – the material clinging to her
in ways that certain specialist websites would pay good money
for. She offers up a nervous grimace by way of greeting. Gives
a little wave, even though they're only four feet apart.

'Mrs McAvoy? I'm Sharon. You know my husband, Harry?
Works here? Bit of a fucking tool but his heart's in the right
place, which is more than you can say for his blood-sugar
levels, which are off the bloody charts.'

Roisin takes a moment to absorb the torrent of words. They
arrived in a rush of Geordie, augmented with so many hand
gestures that it might seem to an onlooker that she is being
beset by a swarm of invisible bees.

'Big Harry?' asks Roisin, and she's surprised to hear her
voice sound weedy and tremulous. She coughs. Hits herself
in the chest. Makes a better show of being a nice middle-class
woman who isn't used to being woken at such an ungodly

hour when she's paid good money for a fancy hotel. 'Receptionist? Right. And?'

Sharon nods, eagerly. She glances up and down the corridor: at the old paintings, the heraldic shields; the locked wooden doors. 'Love the bones of him but he's got a streak of the moron about him a mile wide. Look. Can I pop in? There'll be foreheads and fringes and pearl-clutching old ladies peeping out any second.'

Roisin steps back and Sharon scurries in, gratefully. She smells of cigarettes and rain.

'Your husband,' she says, and makes a face that suggests she's about to deliver unwelcome news. 'Look, he went to help Harry with something and well, look, it's all sort of got away from them. I was asleep, happy in me own little bubble, and then he called and he was all shook up, like Elvis with Parkinson's, and, well . . .'

Roisin feels the familiar tremble of panic; the tremble behind her heart that always seems to jingle, like sleigh bells, when she allows herself to stop believing that Aector is indestructible.

'Look, it's best if I show you,' says Sharon. She looks her up and down. Looks apologetic. 'You'll need your coat.'

A little under fifteen minutes later, Sharon is leading Roisin out the back door of the hotel. Together they crunch down the gravel pathway, wincing against the fading onslaught of rain and wind. Sharon moves quickly, for somebody who seems to be built entirely out of fleshy spheres. Her UGG boots squelch out dirty water with each step. She's lit a cigarette, too. Lit another one for Roisin, which she hands back without a word. Roisin takes it gratefully. Breathes in and recognizes a brand she hasn't smoked since she was fifteen.

'Dad's got a warehouse full,' says Sharon, by way of explanation. 'Bit stale, but if you can sort all this shit out for me you're welcome to a crate.'

Roisin hurries along behind her. She's dressed in the clothes she'd planned to wear for the ramble she'd promised to endure alongside her husband. She's wearing leopard-print leggings, hiking boots, and a big puffy jacket with a fur-lined hood. She's grateful for her furry hat with its earflaps, pulled down low. It's real fur, but she has it on good authority that the animal in question lived a long and fulfilling life before dying of natural causes surrounded by adoring great-grandchildren.

'In there,' says Sharon, waving in the general direction of an outbuilding at the far end of the hotel car park. 'I can only apologize.'

A soft yellow light frames the double doors. Roisin takes the handle and pulls it open. Part of her expects to see Aector within. Her mind begins to fill with horrific imaginings, ugly projections, as if the force she felt in the bedroom were still within her, opening the locked doors and boarded-up dungeons in her subconscious. She shakes it away. Steps inside.

For a moment she's Aladdin, stepping into the cave of wonders. The yellow light comes from an oil lamp and its soft glow illuminates a glorious hoard of treasures and finery. The whole of the far wall is given over to a glittering display of crystals and gemstones: miniature mountain ranges of glittering jewels and quartzes set out to form a perfect simulacrum of the village and nearby moors. It's a colossal work of art: each building perfectly reconstructed in shimmering pinks, purples, turquoises and teals – all set in a great wooden frame that stretches almost from floor to ceiling. The floor is covered with a maze of overlapping rugs: the pattern Persian, Afghan, Mesopotamian. Furs and silks spill out from chests made from fine inlaid mahogany and cherry. Half a dozen guitars hang from hooks in the wall, looking down upon vintage amplifiers, gleaming sitars, goatskin bongos. Three ornate, long-necked hookahs sit atop a small coffee table – a glass ashtray over-flowing with cigarette butts.

Big Harry is sitting on a battered old armchair in the very centre of the room. Part of his beard is missing and his skin is pink and scorched across his cheeks and chin. He's got a shotgun across his knees, like a cowboy sitting on a rocking chair. He's wearing a long nightshirt, and cowboy boots. He looks like a little boy who's made a wish and woken up in the body of a thirty-four-year-old behemoth. He gives a little wave – so incongruous given the circumstances that he starts to giggle at his own ridiculousness.

'Mrs McAvoy,' he says, with a wisp of hysteria in his voice. 'Welcome to my humble home from home. Apologies for the mess. And, erm, for him . . .'

Roisin follows his gaze. In the corner of the room, in the shadow of a grandfather clock and a stuffed capuchin monkey, an older man with nasty yellowing hair is bound in so much gaffer tape he looks like a genuine Egyptian mummy ordered from a selling site. He's glaring up at her with furious eyes – blood leaking from his ears to stain the silver tape that binds his mouth.

'I don't know his real name,' says Harry, conversationally. 'He just goes by Gadgie. But him and his son . . . well, Deon, I mentioned him to you earlier . . . he's seeing Petra, your husband's brother's daughter, if that isn't all a bit complicated, like, and . . .'

Sharon pushes herself into the room behind her. 'Will you stop wittering shit and just tell her what's gan on? Fuck sake, man, the dog's gonna need feeding soon and I've a dream about Daniel Craig to bet mesen back to.'

'You've met the little wife?' asks Harry, smiling adoringly at his bride. 'Love of my fucking life.'

'She don't need to hear any of that, you tool. And could you open a window? It smells of balls in here.'

Roisin looks from one to the other and down to the furious, immobile man on the floor. She gives Harry her full attention.

'Is Aector OK?' she asks, not taking her eyes off the big man.

'He was when he left. Bit sore, I shouldn't wonder. But, fuck, he's hard, isn't he? Fights like the devil himself then apologizes for the mess!'

'Where is he, Harry?'

Harry looks at the floor. 'I don't know. He left me to go see Felix. Left me with this pillock. I didn't want to wait for an ambulance. Didn't know what was for the best. Ishmael asked me to watch all this stuff, see? His little treasure trove in case times got hard. And I didn't want to make a bad decision until I'd thought about what was best for everyone. So I called my little wife here and had her bring us both down for

a bit of a conflab. And she said it were right mean of us to
leave you in the dark about your husband when, well, I sort
of landed him in it, and then he sort of saved my life a bit,
so I just thought . . .'

Roisin nods. She spits in her palm and extinguishes her
cigarette in the little puddle in her hand. The sizzle is lost
amid the sound of the dancing trees and falling rain.

'This man attacked Aector?' she asks, pointing at Deon's
dad.

'And me. Him and his boy.'

'And Aector's gone off with the boy? Deon.'

'Said he was going to Felix's, but we drove past Felix's and
there were no lights on or anything.'

'So you don't know where he is?'

'No.'

'But this man might?'

Harry looks past Roisin. At her side, Sharon gives a little
shrug. She doesn't seem particularly overawed by the
developments.

Roisin pulls out her phone and tries, again, to reach her
husband. It won't connect. She scratches her cheek – a perfect
recreation of her husband's favoured tic when considering his
options. She looks again at Gadgie.

'Well,' she says, giving him a smile that is entirely devoid
of humour. 'You think you've had a rough night so far? If you
don't start talking, you're going to remember what Aector did
to you as the good times.'

She stalks to the middle of the room and picks up the glass
ashtray. Tips the cigarette butts on to the coffee table and
stamps back to where Gadgie lies, eyes wide, like a crazed
horse.

'Now,' she says, hefting it and enjoying the solidity in her
hand. 'Love's all about sacrifice, isn't it? How much of
ourselves are we willing to give up, to alter, to switch off,
in the name of commitment and loyalty? How much of
ourselves do we forfeit for the net gain of caring about
somebody and being cared for in return.' She rolls him on
to his side. Frees his pudgy fingers from the tape and presses
the smallest to the ground, her weight on his knuckles. She

asks the question sweetly, the way her dad used to ask his debtors whether they were really telling him they had nothing to give. 'So you have to ask yourself, Gadgie . . . your boy, Deon. You don't want to drop him in it, I get that. But now's the time to really pose those questions. How much of yourself are you willing to lose . . .'

TWENTY-TWO

The car lurches from one pothole to the next – hailstorms of smashed glass falling from the window frames with each bone-jarring impact. McAvoy's frozen through, skin bone-white, the raindrops in his beard feeling like ice.

'I thought coppers were good drivers,' grumbles Deon, in the passenger seat. He's found a couple of grimy blankets in the back seat and has wrapped himself inside them, hunkered down and pressing his face as close to the hot-air blower as he can manage. He keeps smacking his cheek into the dashboard but he's bearing the indignity with the forbearance of somebody well used to taking a blow to the face in exchange for a little comfort.

'It's the road,' says McAvoy, teeth pressed together. 'I can't see the edge. There's no white lines. And it doesn't help that somebody shot the windows out of the car, does it?'

Deon makes a face. 'None of it were my idea.'

McAvoy doesn't reply. His skull aches. He feels as if his brain is too big: as if grey matter is about to start oozing out of his ears and nostrils like batter. There's no trace of sunrise yet and though the rain has slowed its assault, a thick skein of mist hangs above the glistening road, like a curtain waiting to be swished aside before the true blackness of the countryside is revealed. McAvoy can't work out whether to put the headlights on full beam. They don't make the view any clearer. Nor do the windscreen wipers serve to remove any of the grime that makes the glass appear frosted.

'Did you see that sign?' asks Deon, squinting through the passenger window. 'I'm sure that said Nenthead.'

McAvoy risks shooting a look at his passenger. He can sense himself becoming less agreeable company with each passing mile. 'Nenthead? I've never heard that name before. Why would I be looking for a sign for Nenthead?'

''Cause that's where you turn,' says Deon, looking at him

like he's a moron. 'Fuck, this is shit, innit? It was spring last time I came, and even on a sunny day it was a bitch to find.'

McAvoy doesn't react. He licks his lips. Veers away from the window as the big tyres cut through a great pool of standing water – filthy waves slopping up the panel of the Range Rover. 'Spring?' he asks, as if making conversation. 'You've been back since Ishmael died?'

Deon takes a moment. He's staring out of the window looking for signs. There's a wall of trees either side of the road – a lethal-looking chicane that doubles back on itself before winding towards the little old mining village. The buildings huddle together sullenly, lightless: the front of an old church and the awning of a village shop appearing for a moment in the empty air before McAvoy is swinging the car left and up over a bumpy track. They pass a play park. Pass a mining museum. Bump over a little hump-backed bridge over the swollen river and then squeeze between two rows of cottages. Then they're rising again, up through mile after mile of nothingness.

'Spring,' says McAvoy, again. 'You've seen Ingle again?'

Deon lets his face turn petulant. He looks nasty again, like child caught teasing the cat. 'Aye, course I have. That fucking horsey bitch had it in for me, didn't she? Kept asking and asking. I knew I wasn't going to tell her owt but it didn't do any harm to make sure he wasn't going to drop me in it. I mean, if she did find out where I was, I wanted to know what he'd say.'

'And?' asks McAvoy, slowing down as a sheep skitters across the glistening road, emerging from the fog like a living cloud.

'And nowt,' shrugs Deon. 'Nobody home. I banged on the door for fucking ever but nobody answered. I had a bit of a look-about, same as anybody would. Creepy place, like. Even on a nice day it weren't much fun. Petra wouldn't let go of me. Reckoned it had seriously bad energy.'

McAvoy looks across at his passenger. 'Petra came with you? So she knows you've got an alibi for the night of Ishmael's death.'

Deon's features twist. He sucks spit through his teeth.

'She knows I didn't kill Ishmael. Or the witch upstairs. She didn't know about the urn – just that I'd been selling Ingle some gear. She had to do some quick talking to get out from under her dad's glare, but it was a chance to spend a bit of time together. She didn't like it. I could feel her trembling when I gave her a cuddle.'

'But she's going to tell DI Saville that you knew Ishmael planned to leave you some money? She's going to show her the messages?'

Deon nods, eyes shut. 'It was just talk, man. I mean, I'd rather have Ishmael alive than the few quid he was going to give me. I didn't even know if I believed him. I was just liking the daydreaming, y'know? Talking about our place together, the stuff I'd treat her to. Fuck man, I even set her up an account online – a wish list so she could pick stuff she might like some day. You know how that'll look to Saville? And even if Ingle tells her that I couldn't have started the fire, she'll pin it on my dad. He was guarding the crop the night of the fire: stoned and on his own in a shipping container. You think that'll serve as an alibi? I can't believe she's going to do this to me, just so her dad can stop tearing his hair out. I mean, she's a daddy's girl, but fuck – I thought we were in love.'

'You really don't seem to like Felix,' mutters McAvoy.

'Posh cunt,' spits Deon. 'Her mum's all right, like. Knows more than she lets on, I reckon. Not as soppy as she makes out. She came home one day and found me sitting on the sofa giving Petra a foot massage watching telly. I thought she'd go spare, like Petra had warned me, but she was proper nice. Made me something to eat and came and sat down with me. Asked questions. Took an interest. She even gave me a run home. Nice lady. She and Petra barely talk any more. Fucking shame.'

McAvoy whips his head to the right as an abandoned farmhouse momentarily appears from the fog. The roof's missing: a tree growing out through the last few remaining timbers.

'So many places like that out here,' says Deon, wistfully. 'Like a ghost town in places. Miles and miles of nothing. Some of the farmhouses – they've still got the furniture of the last people who lived there. Dad always said there was silver to be found under Weardale. Reckoned it was more tunnels than rock in some parts. Back in the old days, people would just sink a shaft, work it for a bit, then go bust or jack it in. They'd maybe back-fill the top, or put a cap on the shaft, but really the whole moor is like a big honeycomb once you take the top off. Ish reckoned that if you knew what you were doing, you could probably make your way from Blanchland to Allendale without having to come to the surface more than a couple of times. You couldn't pay me enough money to gan down there, like. Just mud and rocks and stones. Long way to go for a bit of fluorspar, I reckon, but collectors will pay good money for it. Ish's dad bought some of them old fluorspar boxes. Reckoned it was powerful stuff – all good juju, positive energy and stuff. Ish were into some of that. Did you know about the chicken foot? Wore it on a thong around his neck . . . oh fuck, there, turn right . . .'

McAvoy jerks the wheel and steps on the brakes at the same time, sending up a spray of mud and grit and rain. The head-lights illuminate a rusty old farm gate: a pitted track beyond, disappearing up an overgrown slope. Wisps of cloud hang above the long grass like white-robed monks. There are empty oil drums and grain buckets and spools of tattered, rotting rope.

'Did well there,' says Deon, approvingly. 'It's off the latch, look. Someone's been up, or down. Just nudge it, I'm not getting out.'

McAvoy does as instructed, opening the gate with the bumper of the borrowed car. He slips it into second gear and moves slowly up the track. Tall trees cluster in on the driver's side: wet branches protruding in through the smashed window like charred bones. McAvoy peers through the windscreen. Between the puddles he can just make out the tracks of a vehicle in the twin trenches of mud.

'Can you imagine it?' asks Deon, grimacing as a patchy privet hedge shakes a little downpour of icy water into his lap. 'Fucking bleak, innit?'

McAvoy doesn't speak. Something feels wrong. He doesn't believe himself to be touched by any kind of spirit or gift of prescience. He doesn't think he can hear the voices of the lost or commune with wayward spirits. But he has a copper's intuition and a heightened sense of what he can only think of as wrongness. He's been in rooms where people have died bad deaths. He's looked into the eyes of killers. He's watched people die. He knows the flavours of death; the taste of it; the greasy malignant pressure of air that is suffused with suffering.

Deon winces, pressing a knuckle to his temple. 'Shurrup,' he mutters, to himself. 'Shurrup.'

'Are you OK?' asks McAvoy, looking at his passenger. He looks ill suddenly. His eyes are bloodshot, his skin a greyish-green. He's sweating beneath his blankets: the shadows in his face lengthening, the hollows so deep they look as if they've been dug out with a blade.

'Not fucking listening,' hisses Deon, teeth locked, spittle frothing on his chin. 'You can fuck off. Just fuck off . . .'

McAvoy glances back at the track and turns sharply left – the path ahead disappearing into a tangle of solitary trees and the occasional mound of rocks and wire.

'There,' mutters Deon, beside him. 'That's him.'

McAvoy stops the car. Feels the sense of disquiet grow in his belly, in the throb at his temples. Ingle's house is an ugly, hunchbacked thing, squatting like a toad at the end of the track; tucked into a fold hillside and shielded from prying eyes by a stand of tall, thick-trunked trees. It has an air of solidness about it: a home built to withstand attackers, be they without or within. It's a Gothic gingerbread house, all thick stone and red slate: the windows little more than slits in the brickwork. The glass is thick and dark, edged with cobwebs that hang like dirty lace. The path to the door is edged with ragged hunks of twinkling crystal: great splintered rocks of sparkling quartz. In the light of the headlamps, the red door takes on the appearance of fresh blood. There's no garden as such, but at the near end of the property the ground slopes away towards a little patch of waste ground. There's a henhouse behind chicken wire. There's a solitary tree a little further away. Thick bottles hang from the branches. Crosses too: little wooden crucifixes wrapped in thread.

'No,' mutters Deon, again. He kneads his eyelids. Opens his mouth as wide as it will go; clicking his jaw. 'No, shut the fuck up, shut the fuck up . . .'

McAvoy stops the car. Turns off the ignition. Kills the headlights. He turns to his passenger and puts a hand on his shoulder as gently as he can. He tries to put his own face in the young lad's eyeline; tries to show him that it's OK, he's safe, that whatever is chattering away inside his skull can't hurt him.

'Stop . . .' whispers Deon. One eye seems bloodshot; the other leaking tears. 'Stop, I can't breathe . . .'

McAvoy listens to the clinking of the glass bottles in the trees. Hears the pitter-patter of the soft rain falling on metal. Hears the low moan of the wind as it hurtles down from the hilltops. He has a memory of home, of the croft; of those few precious years in the safe and comforting bulk of the white-washed old building. Remembers the smell of the peat fire, of frying bacon and potato scones; of his dad's big strong hands with their smells of sawdust and liniment and wet wool. He suffers a sudden pain, the furnace blast of grief, as he thinks upon all that he walked away from; of all that he lost, of what was snatched away on a false promise. He feels a rage that he did not know lived within him. It's a true fury, an ugly feeling: a low malevolence that growls and snarls and whispers soft, rasping words in the centre of his brain. He suddenly knows the truth of himself. He knows how much of himself is a lie; how many faces he wears for the benefits of others. He finds himself ridiculous; hates his bulk, his blush, his stupid soft eyes and kind hands. He knows himself to be an affectation. Here, now, he feels finally true; finally real. He is wrath. He is sickness and rage. He wants to hurt. He wants to wrong those who have betrayed him. He wants to rip and rend and snap and snarl – to gorge himself on righteous violence and . . .

'McAvoy,' whispers Deon, beside him. He nods, weakly, through the glass. There's a Jeep parked in the shadow of the far wall. 'That's hers,' mumbles Deon. 'He doesn't drive that.'

McAvoy closes his eyes as tight as he can. Forces the feelings back down inside of himself. He realizes he is trembling. He can smell blood. Can smell smoke. Sulphur, at the back of his throat. 'It's whose?' he croaks. 'Deon? Deon. Look at me. Whose is it then?'

'Saville's,' says Deon, huddling inside his rags. 'That's her fucking car.'

McAvoy looks at the house. Sees a soft light flicker into life behind one of the slit-eyed windows. Takes comfort in the fact that now, whatever happens, he'll always know that he had no choice.

'Stay here,' he tells Deon, opening the door and stepping out into the cold, black night.

'On my own?' asks Deon, looking around, wild-eyed. 'Don't leave me here on my fucking own.'

McAvoy makes fists with his cold, numb hands. Breathes out, softly. Opens Deon's door and helps him out, taking his arm like an old lady alighting from a carriage.

'You can feel it, can't you?' asks Deon, softly. 'Feel that . . . that evil . . .'

McAvoy tries to find the right words. Glares up at the sky: thick clouds rolling in and over themselves like a sack full of serpents, devouring, reforming. Looks down at the flagstones that lead up to the front door. They carry inscriptions. Dates. Names. The path is paved with headstones.

'Yes,' he mutters, and begins to walk towards the red door. 'I feel it.'

He's only taken three steps when he hears the scream.

TWENTY-THREE

Roisin leans back against the wet door of the little shed, pressing her sweat-streaked hair against the rotting wood. She feels dirty water run down her neck. Doesn't care.

'Tab?' asks Sharon, appearing at her side. Roisin takes the cigarette. It's already lit. She inhales, hungrily. Breathes out, slowly. Feels her heart slow.

'He OK?' asks Roisin, staring across the long grasses and wildflowers to where the little grassy driveway joins up with the twinkling, half-drowned road. 'Put himself back together?'

Sharon makes a noise that Roisin recognizes as a kind of indulgent scorn: a sort of long-suffering fondness. 'He's actually trained as a first responder,' she says, as if the notion is laughable. 'Once restarted an old lady's heart with his hand, if you can believe it. He's usually OK with blood. I think he's just tired.'

Roisin gives a weary little smile. 'You make him sound like a toddler needing a nap.'

Sharon shrugs, one wife to another. 'Aren't they all?'

Roisin takes another drag. Thinks of her Aector. Feels the warmth of him behind her heart. Were she able to dissolve and reappear at his side, be it at the very gates of Hell, she would not hesitate.

'This Ingle,' says Sharon, nodding back inside the wooden building. Deon's dad is tied to a chair. Roisin didn't have to hurt him much. He gave up the little he knew without the need for extraneous violence. Roisin hurt him more out of a sense of annoyance than in an attempt to elicit any concealed truths. Harry had to stop her before she could do anything irreparable. She'll thank him, eventually. She knows she has a temper. But he was asking for it. There was a look close to mischief-making in his eye when he told her what he and Deon had planned to do to her husband: how he'd woken from a shotgun blast

to find himself stripped and bleeding. She can feel his vulner-
ability, feel his terror. She can sense all that went through his
mind as the two men set about terrorizing him into submission.
She has endured something similar. Has endured something
worse.

'Aye?'

'Harry will be giving himself hell for months, you know that?
Detective Inspector Saville – the horsey bitch looking into
Ishmael's death . . . she was bugging him a few days ago about
the CCTV. Something about one of the vehicles being registered
to somebody's ex-wife and having a different name to one
of the guests? I mean, if he goes by Ingle, that's his lookout,
isn't it? Ingle, Nightingale, you can see how one might be a
nickname for the other. Harry only ever knew him as Ingle – bit
of a sad sack who used to hang around up at Ishmael's place.
Hero-worshipped Ishmael – had every recording of his dad's,
even the bootleg shit; the underground stuff. He was always
bugging Ish, asking him about his dad's bad old days – the
Seventies, when him and Bowie and Glenn Whatsisname were
trying to summon up the spirit of Aleister Crowley and put
hexes on Freddie Mercury and whatnot. I mean, Ish indulged
him, but once he got ill and he couldn't always remember what
was what, he had less patience. He didn't want people up at
the house all the time. He wanted to be with the people he
loved. I think he was making his peace, you know? He was
never going to be an old man but he was trying to put his energies into being there as long as he could for his little girl. Heloise
was all right too. She and Joy did their best to make it work. I
dunno about you but I'd be a bit less cool with inviting my
husband's bit of fluff to move into the house.'

Roisin lets out a little laugh, picturing the scene: Trish
Pharaoh taking up a great chunk of the marital bed, snoring
away in her ear, waking her at two a.m. to demand cups of
tea and crumpets and a two-minute go on her husband. She
shudders. Decides to never think of it again.

'You think he'll be OK?' asks Sharon, trying to put her face
in Roisin's eyeline. 'I mean, I know he's a big bugger, but he
can't trust Deon, can he? And if Ingle did it . . . I mean, he's
dangerous, isn't he? That's a proper psycho.'

Roisin replays all that Deon's father divulged. Deon stole an urn from Ishmael Piper's house. He delivered it to Ingle. Deon made his way back to Consett and joined his dad picking up a re-supply of weed, Spice and MDMA from a source just outside Ponteland. They were together all night. Ingle returned to his room at the hotel. During the last round of questioning, DI Saville shoved a printout under Deon's nose. It showed all calls made to and from the mobile that had been in his pocket when he was picked up on drugs charges. One of the numbers he had been in contact with was registered to a Leonard Nightingale. And the ever-so-obliging phone company had triangulated the position of the phone at a little before midnight on 11 February. Nightingale's phone had been active within 400 metres of Ishmael Piper's house on the night of his and Heloise's death. Deon hadn't reacted. His dad had taught him well. Instead he'd stuck to silence. The only person other than his dad he told about the new development was his girlfriend: Felix Darling's daughter, Petra. And now Petra was going to drop him in it and tell the police that Deon had been secretly plotting to bump Ishmael off in order to get his hands on the nice chunk of cash he'd been promised in return for treating his goddaughter with a bit of respect.

'You've tried calling him, I suppose?' asks Sharon, grinding her cigarette out under the sole of her UGG boot.

Roisin nods. She knows that she shouldn't – that whatever he's doing, the last thing he needs is distraction or a sudden trilling alarm. But she can't wait any longer. She needs to know he's safe. As much as that, she needs him to know what she's about to do. She needs him to be aware that by the time he comes back, she'll have banged on Felix's door and told him just who killed his best friend, and why.

'What are we doing with him?' asks Harry, weakly, from inside the garage. Roisin takes another cigarette from Sharon. She's starting to like the taste.

'Him?' she asks.

'Laddo,' he says. 'Our guest.'

Roisin shrugs. 'Whatever you like. If you've got a pipe and some barbed wire, feel free to be creative.'

Sharon and Roisin share a grin as they hear Harry heave.

He's been throwing up in fits and starts since the tough old bastard came clean about what they planned to do to Aector and him, given half the chance.

'Will you be wanting company?' asks Sharon. 'I can hold your hand if you're going to see the lord of the manor. Not that I think you need much in the way of help. Reckon there's nowt you couldn't handle.'

'Don't go off without me,' pleads Harry. 'I need a lie-down and some soup.'

Sharon rolls her eyes. 'I'll be tending to the hero of the hour, it seems. Take my number. If I can help, just call me.'

Roisin puts the number in her phone. Takes another cigarette and puts it behind her ear. 'End of the road, yeah? Old church?'

'Can't miss it. Follow the smell of money and bailiffs.'

'Bailiffs?' asks Roisin, confused.

'Hard times for the Darlings,' shrugs Sharon. 'Poor Harry had to cut off his credit at the bar a few months back. Gave directions to a civil enforcement van a while back. Nobody's as rich as they were, are they? Even that Petra's been pulled out of the posh school and chucked in with the plebs. No bloody wonder she fell for Deon. At least he could buy her the kind of presents that Daddy used to.'

Roisin starts to count backwards from ten. Gives up at nine.

'Tell me all that again . . .'

TWENTY-FOUR

McAvoy puts his boot to the door just below the handle. It explodes from the frame in a riot of splinters and dust and paint. He stumbles as he spills over the threshold. It feels, for a moment, as if some invisible force is pushing him back. He feels a sudden agonizing pain in his chest, a crushing weight, as if his ribs were being squeezed together by some colossal unseen force. His head reels, ears thudding. He feels as if he's underwater, the lights of the surface diminishing, winking out.

The scream again. The desperate cry.

McAvoy shakes his head clear, holds himself steady. A splinter of wood skewers his palm as he grabs the doorframe. The pain is sharp and bright and the fog in his head lifts long enough for him to make sense of what he sees.

Kate Saville is naked. Blood-soaked. Her hair has been crudely hacked away from her skull. Bloodied ropes dangle from her wrists and ankles. They have the appearance of tree roots, of snakes: ugly white serpents risen from the earth to clutch at her exposed skin.

She has her thumbs in Leonard Nightingale's eyes. She's hissing into his face, inhaling his screams as he wriggles and writhes, pushing himself back against the rotting leather of the sofa. He's dressed in a dirty hessian robe: barefoot. Piss and mud runs down his calves to his bare feet, puddling around the knife that lays atop an ancient-looking book, its pages fluttering in the breeze that barrels down the soot-caked chimney.

Later, McAvoy will ask himself whether there was a moment when he considered taking his time. He will force himself to re-examine his every thought and word and impulse. He will lash himself as he searches his conscience for any indication that he took his time; that he allowed her to push a little deeper, to inflict a little more pain upon the creature that has bound her, stripped her, hurt her.

Here, now, he doesn't pause. He throws himself across the space between them, taking the detective around the middle with his left arm and cushioning her fall as he thuds, painfully, on to the ground. He feels a burning candle snuff out against his cheek. Something pops in his knee.

She fights him. Struggles. She's all kicks and elbows. She smashes her head back against his jaw, his cheekbone.

'Police,' he yells. 'Please . . . you're safe, don't . . .!'

He holds her tight, arms around hers. Her blood is on his lips, in his nostrils, on his face.

McAvoy looks up. Sees Nightingale pulling himself upright. Blood pours from his eyes. He stumbles as he makes for the door. Clatters forward, slipping on candlewax. One of his feet tears a page from the fluttering book. He screeches like an owl. His hands scrabble upon the floor. One hand closes upon the handle of the knife. He drops it again, the handle bloody. Scrabbles again amid the piles of paper, of broken glass. Seizes the handle of an old mirror and holds it to his face as if about to sup from the grail.

His face twists. First fear, then something close to bliss.

'You fucking evil bastard, Ingle.'

McAvoy turns towards the voice. Deon stands in the doorway, a look of pure disgust twisting his features. He's holding the knife that Ingle discarded. He's looking at his pale, grimy neck.

'No, Deon. No, don't!'

Deon lunges. Brings the knife down. Ingle swings instinctively. The blade strokes the surface of the mirror. There is the sound of breaking glass.

Deon stumbles backwards, cursing, shaking his bleeding hand. Ingle stares at the mirror. One great shard of jagged glass slips from the frame: Ingle's open mouth and horrified features reflected in its darkened surface.

McAvoy wriggles free from beneath Saville's weight. Throws himself at Ingle's back and pins him to the ground. Shields him with his bulk. If Deon or Saville want to kill him, they'll have to dig their way through McAvoy's big, unyielding back.

'Leonard Nightingale, I'm arresting you for the murder of Ishmael Piper and—'

'No!'

McAvoy turns his head. Stares at DI Saville. She's sitting up, arms wrapped around herself, shivering, bleeding. But the madness has left her eyes.

'No,' she says, shaking her head. 'He did this,' she stammers, pointing at herself, at the ropes, at the blood on the floor. 'Did all this. But not that.'

McAvoy feels like his head is caving in. He hears Deon move. Turns his head and sees the young man take off his coat and wrap it around the shoulders of the police officer who thought he was a murderer. She takes it without a word.

'Told you it wasn't fucking Nightingale,' mutters Deon, sitting down with a thump. He takes a handful of papers from the pile by the fire. They're printouts. Accounts. Red-headed letters. Final demands. He reaches over to the fireplace and picks up the laptop. Opens it up and looks at the picture on the screen. His eyes darken. Fill with tears. He leafs through the papers. Finally, he gives a tired little laugh. Holds up the printout and slaps a bloodied fingerprint on the heading. It's for Felicia Holdings.

'Your fucking brother,' he spits. 'Fleeced Ish for every fucking penny.' He looks down at the floor. Shakes his head. 'Fuck, man – that's why he wanted the Spice . . .'

McAvoy doesn't need him to say any more. He takes Ingle's wrists in his palm and holds him tight as he wriggles his other hand into his pocket. Finds his phone. There's a missed call from Roisin. A text message too. She's going to see Felix Darling. She thinks she knows what happened.

McAvoy looks to DI Saville. She reads the look in his eyes. Gives the faintest of nods.

And McAvoy is up and out and tearing across the gravel, phone to his ear, begging her to pick up, to answer, to not do what she's about to fucking do . . .

He's back in the car and halfway down the track before he even notices that he's holding the knife.

TWENTY-FIVE

Petra's mouth is dry, her tongue swollen: pain digging a trench across her brow. She's barely slept. She feels sick and jittery and, beneath her T-shirt and onesie, she's slick with sweat. Her nerves are jangling the way they were that first day at new school, mind full of dark imaginings of all that is going to go wrong. Being proved right had come as no comfort. The people were every bit as bad as she'd imagined. She was picked on mercilessly for her accent, her designer labels; her jolly little anecdotes about ski-trips and the holiday home in the South of France. Her name was the funniest thing any of her new classmates had ever heard. Petra, they laughed, repeating it over and over, until it lost all its meaning. Like Petrified? Fourteen years old and they were using playground catcalls.

'*Petra, Petra, we're gonna get ya.*' Christ, it had been so humiliating.

Today will be worse, she knows that. Facing Daddy. Facing the police officer. Telling them what everybody needs to hear.

Through the fog of tiredness, she becomes slowly aware of voices from downstairs. She knows this house and its echoes; knows how Mum and Daddy sound when they're chatting, when they're fighting, when they're drunkenly doing it in Daddy's office. This doesn't sound like any of those familiar sounds. Something's wrong. There's somebody in the house – somebody who shouldn't be.

Petra slips out of bed and strips off her onesie. She pulls on jogging trousers, vest top and hoodie. Pulls on a pair of trainers she outgrew a year ago. Picks up her phone and feels her heart thud against the inside of her chest as she sees the huge number of missed calls and text messages. She scans the messages first of all. They're all from Deon. All sent within the past hour. All telling her that she needs to get her story straight. He forgives her. He understands why she was going to tell lies to DI Saville.

She had to protect her dad, right? He gets it. But the copper is on his way. He knows what Felix did. Her dad needs to hand himself in. She needs to warn him . . .

The voices from downstairs grow louder. She runs to the window and pulls back the curtains. The sun is struggling to rise through the grey-black wall of cloud. The air is slick with a squally, persistent drizzle. Birds and dead leaves whirl upon the twisting gale. She scans the car park. There are no new vehicles. No cop cars.

'. . . know what he's been through, you prick? What he's had to do just so you could rest your pampered head a little easier? Fuck sake, what is wrong with you people?'

Petra opens her bedroom door. Crosses the landing silently. Peers down. There's a small, dark-haired woman standing in the kitchen. She's soaking wet and her hair is clinging to her flushed face, but she's strikingly beautiful in a dangerous, bewitching sort of way. She's petite, but somehow buxom too. Sparkly rings flash at her fingers and neck. Her nails look expensive; her smudgy tan painted on. She recognizes her. Roisin. His wife.

'You can't come barging in here shouting the odds, I'm afraid,' says Daddy, iron in his voice. He's towering over her, face wan, eyes dark, still dressed in his bedclothes of rugby shirt and jogging trousers.

'Shall we all calm down a little? I can make coffee.'

Petra cringes at the sound of her mum's pathetic, wheedling voice. God, she disgusts her.

'Don't you dare touch that fucking coffee machine! She's not a guest, she's a blasted intruder!'

Roisin laughs, the sound bitter. 'Coffee would be lovely,' she says, sounding suddenly sweet. 'Two sugars, please. Biscuits would be nice.'

Petra cranes her neck. She can see Mum standing by the sink. She's wearing one of her baggy T-shirts and a sad, faded pink dressing gown. Her hair's sticking up and the varicose veins in her chunky white legs make Petra want to heave. She's not even wearing slippers: just standing there with her pudgy feet on show, nails unpainted, making her silly noises as she waits to be told what to do.

'You let him talk to you like that, do you?' asks Roisin, shaking her head. 'How much did Daddy pay for your education, Felix? All that cash and they couldn't even afford a tutor in basic manners.'

'I'm wasting no manners on you,' hisses Daddy. 'You may have fooled that bloody simpleton of a husband, but I see through you. Daddy too.'

'Do you know what you sound like?' laughs Roisin, dripping scorn. 'You're a fifty-year-old man and you call Crawford "Daddy". I mean, fuck off, Felix. And if Aector's this simpleton, how come you've gone out of your way to get him up here? To chase around like a dog after a rat? You fecking sicken me.'

'I never wanted the duffer up here!' spits Felix, aghast. 'Good God, I forget the fellow exists until somebody reminds me! Don't go flattering yourself that he was some guest of honour. I don't even know what Daddy's playing at with this silly party idea. Why here? Why at the hotel? It's not as if we haven't got enough problems to contend with. Your great bumpkin husband is really the last thing on my mind.'

'It's money, isn't it?' continues Roisin, as if he hasn't spoken. 'I don't blame you really. You saved his life time and again, didn't you? Kept dragging him out of the mire, cleaning him up, putting him on the straight and narrow. Never had to worry, did he? Always money in the bank, always another great fat royalty cheque just around the corner. And you as the only person he trusted. You and the wife, executors of his will, responsible for his finances. You did it well, I think. Really, I do reckon you had his best interest at heart. But then he had a kid. And he got ill. And he started planning for what would happen when he wasn't going to be here any more. He started asking questions about what he had left, about the best ways to set up a trust for Delilah; how to keep Joy safe and secure – Heloise too. He wanted his financial adviser, his best friend, to be open and honest with him.'

'You don't know what you're talking about!'

Petra realizes her heart is beating too fast. She's sweating, palms clammy. Daddy's wrong. She does know what she's talking about. She knows almost all of it.

'How much did you spend, eh Felix? How much did you take? And he wasn't dying quickly enough, was he? Such a bastard of a disease, Huntington's. Could drop tomorrow or live for another twenty years. There was no way he wouldn't work out what you'd been doing with his money.'

'Look around you,' spits Felix, waving at the expensive appliances; the high ceilings, the exquisite art. 'We're not exactly paupers ourselves, my dear. Do you know how much Daddy is worth? I've managed hedge funds worth tens of millions of pounds!'

'Managed them into the ground, Felix,' says Roisin, pushing her hair back from her face. 'Jesus, if Aector wasn't so feckin' nice he'd have made it his business to know as much about you and your daddy as I do. You're a fuck-up, mate. That education Daddy paid for? The one he thought Aector should be so bloody grateful for? What did you do with it, eh? Got yourself a job at a City bank and messed it all up because you couldn't stop putting your profits up your nose. And then the big financial adviser; the consultant with the multimillion-pound portfolio? How come you've got the bailiffs after you, then? How come you're behind with your council tax?'

Felix waves a hand, bored by the attack. 'We've had setbacks. We've made sacrifices. But if you think I would kill my best friend just to get my hands on his money, you're every bit the poisonous Gypsy bitch that my stepmother took you for!'

Petra jerks at the sound of glass smashing, crockery falling from the drainer. She pokes her head over the balcony. Mum is holding the handle of a glass coffee pot. The pot itself is in pieces all over the hard floor. She's staring at Roisin as if she's drunk. She looks dizzy. Looks sick.

Please Mum, thinks Petra, making fists with her hands. Please don't tell . . .

Roisin looks past Felix. Holds Mum's gaze.

'He was going to die . . .' begins Hattie, dreamily. 'How do you murder a dying man? He'd have wanted it to happen as it did, I know that. If we'd asked, he'd have agreed. But Felix couldn't ask. He's too proud a man for that. What choice did I have? She's so unhappy at that school. They pick on her.

Call her such terrible names. She started seeing that dreadful boy just to spite us. And it would all stop, wouldn't it? It would all stop if Ishmael just fell asleep and didn't wake up. Split down the middle, like we'd always agreed. Half for Felix, half for Delilah and Joy. It was a good chunk. Enough. She could be back at a good school, back with the right people . . . she could stop hating me . . .'

Petra watches her father's face change as he digests his wife's words. Sees the crease appear between his eyebrows. Sees his eyes fill with tears; his lip quiver.

Hattie glances up. Glances past Roisin to where Petra sits, arms around her knees, rocking herself back and forth. Roisin turns. Follows her gaze.

Petra looks down at her trainers. They're too small for her. They can't afford a new pair. Can't afford for her to go on the German exchange trip. They've sold her laptop and her digital camera. Sold her horse. Sold her skis and spent the money on having the railings of their posh new house painted to a suitably splendid black. They've sold off everything she thought of as her own, just to keep up appearances. And all the while Ishmael was up in his villa, frittering money away on his stupid projects: his crystal boxes and old guitars; solar panels he'd never install, and digging out old mineshafts for museums that would never become more than a whim. He was only alive because Daddy got him clean; got him off the drugs, brought him back to Weardale, and stayed close enough to keep him sober and safe. And he was dying anyway. Deon saw the sense in it. His dad too. It was cruel of him to sit in his throne in his crumbling palace while there were so many people struggling to get by. All he had to do was give in to his illness and all the problems would be fixed. But Deon didn't want to hurt somebody he liked. He'd have worked twelve-hour days and grafted until he dropped to provide her with whatever comforts she craved, but he wouldn't do the one simple thing that would make it all better. He wouldn't spike Ishmael's weed with Spice. He wouldn't give him a little nudge in the back as he pottered around in his crystal garden.

Petra meets her mum's eye. Roisin looks from one to the other. Sees. Knows.

'Oh you silly girl,' says Roisin. 'You silly spoiled, silly little girl.'

Petra buries her face in her hands. Lets it out. Lets go of the feeling that has been eating away at her for months. Allows herself to remember the moment of impact; the crunch of stone and glass into the brittle bone of his skull; the way he slumped and slithered, tipping the cement sacks on top of himself; the way he'd blinked and gasped, blood running from his eye, his ear. She remembers sitting at his side, watching his breaths dissipate; watching the concrete harden on his skin. Remembers the mad giggle that erupted as the word presented itself to her. Petrified.

It would have been different if Delilah had been out of the house the way she was supposed to be. And she hadn't even given a thought to Heloise. She knew that Uncle Ish had paperwork in the house: printouts of accounts, copies of his legal agreements and holdings; the letter from the record company telling him about the next bumper payday, having sold the rights to his father's story. And Petra had known that the only thing that would make it all go away was a beautiful cleansing fire. She set it in the living room. Watched it grow. Delilah was being a good girl, staying where Daddy told her to. She was still standing in the doorway when the flames started taking hold. Petra just slipped out the back, pretty certain that Delilah would scarper once her back started getting warm. Then home to Mum. Home to silly sad Mummy in her pink dressing gown, downing her wine, doing her word searches. Mum, who saw the blood on her daughter's hands. Mum, who wouldn't let up until Petra told her everything.

'What?' demands Felix, glaring at the three women, one after the other. 'What am I missing?'

'Couldn't leave it alone, could you?' asks Roisin, quietly. 'Had to start a witch hunt. Had to know who killed your best friend. And all the fucking while . . .'

'I did it,' says Mum, softly. 'I hit him. Killed him. Set the fire.'

Petra thinks about Ingle. About the man called Mr Nightingale. The man who saw what she did. Who saw it all from his safe little place at the entrance to the mine. He saw it all. He got in contact with her just days after the news broke about Ishmael and Heloise's deaths. The email came through when she was at school, a simple missive, written without emotion. It was almost complimentary. She had, he said, burned a witch. They were kindred spirits. Ishmael's death was unfortunate. It was a source of regret. But Ishmael could have avoided the wrath of the spirits if he had just been willing to share a little of his father's remains. He would keep her secret, he said. And all she had to do to secure his silence was remain pure. Remain vestal. But he needed something in return. Needed some of her essence, to help him track down those other dark forces that had cursed him, bewitched him, turned his face to a cauldron of simmering boils. She'd done what he asked. Photos first. Then the weird stuff. Just a few drops of blood. Some spit. Some piss. She didn't ask what he did with it. Didn't want to know. She felt no guilt about Ishmael's death. Heloise's neither. Delilah's injuries were regrettable but the little princess was going to inherit half a fortune so she couldn't see that there was much to complain about, scars or not. But Mum couldn't relax. Mum couldn't keep her mouth shut. Couldn't stop her lip from wobbling every time Dad started to sob and cry and demand answers about who had killed his friend. He wouldn't release the money either. He'd convinced himself that one of the beneficiaries in Ishmael's will had done him in. He used the family name, the old school ties, called in favours. He moved heaven and earth to find out who killed Ishmael: all the while his wife coming apart with the pressure of keeping her secrets. It was Petra who brought up McAvoy's name. He'd been in the news for his part in catching killers. He had bravery medals. Even Daddy said he was the most decent of men. Why not ask him to sniff around? If he found no signs of criminal activity, they could relax. And if he found the opposite, well . . . he was family, wasn't he? And if all else failed, she'd serve him Deon on a plate. She wouldn't want to, but until Daddy had somebody to hold accountable, they weren't going to get a penny, and she certainly wasn't going back to her old school with her old friends. So she told Grandad about her brilliant idea. Wouldn't it be a lovely surprise for Grandma if her Scottish son, the policeman, came along to celebrate her big day? Wouldn't that be so special for everybody – a chance to bury the hatchet, start over. And the old fool had gone for it. Moreover, so had Aector McAvoy, the poor sad sap.

'Petra?'

Daddy's voice is small. Distant. Far-away. Petra despises it, suddenly. Despises all of them.

'It was me,' says Mum, again. 'I swear.'

'Shut up, Mum,' spits Petra. 'God, you're pathetic. The pair of you. Fucking pathetic. You don't get credit for this. You aren't even capable. Do you know how it feels to smash a man's brains in with a rock? To feel his blood on your wrist? To see the light go out in their eyes. I did that. I did what you were too fucking weak to do!'

Roisin stares up at her. There's no anger in her eyes. If anything it's sadness: a boundless mercy. It's with regret that she pulls the mobile phone from her pocket and holds it aloft.

'Did you get that, babes?'

The back door swings slowly open. On the step is Aector McAvoy. He's bleeding; clothes torn, bruised across his face and neck. He has a mobile phone in one hand and a ceremonial blade in the other. He looks to Petra, then slowly, to Mum. Finally, his gaze lands upon Felix. Felix looks away first. McAvoy nods his head. There's no triumph in his voice when he speaks.

'Every word, my darling. Every last word.'

TWENTY-SIX

Audio transcript, 29.05.23
Harriet Brett-Fethering, D.O.B 22.01.1978

' I don't know what you expect me to say. She's not a bad girl. I know you won't believe that and you'll be wondering what sort of person would do that, but honestly, she's been through so much and I really think she thought she was helping. Her dad – he's not her real dad, you see, but she's always idolized him. Felix and me got together when she was only six and he changed our lives, he really did. He had money and influence and power and I was barely keeping things together. He swept in to our lives and made her feel like a little princess and it was all luxury and money and every type of advantage. Imagine that being taken away – imagine seeing all the riches and getting used to that life and then suddenly you're facing up to going to a state school again, and your old friends don't want to know . . . it's no excuse, but, he was dying, wasn't he? And if he'd just died a little sooner . . . Felix didn't even know how bad things were. It was me who kept topping up our family finances from Ish's money. But for all that I'm grieving for him, you have to remember that it was us who kept him alive. Before Felix sorted him out, he was living in squats, off his head, dying in stages. Even Joy – she's no holier than thou, believe me. Felix had some bad luck, that's all. It would have picked up. He was just too bloody proud to ask his daddy, or to tell Ish. I suppose Petra just did what seemed the obvious thing to do. And it's me that's spoiled it, isn't it? She'd never have told, I'm sure. It was me who couldn't stop panicking, had to keep jittering. Bringing that poor man to the valley, that was all for me. I needed to know if we were ever going to be found out. Didn't take long to get an answer, did it? Look, we're family, Aector. There has to be a way forward. Is Felix OK? Is he talking to you? He's good in a crisis but . . . please, tell Aector

I didn't mean for it to happen this way. I really didn't. Is there no way you can just put it on Deon? I mean, Petra's bright. She's got her whole life ahead of her. Should she really lose out on all of the opportunities just because she made one silly mistake . . .?'

ENDS

EPILOGUE

McAvoy winces as he shifts in his seat. Takes a look at the bill, nestling under the chocolate-smeared plate. Winces again.

'This decimal point?' he asks, looking pained. 'We're sure this is in the right place, yes?'

Roisin leans across from her side of the little table. Puts her palm on his cheek and smiles into him. 'Just enjoy yourself, my love.'

McAvoy scowls. He doesn't like to conform to cultural stereotypes but just this once, he'd like to allow the measly, Presbyterian side of his nature to show on his face. Truth be told, he doesn't begrudge the little tea room its eye-watering pries. The soup was good, the sandwiches better and the Malteser slice was big enough to use as the foundation of an ambitious building project. He's being difficult because he's nervous. He wanted to go home yesterday. It's been nearly two days since Petra was arrested. Her mum's been released but McAvoy has no doubt that charges will soon follow. Petra's still being questioned, police having applied for an extra twenty-four hours to continue grilling her. She's got a good solicitor – the best Ishmael's money can buy. Nightingale's been charged. Remanded. He's being assessed by mental health professionals. McAvoy's pretty sure he'll be found wanting.

'You don't have to do this, y'know,' says Roisin, for what must be the tenth time. 'You shouldn't have to explain yourself. You're the one who was manipulated. It's not your fault that they thought they knew you when they didn't.'

McAvoy sits back in his chair. The tea room is pretty and quiet. They're in the back room, seated at a circular table. McAvoy's battered and bruised, but he's scrubbed up OK for his peculiar date with Mum and Crawford. Roisin's been taking advantage of the Darling credit card, charging everything she can think of to their account. They're bringing home more lotions and soaps than they can use in a lifetime. Roisin plans to reverse-engineer them – to work out whether they're really worth the money. Big Harry has already promised that the hotel will stock her massage lotions as soon as she can manufacture them in sufficient bulk. She's bought him and Sharon a voucher for a five-course tasting menu at the hotel, by way of a thank you. She's charged it to Crawford, of course.

'Do you think he knew?' asks Roisin, re-applying her lip gloss. 'Ishmael, I mean. He was a grown man. He wasn't daft. He must have known they were fleecing him.'

McAvoy picks a crumb from his waistcoat. He's looking dapper in soft cords, collarless shirt and tweed waistcoat. He's got a new pocket-watch: a gift from Roisin. His tan boots shine like moonlight on water. He asks himself what he really believes, hoping he'll come up with a decent answer. He still doesn't know.

'I don't think Ishmael took notice of the same things that bother other people. I think he probably knew and didn't care. There's a new royalty deal being cut at the moment. The estate of Moose Piper is going to be getting a nice fat cheque, so even if they'd emptied the pot, it'll fill back up.'

'Will they get it, you think?' asks Roisin, fiddling with her phone. 'The money?'

McAvoy shakes his head. 'I don't think there's much money left in the pot. There'll be royalty monies coming through for years, but they'll go straight to Joy and Delilah. It'll be hard for Felix to inherit anything, even as executor, given that his daughter's responsible for Ishmael's death. There are rules about that sort of thing.'

'But he didn't do it himself, did he? He wouldn't be profiting from his own crime.'

'That's all up to the lawyers,' says McAvoy, his face clouding. In his experience, lawyers keep squeezing until whatever it is they're juicing has run dry. 'It'll be like *Bleak House*, I shouldn't wonder.'

'And in the meantime?'

'In the meantime, Harry will slyly sell off a load of Moose's old stuff. He'll take a cut, like Ish promised, and the rest will go to Joy and Delilah.'

'And Mr Nightingale had nothing to do with any of it?'

'I wouldn't say that. He manipulated Deon into stealing Moose's ashes and then blackmailed Petra into giving him everything he asked for. The photos he took – they must have been taken from the mouth of the mineshaft. He saw what she did and used it to his advantage.'

'Was he trying to summon witches or kill them off?'

McAvoy sighs, tired of death and insanity and working people out. 'I think he's a very ill man.'

Roisin reaches out and puts her soft hand upon his big, scarred knuckles. 'And what's next for Felix?'

McAvoy scratches at his beard. He thinks again of Felix as a teenager: as the rich kid with the floppy fringe and the cocksure confidence; the kid who made fun of his accent and told him not to touch his things; who told him that his mum didn't even want him here but that she couldn't stand the thought of him having a decent relationship with the father who'd tricked her into marriage and reduced her to the status of a drudge. McAvoy has never let himself forget that phrase. He'd known Felix wasn't lying. It was exactly what she'd say. It was what she thought. It was what she said in interviews to the trade presses as she worked her way up the corporate ladder and agreed to participating in profile pieces about her rise to the top. A marriage she deeply regretted, with a farmer who'd made her think that life in a little white-painted croft on a hillside would be enough to compensate for the curtail-ment of a flourishing career.

'You're thinking,' says Roisin, staring into him. 'You're being unkind to yourself, I can tell.'

McAvoy runs his finger around his plate. Eats a crumb of cake. Checks his watch. She's late. They're not bringing the helicopter, as it turns out. They're driving down. They'd never had any intention of coming to the village to celebrate her birthday. They'd planned to blame bad weather, and make it up to him some other time.

'Trish keeps sending laughing emojis,' says Roisin, glancing at her phone. 'Apparently she's getting a tonne of messages from Saville's boss. Can't praise her underling highly enough for his contribution. There's going to be a press release. Don't worry, you won't be named. Apparently you saved her life. Saville, I mean.'

'She was doing fine,' he says. 'I just made things more complicated.'

'You're a hard man to praise, Aector McAvoy.'

McAvoy sighs. Checks his watch again. He doesn't know what he's doing this for. Doesn't know what he has to say. He wants to go and see the kids. See East Yorkshire. Wants to breathe in the salt and diesel and cocoa powder of Hull's complicated air. Wants to eat an ice cream in the cold of Hessle Foreshore. Wants to take a walk in the woods at Brantingham, holding Roisin's hands and naming the trees for his son and daughter.

'We could go,' says Roisin, quietly. 'Feck 'em, I say. What good is there to come of any of this?'

McAvoy considers the opportunity. He knows what he wants. He wants his mum to meet his eyes. To tell him he's a good lad and that she's proud of him. And she won't do that. She'll never do that. She isn't made that way.

'I love you,' says Roisin. 'I'm so fecking proud of you. Kids too. Even Trish.'

McAvoy lets himself smile. Imagines his mum and stepdad slithering in through the big wooden door to find that McAvoy hadn't been kidding when he said he didn't tolerate lateness. He decides he rather likes the mental picture. Gives a nod.

'Aye,' he grunts, and his accent is, briefly, the one he was raised with: an echo of his dad's. 'I reckon we're long out of the will anyway.'

'The will?' asks Roisin, grinning. 'You think you were ever in it?'

McAvoy shakes his head. He realizes that he truly, truly doesn't care.

'Howay,' he says, in his best imitation of a Geordie accent. 'We've got the room for another night. I reckon we've time.'

'Really?' asks Roisin. 'The long-awaited threesome?'

'You, me and the massage machine, my love. Hold on to your hat.'

McAvoy leaves a generous tip. Pays the bill. Steps out of the old school building and stands for a minute in the cold blue light. Blanchland's beautiful. It glistens in the light: the old honey-coloured stones looking clean and new after the downpour. He takes Roisin's hand in his. Looks over the crossroads to the arch. Joy and Delilah are standing chatting with another mum and daughter. Mum's got fiery hair and bright eyes: multi-coloured overalls and hand-painted boots. She's laughing at something Joy's said. Delilah is talking with a five-year-old girl. Bunches, brown eyes, leather jacket and wellies. They're laughing too.

'Better day, eh?'

A handsome older man with grey hair and a silver beard waves a hand as he crosses the road and makes his way into the church. He's walking with a staff. He looks a bit like a wizard. The woman in the archway looks like she could do more than bewitch.

'Imagine what he'd have made of me,' grins Roisin, reading his thoughts. 'Your Nightingale. Imagine if he met the real thing.'

McAvoy holds her close. Kisses her head. He doesn't need to be promoted. He's imagined nothing else since he realized that a bad man was trying to do harm to those with the gift of seeing beyond the veil.

'It'll happen again,' says Roisin, softly. 'There'll be another Burning Time. It might look a little different, but some people will always need to set fire to the things they don't understand.'

McAvoy holds her. Kisses her. Breathes her in. For a moment, he sees dancing flames upon the lenses of her eyes. Smells smoke and sulphur and flame.

'And what will that mean for you?'

Roisin grins. Bites his lip. Plucks a red hair from his crown and winds it around her finger like a garrotte. 'I'll keep you bewitched, my love.'

'You're enchanting, Ro—'

'Aye. I know.'